I0779720

GRULEN
SVESTI FATED MATES   BOOK 7
WAVY MARTIN

ISBN (Paperback): 978-1-959469-16-2
ISBN (Ebook): 978-1-959469-17-9
ISBN (Large Print Paperback): 978-1-959469-18-6
Library of Congress Control Number: 2025901994

This is a work of fiction. Names, characters, places, and incidents either are the product of the author's imagination or are used fictitiously. Any resemblance to actual persons, living or dead, or locales is entirely coincidental.

Any trademarks, service marks, product names, or named features are assumed to be the property of the respective owners and are used only as reference. There is no implied endorsement if we use one of these terms.

Catalyst Publishers
P.O. Box 1232
Aliquippa, PA 15001
publisherscatalyst@gmail.com
Author website: wavymartin.com

OTHER BOOKS BY
Wavy Martin

SVESTI FATED MATES SERIES
Vared

Devik

Ash'n

Ronan

Karid

Traxen

Table of Contents

Prologue

All dates mentioned use Earth's calendar.

The Svesti, an alien warrior race, have guarded Earth's region of space from the Zuvgran since the early 1900s. Ruled by an Emperor, the Zuvgran invade worlds, kill the elderly, the very young, and some of the males. Those left living become unwilling slaves or subjects for medical experiments. The Zuvgran strip conquered worlds of their natural resources and move on. They attack anyone believed weaker, so ships or colonies are unsafe as well.

Zuvgran who disagree with the Emperor's expansionist policies or the pervasive cruelty to other species find ways to escape or aid others. Unfortunately, there are far too few of them and they are without the resources to do more.

In the early 2000s, the Zuvgran released a devastating virus on Costonia, the Svesti home world. The virus killed eighty percent of the Svesti females, as well as all female young, and rendered the remainder infertile. It's now 2037 and Svesti scientists discover the first biologically compatible beings—human females.

Ruled by a King and a Council representing their twelve Houses, the Svesti also worship a deity called the Goddess. The Svesti culture mixes old world gentility with superior technology. With their toned bodies clad in tight black pants and leather, most Svesti males tend toward overprotectiveness and a fierce sense of loyalty.

A divided Svesti Council creates discord on Costonia. Some want to invade Earth and take whatever females they want, while others believe any young born of a Svesti-human couple would no longer be Svesti. However, King Traxen Sovex wants to open up negotiations with Earth to receive willing human females for breeding or troth contracts.

A troth contract is similar to a short-term marriage. A breeding contract, now called a birthing contract, is specifically for the bearing of Svesti young. True mating, where the Svesti experience the biological urge to bite their partner and mate for life, supersedes both contracts. Fated mate bonds, where it is believed the Goddess blessed a couple by gifting them the one being in the universe who is their other half, were last recorded over a century ago. Upon meeting the first human females, the bonds begin to spark again and offer hope of lasting love and companionship for the Svesti.

King Sovex sent Commander Vared Durek of the *Invictus*, a space cruiser holding 3,000 warriors, to Earth to initiate first contact. Durek's long-time best friends serve on the *Invictus* as well—Lieutenant Karid Wurvez, head tactical officer; Lieutenant Devik Tolvex, head security officer; and Healer Ash'n Rivezt, head healer.

Durek initiated first contact with six countries based the size of their territory or influence after initial research of Earth revealed humans continue to be fragmented in their joint leadership. Each country convinced or ordered one woman to take the two-month trip to Costonia, live there and gather information for fourteen months, then return home. True to human nature, Earth's leaders instructed the women to focus on Svesti military capabilities, weaponry, and technology.

Earth's leaders allowed the Svesti to believe the women volunteered to be part of a Choosing at the King's Court, where they would choose a male for a breeding or troth contract. The women discovered the truth while traveling in space and didn't take the news well. Despite the rocky beginning and being unwittingly manipulated by Earth's leaders, the Svesti and the human females found common ground and proceeded to work together.

Talia Sullivan, the American President's secretly appointed Ambassador, worked with the Svesti on a fair treaty. During their travel to Costonia, Commander Durek, his trusted friends, and the women realized a Svesti traitor traveled onboard the *Invictus* and communicated with a Svesti noble on the home world. In a temporary alliance with the Zuvgran, these traitors attempted to kill human fertility via another virus. What the traitors didn't know was that the Zuvgran constructed the virus to also kill Svesti male fertility. Fortunately, with the help of the human physician and botanist/biochemist, Natasha Petrov and Lin Chang respectively, the Svesti developed a vaccine to protect humans and Svesti before the virus spread and both races suffered a slow genocidal attack.

About a month and a half into the trip, Durek received word from the *Defiant*, the ship they left to protect the space near Earth, that Earth's leaders publicly proclaimed the Svesti kidnapped the six women. Those same leaders called for increased military funding and gave the appearance of gearing up for war.

Talia developed an idea to get the correct information to Earth. King Sovex approved the plan and allocated resources. When all was said and done, King Sovex named Durek and Talia the Svesti Co-Ambassadors to Earth.

Despite the ongoing efforts of the loyal Svesti and women, the traitors remain unidentified. Based on information they did know, Durek sent Wurvez and another warrior, Grulen Jevax, on a secret mission.

Along the way, the *Invictus* received a distress call about a mine collapse on Talonka Six. While there assisting, Natasha met a Svesti-Zuvgran hybrid, Ronan d'Olorg, and became aware of a measles variant spreading across planets. Ronan and his adopted Zuvgran father, Largon d'Ayen, rescue Zuvgran hybrid younglings and help relocate to hidden colonies those few Zuvgran who wish to escape the Emperor's cruelty. King Sovex offered temporary sanctuary on Costonia for the hybrid younglings and his assistance in finding a permanent safe location so they can all be together.

The Zuvgran captured Natasha and Ronan on their return from distributing vaccines to the hidden colonies. The pair discovered Wurvez already imprisoned at the same location. The Svesti rescued all of them shortly thereafter and they rejoined the *Invictus*, which now carried the hybrid younglings and their caretakers. The group subsequently arrived safely at Costonia. Four of the human females formed fated mate bonds before reaching the planet.

The Zuvgran destroyed Jevax's ship not long after Wurvez became a prisoner, and his status remained a mystery...until now.

- Wavy

Chapter 1

Twenty-nine years earlier
November 22, 2008 *(Earth calendar)*
Nestune *(village on Costonia)*

Twelve-year-old Grulen Jevax stared dry-eyed at the newly turned soil. After weeks of screaming agony, the bodies of his mother and five sisters lay eerily silent. A virulent virus swept through their village and every female suffered terrible pain before succumbing to death. His family was the most recent to be laid to rest. The weight of his father's hand rested on his thin shoulder as they gazed upon the caskets of his older siblings—Yopa, Fliva, and Riba, his mother, and his little sisters, Muri and Hadili, for the last time. He already missed the scent of the female that gave him life. Everything about her, from the warmth of her embrace to the steadfast support when he was sad, embodied love and safety to him. *I'll never hear their voices and laughter or feel their hugs again.*

A broken rumble emanated from his father's chest. Grulen looked up at the reddish bronze male who appeared to have aged three decades in a month and noted tears in the brown eyes so like his own. *I've never seen my sire cry before this virus. I stopped crying a week ago. I just can't anymore.*

Remembering his father's sobbing prayers to the Goddess to spare the females and let him bear their pain pinched Grulen's heart. Hearing a decorated warrior repeatedly plead for those he loved broke something in his young soul. The only mercy is they no longer suffered. *Goddess, please take good care of all our females. They did not deserve this.*

His father's fingers squeezed Grulen's shoulder.

"It's time, my son."

Taking a shovel from his father, Grulen nodded. Mounds of dirt thunked on the wooden boxes as they worked in silence. An occasional grunt of exertion punctuated the quiet. Even the birds refrained from song as if in respect for the solemnity of their grief and toil. When the graves were full, they cleaned the area and carefully planted the favorite flowers of each family member over their final resting place. His nose twitched at the irony of the smell of life covering the death below. The vibrant colors assaulted Grulen's eyes, and his vision blurred. *Guess I do have more tears left in me.*

Years later, the memories of the broken village males trying to move beyond the devastation to provide and care for the surviving younglings while dealing with their own grief stayed strong in Grulen's mind. It seemed like forever before Grulen's father began to genuinely smile and stand tall again.

Every morning, his sire taught him training forms. When Grulen no longer needed instruction, they exercised silently side by side. Grulen found peace in the flowing movements and increasing control of his growing body. He found memories of their lost females turned from their painful end to earlier ones. His mother making his favorite dessert and teaching Yopa, Fliva, and Riba how to cook. Holding Muri and Hadili in his arms when they were born. The tinkling laughter of all of them when their father splashed them in the nearby lake. Tugging on their hair and teasing them. Overhearing Yopa tell their mother when a male kissed her.

When the Warrior Academy accepted Grulen, he and his father moved away from Nestune. More females had survived in the populated area, but all could no longer bear young. He met females of other species at the spaceports. With his classmates, he visited erotica establishments and learned to physically please a variety of females. He teased all and flirted shamelessly, but he kept his heart closed to more. The memories of shattered male hearts remained, and he vowed never to be in the same position.

Five years earlier
February 2, 2029 *(Earth calendar)*
Trezoura *(Capital city of Costonia)*

Standing at attention with his tail relaxed and still, Grulen waited for Commander Vared Durek of House Ruxila to speak. He surreptitiously took in the large male's golden bronze skin and scar across one cheek. Lavender eyes indicated a familial connection to the royal House Davelk. Like Grulen, Durek preferred to keep his dark hair short. The Commander had a reputation for a fiery temper but was also known to be fair. Grulen had no idea why he had been ordered to appear before the male.

Lieutenant Karid Wurvez of House Binova stood next to Durek. Known for his humor and tactical skills, the reddish bronze male's ponytail kept his long brown hair out of his gray eyes.

"Warrior Grulen Jevax, thank you for coming." Grulen refocused his gaze on the Commander.

"Sir, thank you for inviting me."

The males stared at each other. *I won't ask why I'm here.*

Durek grunted and leaned his elbows on the desk.

"Sit, Warrior. You aren't in trouble."

Grulen sat and waited.

"I've recently been assigned to the *Invictus* and am interviewing potential crew. Lieutenant Wurvez will be my second-in-command and head tactical officer. Your commanding officer recommended you."

"Sir, I am just a warrior with no special skill sets."

Wurvez snorted.

"With the exception of programming computers, you excel at your assignments, Jevax, remain levelheaded in stressful situations, and somehow manage to maintain friendly relationships with those around you without obsequious fawning."

Grulen inwardly flinched as an unbidden memory of Fliva trying to unsuccessfully teach him to program a synthesizer entered his mind.

"You seem to have no political biases that interfere with your duties, other warriors respect you, and according to your commanding officers, you are patient when instructing others to improve their skills. In fact, your team leader said you routinely offer helpful suggestions to your fellow warriors when you notice they may need guidance, but you do so in a manner that lifts their self-esteem, without drawing attention to their lack."

Durek frowned, his scar taut and white.

"I must keep most of the current space cruiser's crew. I want solid, proven warriors to join us. I believe you will be a good fit, Jevax."

"As the flagship of the Svesti fleet, what types of missions could we expect, Commander? I'll be honest, I would not be happy solely escorting dignitaries." Grulen leaned forward when Wurvez grinned, his fangs white against his lips.

"We will be on extended duty protecting various planets from the Zuvgran."

"I see." Grulen nodded. "If you believe I will be an asset, I am honored to accept reassignment to the *Invictus*."

"Expect new orders by tomorrow, Jevax. You will have a *lunar* leave before you report since we will be away from Costonia for at least a *solar*."

Grulen stood.

"As you will, Sir."

"Dismissed."

As he walked down the hall, he decided to try to talk with his commanding officer. *If he needs me to stay a couple weeks, I can shorten my leave. Father doesn't return from Nestune yet. I would hate to make him cut short his annual trip.*

Exiting into the bright sunshine, he looked up at the periwinkle sky and inhaled deeply. *I should visit their graves before I report to the Invictus. I'll go alone as usual. I feel closer to them that way.*

After Grulen finished his training forms, he picked up the towel and water pouch from the blue grass next to him. Muscles loose and limber after his workout, he wiped the sweat from his face and chest before rehydrating. Even after being on the *Invictus* for five *lunars*, he was still amazed by the aquiponics area.

Staggered levels with produce and herbs growing surrounded the enormous space. A pink gravel path circled the lower perimeter with fruit-growing bushes and trees scattered about the area. Smaller clearings dotted the central space such as the one he just used—some with benches and flowering plants.

Tail swaying, his nostrils flared as he drew in a deep breath enjoying the fresh scents of Costonia on the space cruiser. The aquiponics area served multiple purposes. Fresh food production and cleaner air meant healthier, happier warriors. Whenever possible, Grulen liked to conduct his forms here and used the designated training areas for sparring and other physical activities. The routine also helped him meet more of the three thousand warriors stationed on the *Invictus*.

"Warrior, come here!"

Grulen looked around and saw the older male who seemed to always be working among the plants gesturing to him. Dark brown hair laced with silver, brown eyes, and a strong body housed the irascible male who seemed to be a similar age to Grulen's own sire.

"Me, sir?"

"Do you see anyone else?" *Grumpy male.*

Tucking his water pouch and towel into a pocket, Grulen jogged across the grass to meet the other warrior.

"I require another set of hands to help harvest a section of *lobile.* The warriors scheduled to assist me are being disciplined by their team lead for their drunkenness last evening."

"Would those be the warriors that let loose some training bots into one of the hangar bays?"

"Yes. *Crekkin' naroons.* Fortunately, none of the ships were irreparably damaged or Commander Durek would be handling their discipline personally."

"Then the healers would have extra work as well." Grulen chuckled.

The older male grinned, his fangs white against his face.

"Have you been on the receiving end of the commander's ire?"

"No, sir, I've managed to avoid that type of attention. I've heard rumors though."

"Yes, he likes to reinforce his lessons with a heavy dose of sparring. What is your name, Warrior? I'll comm your team lead to let him know you're aiding me."

"Grulen Jevax, but I'm not on duty. I'm happy to help."

"Merix Hunnek." The old male grunted, kneeled, and proceeded to show Grulen how to properly harvest the purple tubers. Grulen didn't tell him he already knew how to do it from his time in Nestune.

"*The* Merix Hunnek? The one that invented aquiponics areas?"

His brown eyes widened.

"How would you know that?"

"My last assignment was onboard the *Diligence*, a science vessel. We had a much smaller aquiponics area based upon your research. One of the exobiologists extolled your work."

"Are you a scientist?"

Grulen shook his head as he pulled a tuber from the dirt and lightly tossed it into a container.

"No. The ship traveled to many planets, and I primarily took a protective role on away missions. Otherwise, I assisted wherever there was a need. Only one hundred of us made up the ship's complement."

"A big step from the *Diligence* to the *Invictus*. Were you not happy?" Hunnek dug out a tuber. His fingers looked misshapen and painful.

"I enjoyed my time there, but when Commander Durek offered me a place on the Svesti flagship, I chose to accept."

"Have you settled in with the crew? I notice you practicing your training forms here regularly."

"I believe so. I like the peace of this space when I meditate. Now that we're in the Quon system protecting Urdite space, I hope I will have more to do beyond learning about space cruiser operations."

"Be careful what you wish for, Jevax. If we're lucky, the Zuvgran will ignore Urdita and the other planets in this system."

Grulen noted Hunnek occasionally wincing as his fingers dove into the soil.

"May I ask a personal question?"

Hunnek grunted and his tail stiffened before resting on the ground.

"What happened to your hands?"

The older male rotated his head cracking his neck before he looked at his companion from the corner of his eye. He sighed and returned his attention to his work, speaking quietly.

"When the virus took my mother, my mate, and my daughter, I volunteered for the riskier missions to allow warriors with young families time to recover. Consumed by sadness and anger, I took chances I shouldn't have. The Zuvgran captured and tortured me. They broke my fingers early on. I finally escaped, but it was almost a *lunar* before I could return to a Svesti ship. The healers did what they could, but they had to break my digits to set them correctly and the cartilage deteriorates more rapidly now from the residual damage. It's bearable and an unfortunate reminder of the consequences of making important decisions with emotions rather than reason."

"I'm sorry," Grulen said softly. "I was a youngling, but my mother and five sisters succumbed to the virus, leaving only my sire and myself. The anger and grief affected everyone."

"That experience marked us all."

Lost in their own thoughts, they continued harvesting and collected five large containers of *lobile*. Hunnek stood in a single fluid moment. *The male may have damaged hands, but there's nothing wrong with his strength and mobility.*

"What's next, Hunnek?"

"If you want to help me doublecheck the programming for the water reservoirs, you're welcome to join me."

Grulen grimaced and shook his head.

"Programming anything other than coordinates for flying or weapons is beyond me. I have difficulty with equipment as simple as a synthesizer."

"Interesting. I could try to teach you."

"Many have tried and failed." Grulen's tail flicked behind him, and he grinned to soften his refusal.

Hunnek slapped Grulen's shoulder.

"Thank you for you assistance."

Grulen smiled as he headed to his shared quarters. Despite Hunnek's initial grumpiness, he enjoyed his time with the older male. *I think I could learn a lot from him.*

Chapter 2

Three years earlier
May 12, 2034 *(Earth calendar)*
Oklahoma City, Oklahoma

Morgan Calloway burst into laughter when she pushed aside the colorful tissue paper revealing a silky white button-down blouse accompanied red accessories—an engraved leather belt and a lacy push-up bra with matching thong. She shook her head in fond exasperation at the remaining black items—a narrow skirt with a side slit, sheer pantyhose with a prominent back seam, and fuck-me heels—before placing the enclosed oversized eyeglasses on her nose. Her now-former coworkers grinned at her.

"Really, ladies?"

"There's more," said Candi Torres. Her brown eyes lit with humor and anticipation. The other dozen women encouraged Morgan to continue exploring the contents of the gift box while the ten men smirked. She slapped her palm with a wooden ruler before holding up a pencil and a *Hot for Teacher* sign.

"You've kept long hours working here while getting your degree. We want you to start making time for relationships. And remember to have fun. You deserve it." Beth Weston, a blue-eyed blonde, smiled.

"None of us want a guy who regularly seeks out stripper entertainment," Danae Stefano said with pursed lips.

"It's not like Mr. Right hangs out in places like this, even if ours is a thousand times better than the Carmine Canine," Penny Lockhart added, her hazel eyes glinting. The other women nodded.

Morgan snickered at their nickname for a strip club on the other side of town. Years ago, some of them had gone there one night to scope out the competition. They'd left in disgust after visiting the ladies bathroom. The lack of cleanliness sucked, but even worse was the realization that the strippers weren't afforded a separate dressing room. They had to change in the public restroom.

Morgan glanced around. Her best friend and boss, Sophia Pratoria, had successfully combined a ritzy gentlemen's club with a high-end strip joint.

A large stage dominated the far end of the main room. On either side, dance platforms surrounded center poles and hovered about eight feet in the air. Rather than cages, thick, clear acrylic tastefully decorated with fake gemstones encased the mini-stages and glittered under the bright lights. Two long bars ran the lengths of the space and the black marble countertops gleamed. Solid oak tables with plush chairs in red, black, and gold filled the parquet floor while the upper level contained VIP areas. Sophia even had a chef on staff and offered gourmet meals four nights a week.

"I'll be too busy setting up my classroom and writing lesson plans."

A chorus of boos answered her comment.

"Keep yourself open to the possibility," said Beth.

Morgan nodded. Opening the remaining cards and gifts, eating, and accepting well wishes filled the next two hours. Laughter rang loud when Penny's acerbic commentary about customers caused Candi to snort her soda.

As the event wound down, Jake Broussard and Tony Dixon, a bartender and bouncer respectively, offered to load the gifts into Morgan's fifteen-year-old car while she returned goodbye hugs.

Jake frowned, his blue eyes concerned.

"Your car is stuffed to the brim. Are you leaving right away?"

Morgan nodded. "Straight from here. I've got about twenty-five hours of driving ahead of me."

"Be careful. Find a hotel if you're tired."

"Yes, Dad." She stepped into his embrace. He bent his lanky six-foot frame to look into her eyes.

"I care about your safety." He kissed her cheek. "I ought to paddle your sassy ass."

"You and what army?" Morgan's grin at their usual banter faded. "Thank you for looking out for me all these years. You've been the big brother I always wished I had." Tears welled in her eyes when his expression softened, and he gently tugged her ponytail.

"I'm proud of you. Those students of yours are luckier than they realize."

"Thanks." She ducked her chin.

"Are you going to miss this place, even a little?"

Morgan turned at Sophia's husky comment. A decade older than Morgan's twenty-six, Sophia exuded high class with her lush form dressed in a teal silk dress, designer heels, and manicured nails. She impatiently pushed at a lock of her wavy black hair falling across her eyes.

"I'll miss you and the staff, but I'm not going to miss the work." Morgan tilted her head and smiled. "Exotic dancing was never going to be my career, but I'm grateful you hired me."

"You love performing with the silks." Sophia gestured with an elegant hand.

Morgan's auburn ponytail swung when she shook her head.

"I enjoy the exercise and choreographing routines. I only tolerated performing." Wagging a finger at her friend, she said, "Your bottom line isn't going to suffer. I've been working with some of the girls to teach them some easy moves that look complex."

"Even though your acts have always pulled the clients in, I'm not worried about the money." In a rare moment of visible discomfort, Sophia bit her full lower lip, and her long dark lashes shimmered with moisture. "I'm going to miss you. And you're going to be alone when you start your new job. Why couldn't you apply for positions closer?"

Morgan sighed.

"Now that I finally have my degree, I want to teach. School administrators in Spokane aren't as likely to realize that the Manor House on my resume is a strip club."

"You'll keep in touch?"

"Of course. You're my best friend no matter where I am." Morgan's eyes welled as she returned Sophia's fervent hug.

Twelve hours later, Morgan's eyes watered again, and her jaw popped when she yawned wide. She exited Interstate 25 somewhere in Wyoming looking for a cheap motel.

Streetlights would be nice. I can't see shit.

Her engine suddenly quit, and she pulled over.

What now? I'm too tired to deal with car trouble.

With a heavy sigh, she zipped her hoodie, popped the hood, and grabbed a flashlight. Grumbling under her breath, she opened her car door. The cool night air smelled fragrant, but her nose wrinkled when another scent registered.

Ugh. Is there an open septic tank nearby?

All-encompassing pain spread from Morgan's shoulders throughout her body. Back involuntarily arching, she shook uncontrollably before falling to her hands and knees. Nose bleeding, hair awry, she slowly raised her head and peered behind her. Four large orange beings with three bulbous black eyes aimed weapons at her. Her eyes widened and a broken gasp left her rasping chest.

One spoke in guttural tones. She shook her head groaning with pain. It...he gestured at one of his companions who stepped forward and grasped her upper arm. Effortlessly he lifted her to stand unsteadily. *Claws. They have fucking claws. And they stink.*

Another placed a collar around her neck. *What am I? A fucking dog?*

She struggled weakly as they led her into the tree line. They spat harsh words at her, and she increased her efforts. When the first one backhanded her, the world went black.

As Morgan regained consciousness, her body screamed at her. A cold metal floor thrummed underneath her as she catalogued her injuries. Tentatively, she touched her tender swollen jaw and cheek. Dried blood flaked off under her nostrils, a headache pounded behind her eyes, and her left ear felt like a hammer had struck it. Her muscles ached like she'd worked on the silks every waking hour for a week straight. Her stomach churned as she slowly sat up and took in her surroundings.

She estimated a hundred people, mostly women, filled a large low-lit area. Only a single section remained clear. The reason became clear when two women moved there. One stood guard while the other dropped her pants and squatted. Morgan's lips twisted. *Guess that's our litter box. Fucking wonderful.*

An older black woman sitting near her spoke quietly "How ya feelin', sweetie? Most are thrown in here screaming or in shock. I worried because you were bloodied and unconscious."

"I feel like I went ten rounds with a bus." Morgan grimaced and rubbed her arms.

"Who got ya? The orange or the gray dudes?"

"Orange. There are gray ones, too?"

"Yep." The woman extended a hand. "I'm Faith Roberts from Atlanta. Bastards picked me up at my boyfriend's cabin." Her face fell. "They killed him when he shot one."

"I'm sorry about your boyfriend." They shook hands. "Morgan Calloway. I was driving from OKC to Spokane when my car broke down somewhere in Wyoming. How long have you been here?"

"Three days." Faith pointed at a group across from them "They were here when I arrived and said they'd been picked up four days prior. You were one of the last."

Morgan fingered the contraption around her neck.

"What's with these collars?"

Faith's brown eyes hardened.

"They're pain collars. The aliens use 'em to control us."

"How do you know that?"

"An orange one explained it, then demonstrated it." Faith nodded at a burly guy. "Dropped the man to his knees. After he recovered, he said it felt like a thousand needles spiking into his neck and electricity coursing through his body. He was pretty shaken up. And pissed."

"You can understand them?"

"You can too, now. They implanted translators in everyone." She tapped behind her ear. "Hurt like a bitch when they did it."

Morgan fingered her own aching flesh near her ear.

"I'm not dreaming, am I?"

"No, sweetie. We've been abducted by aliens who stink like an outhouse that needs relocated."

"Why?"

Lips pursed and eyes shadowed, Faith said, "They're going to sell us as slaves. And since we're mostly female, I suspect it'll be even worse for us." She patted the younger woman's arm.

All Morgan could do was cry.

Elbows resting on her bent knees, Morgan raised her weary head when the hum of the ship changed. She scanned the cargo hold and frowned at the condition of her fellow hostages. Jim, the big guy Faith pointed out on Morgan's first day, leaned bare-chested against the wall. His long legs stretched in front of him with his shirt wrapped tightly around his right knee. One of the orange aliens—Durelians she now knew—had struck the man with a shock stick when he fought to keep them from taking a woman from the cargo hold two days ago and his limb twisted wrong when he fell.

Everyone had lost weight. Their captors mostly left them alone except for when a disgusting gruel showed up once a day as a meal, although water flowed easily from dispensers around the space. Every couple weeks a weird green light slowly swept the space for several minutes leaving the faint smell of ozone in its wake. She believed it probably cleansed them in some fashion, otherwise they would smell even ranker than they already did after almost four months of this unrelenting hell.

They learned the gray aliens were called Frezzians, but a Durelian named Krutus captained the vessel. He showed up after a group of their captors removed Lisa from their prison and returned her battered, naked body. With his claws, Krutus sliced the ringleader of the group until he bled to death while coldly explaining profit loss because of a slave was unacceptable. He then shot the other perpetrators with a high-tech weapon. That was about three months ago. Unless someone fed Lisa or made her drink water, she remained quiet and still, huddled in Morgan's hoodie and a large scarf wrapped around her waist that another woman gave her to cover her nudity and flinching whenever someone came near her. *Poor Lisa. She hasn't uttered a word, and she's retreated so far into her head that I don't think she'll ever come back.*

Her ponytail holder long gone, Morgan pushed her lank hair from her face. Despite Krutus' punishment of the first group, two others had pulled women from the humans to rape them. The captain's reaction remained the same, reducing the number of crew each time. Morgan turned her head to look at the second victim, Bree, comforting Evelyn, who was the one Jim tried to save. Fortunately, the dozen human men didn't try to force themselves on the women, instead they behaved respectfully. *I wonder if they would've acted differently if Krutus supported his crew. Four months without sex can feel like a long time for some.*

Not even a little concerned about her cynicism, Morgan focused on what the change in the ship's sounds meant for them. Her hands shook. *Are we getting close to our destination? Will we be sold? Will the rest of us be raped?*

"I think shit's gonna get even more real soon, sweetie." Faith wrapped her hands over Morgan's, warming them.

Morgan blew out a long breath at her friend's quiet words.

"I know."

"Do what you can to survive. Humans are stronger than these fucktards believe. And we have a collective history of rebelling against injustice."

Morgan flashed a tired grin.

"I don't know why it continues to surprise me that while you look like a sweet grandmother, you have the mouth of a drunken sailor."

Faith patted her unruly hair and tilted her head.

"A particular talent I've cultivated over the years."

Softly, Morgan said, "Thank you. I'm not sure I would have made it this far without you."

Faith's mouth firmed.

"Someone who grew up fatherless, dropped out of college to care for her mother while she fought cancer, then chose exotic dancing to pay for her education as quickly as possible and graduating with honors after her mother's death is already a survivor. Do not doubt you have what it takes, Morgan. You could've broken long before now with everything you've dealt with, but you haven't. You won't now. Trust yourself."

"I bet you're a great advocate as a social worker."

Eyes sad, Faith's lips tipped up.

"I like to think so. I worry about the kids I was helping. Is my disappearance going to set them back?"

"You have a huge, giving heart. That's what those kids will remember."

Faith bumped her shoulder against Morgan's.

"You're good for my ego, sweetie."

They sat in silence for long minutes as the green light appeared and did its thing.

"We're probably going to be separated, aren't we?"

A dozen armed aliens entering their prison interrupted Faith's response.

Two Frezzians dumped containers on the floor. Sheer white material overflowed from the boxes.

"Everyone strip and put on these clothes," a Durelian ordered. He waved his weapon at the two humans closest to the boxes. Distribute those to the other slaves."

Cautiously, Moe and Renee pulled tunics from the first container and silently handed them to those around them people passed them back. Morgan couldn't be sure who spoke but heard, "Oh, fuck, no." Whispers and grumbling filled the space as everyone realized the clothing would leave nothing to the imagination. When no one moved, shock collars activated, and people screamed.

When Morgan could move again, she crunched the material in her fingers and looked at Faith who pulled her shirt over her head and slowly unclasped her bra. Staring at each other for courage, they stripped and tugged the tunics over their heads.

"Survive," Faith whispered under her breath and Morgan squared her shoulders.

Survive.

Chapter 3

Eighteen months earlier
November 9, 2035 (Earth calendar)
Delizas *(pleasure planet)*

Morgan adjusted her leotard after it rode up her ass crack...again. Royal blue cloth barely covered her nipples and groin over the sheath of glittering nude fabric holding it all together. *Damn Slovis, I swear he deliberately orders my clothes too small to irritate me. He took great pleasure in ordering me to attend to the high rollers in this latest costume. I'm glad he saw reason about the ridiculous headgear. I'd probably decapitate myself.*

She had a tolerate-hate relationship with her eight-foot-tall green owner. Instead of legs, six tentacles formed the Cephation's lower body, while two arms rested high on his torso and a single red eye sat above a fat nose. Fourteen months ago, he purchased all the humans on Krutus' ship to serve in his row of brothels on the pleasure planet Delizas.

The tolerate portion began early when Slovis ordered medical care, food, and decent clothes for everyone, as well as time to recuperate and adjust. He held a meeting and explained that each could earn their ownership papers by taking on various jobs and earning a percentage toward the cost of their purchase. All were sex slaves for the first *solar*, or year, for a smaller percentage initially. After that time, those willing to continue prostituting themselves earned a higher take than cleaners or waitstaff.

During their first two weeks of captivity, he encouraged them to speak with other slaves and understand what would be expected of them. Surprisingly, his establishments were clean, medical care mandatory, all slaves protected from significant harassment, and he eschewed regular use of pain collars. Fine golden chains replaced the bulky circles around their necks. While they still could be used to inflict pain, the levels were lower and Slovis rarely pushed that button. In fact, the only time she witnessed it was after a reptilian male slave attacked one of the females.

She and Faith asked lots of questions of the female slaves. Slovis provided birth control as well as lubricants for those who needed them, did not require them to perform sex acts that caused pain—unless the slave wanted it, and he refused all clients of species who killed after sex. Addictive mind-altering substances were prohibited. Anyone who hurt one of his slaves received retribution. If a slave performed well, he wouldn't sell them to a new owner unless the slave concurred. Compared to sex traffickers on Earth, Slovis treated his slaves like royalty. *And that gel he gives us has probably saved me from being split open—more than once.*

Fortunately, Morgan had piqued his interest after three months—*lunars*—when she told him he didn't think big enough. She and Faith informed him anyone could sell bodies, but only true visionaries could sell fantasies. His ego allowed them to manipulate him into a test of a new entertainment house where no slave was expected to sexually service the clients. They modeled the facility on the Manor House but bigger and grander. Morgan worked with Tarqel, Slovis' Ladortan assistant, to set up *Fantasia*, while Faith learned everything she could about the various species they could expect and what appealed to them beyond what their personal experiences had taught the women. Taking into consideration everything from food, liquor, and games of chance to what each found sexually arousing—colors, clothes, even scents, the women planned every aspect of the new establishment. *Anything to keep from having to sexually service anyone with credits.*

Being a slave constituted the hate portion of the relationship, as did being forced to have sex with random aliens. While some of the females used a non-habit-forming aphrodisiac provided by Slovis—for a price—to get through the prostitution, Morgan only used the lubricant gel and healing salve. Too many times she cried herself to sleep when a shift was over, sometimes even wondering why she tried so hard to survive.

She shuddered to think how many different beings they'd been made to service. The only exceptions she knew of were Orkites, Jalaxians, and Svesti males. From what she understood, they worshipped goddesses and using a slave for sex was an affront to their beliefs. There were other brothels on Delizas where females worked by choice and those males went there instead. *Oh, let's not forget arachnids and the insectoid and reptilian species who kill after sex. So glad we don't have to deal with them. The avian one who pecked at her hair was scary enough.*

At least we convinced Slovis about the credit-making opportunities of Fantasia. And we took a bunch of females and several males out of the brothel pool sooner rather than later. Now if I could just figure out how to keep him from auctioning me off every couple months for a night with his star performer. The extra credits toward freedom are not worth it, but his excuse that I didn't do my full solar is difficult to refute.

Morgan nodded at the Crestillians guarding the stairway to the performers' upper level. While VIP areas encompassed the second floor, the third floor contained dressing rooms and access to the floating discs. Not only humans staffed *Fantasia*. Faith found females of other species who wanted to dance, and Morgan trained them. They were also considering adding male performers one night a week. Cooks, waitstaff, bartenders, and cleaners of all sexes and species helped fill the needs of the establishment. Several could play instruments and sing. Reeva, a red-skinned Wrestikan, currently sat on the large center stage, her four hands caressing the keys of an instrument similar to a piano performing a bluesy-type number. *Damn, she's good.*

Unlike the Manor House, *Fantasia* had five circular floating discs, with the largest over the center stage. Currently, all of them sat at the third level with lights streaming down from their transparent floors, hiding Morgan and the others from the clientele. When the discs lowered, the lights would rotate upward to spotlight a female and change colors as a special effect.

Morgan removed the ridiculously high heels from her feet and scurried up the ladder to check the valadium hooks and support beams. Slowly sliding down the white material she'd found to replace Earth's aerial silks, she ended up in the middle of the largest disc and continued to examine, tug, and stretch the fabric looking for signs of wear and tear. Pulling the two lengths taut and lining up the carefully hidden marks in the fabric, she threaded them between her legs and around her waist before she raised her arms and slowly spun so both pieces of fabric covered her from thighs to underarms to the other hidden marks. Tapping the remote for the levitation modules adhered to the backs of her shoulders and her hips, she ensured they worked as designed. While confident in her preparations, the additional safety measure reassured here. *I certainly don't want to fall to my death for the opening number...or ever.*

She looked at the other discs and nodded to the females taking position. A lithe Praxite with lavender skin and three breasts, a small Pellotian with green skin and wings, a Crestillian with dark scaly skin and a short crocodile-like snout, and a blue Jalaxian with long black hair wore costumes similar to hers in varying colors although their nude leotard fabric matched their skin tones. The Praxite and the Jalaxian would dance around the poles on their discs, while the Pellotian and Crestillian would maneuver without poles in their spaces.

The music changed to an old Earth song with an alien undertone. Although she couldn't see through the lights, she knew a hidden track on the stage would be sliding to remove Reeva and her instrument from view and clear the area. While the lights on the other discs changed color and rotated upward to showcase the other females as their mini stages lowered, the ones on her discs dimmed to a soft glow. She took a deep breath, grabbed hold of her aerial silks and rotated so her body was airborne and parallel to the floor. She waited as her disc silently descended without her, the lights beginning their programmed routine, mimicking the music's tempo.

At her cue and the song's crescendo, Morgan let go of the silks and twisted her body to drop suddenly, unrolling from the silks to halt a mere foot from the floor with her body facing upwards and her hair brushing the disc. The levitation modules ensured she didn't hit the floor at high speed if the silks tore.

Seductively, she rotated and dropped to her hands and knees arching her back. Intentionally hiding and teasingly revealing her outfit, she unwrapped herself from the remaining fabric. Using her hands on the silks, she pulled herself up and began a complicated routine. She primarily used one length for support while the other tantalized the audience as she straddled it or slid it suggestively around her body.

Sweat formed on her brow as she exerted herself in time with the music. Her nose wrinkled when it registered Durelians and Frezzians in the audience. She kept a small smile on her face even as her costume rode up her ass again. She closed her eyes when the song changed to a slower beat and pretended she was back at the Manor House on Earth. For a brief time, she savored the illusion of freedom and choice.

The finale had her spreadeagled in the silks with them wrapped around her wrists and ankles. She held the position as the other discs rose before hers lifted to meet her body and she rested in an uncomfortable split. The tension in the silks relaxed. The lights focused on her and dimmed the higher she went. Breathing heavily and disengaging from the fabric when she was no longer visible to the audience, she pulled herself into a more comfortable position. She rapidly blinked to keep the sweat from her eyes. At the top, Faith waited with a towel.

Morgan smiled tiredly at her friend as she wiped her face and adjusted her leotard...again.

"You gave them their money's worth tonight, sweetie."

"Yeah, I love to serve." Morgan pursed her lips.

Faith's forehead wrinkled.

"Slovis sent me to tell you to put on a slinky dress after you clean up and meet him downstairs. It sounds like he's got a John for you."

"Dammit." Morgan's face hardened.

Faith shook her head.

"I tried to make the case that you're exhausted from training the dancers and choreographing routines for everyone, not to mention performing. We're making him credits hand over fist and he still wants more."

Morgan blew out a breath and tilted her head back as she stretched.

"I was hoping he'd lose interest. It's been almost three months since the last one."

"I feel guilty he's not pushing me to do the same."

"Don't. Don't feel guilty. If any of us can avoid it, it's a good thing, Faith. Besides, you're doing a phenomenal job running this place. You've got a gift for managing people. Fortunately, he sees that."

"How much longer until you earn your freedom?"

"At this rate, without the Johns, I estimate another decade or so." Morgan huffed in disgust. "Unfortunately, humans cost more because we're so fucking desirable as slaves. At least he's not taking offers right now."

"Better the devil we know." Faith waved her hand. "The whole situation sucks, but he's far from the worst owner we could have."

"I wish I could hate the slimy bastard more." Morgan grabbed her discarded shoes and walked barefoot toward the dressing room. She tossed the towel into a refresher and headed to the showers. *At least we designed it so we could have individual stalls.*

"Want me to pick something out while you get cleaned up?"

"If you have time, that would be great. Any idea of what species I'm meeting?"

"No, he was pretty tight-lipped."

Morgan sighed.

"I guess I'll be surprised."

Damn, I hate being a slave.

Morgan checked her appearance in the viewer. Her long auburn hair was in a messy bun and scattered curls framed the hard blue eyes in her tired face. A light dusting of glittery powder highlighted her cheekbones while raspberry-colored gloss stained her lips. Tiny hoop earrings shimmered above her gold slave collar. She centered the stone of the collar over her throat where there was a cleverly hidden panic button for if she felt her life was in danger. If a client attempted to strangle her, he would set it off unknowingly. She believed the panic buttons were installed more to protect her owner's investments rather than any serious concern about each of them as individuals.

She smoothed the strapless navy-blue cocktail dress over her hips. Somehow the clothing Slovis provided lifted and supported breasts comfortably. *Although, as usual, the material seems thinner over the nipples. Fucking pervert.*

Sheer stockings topped with white ruffled fake garters peeked out under the short hemline when she walked in another pair of skyscraper heels. Her small bag contained several capsules of the lubricating gel. She didn't know how it worked, but the small amounts expanded after insertion to provide copious amounts to protect her innards. Pulling out a small tube similar to a lipstick, she applied the unscented substance under her nose. *Whoever invented this smell-blocking shit was a genius. Puking on a John because of his body odor would probably not go over well.*

She sighed when she saw Tarqel appear behind her.

"I'm ready."

The Ladortan gestured for her to precede him to a hidden lift. They rode in silence to the second floor. He indicated she should turn right when the doors opened. Her heels tapped lightly on the tile. Then she waited outside Slovis' office until Tarqel nodded.

"Morgan, you look stunning as usual." Slovis' eye traversed her from head to toe.

"Thank you."

"You'll be entertaining two Svesti at their hotel this evening. They were quite interested in you. Upon your return in the morning and confirmation that they have no complaints, I will apply additional credits to your outstanding balance."

Morgan breath hitched.

"Two? All night?"

His red eye narrowed and two of his tentacles waved menacingly.

"Is there a problem?"

"Not exactly. You rarely allow any of us to leave your establishments, let alone in the company of multiple males. I've never serviced more than one at a time. Perhaps someone else would be better suited for these clients."

"They were very specific that you were the one they wanted. In fact, they questioned me about your ability to handle larger species."

Oh, that doesn't make me feel safe at all. Especially if they are Svesti going against their Goddess' teachings. Fuck.

"If I am working all night, I will be too tired to train the newer females tomorrow."

"That's fine. I'll ensure you have an adequate rest period. Tarqel will accompany you."

Morgan suppressed a sigh and gave a short nod. *At least Tarqel will remain nearby, just in case.*

After a short flitter ride to a nearby hotel, she waited silently next to the Ladortan as he activated the chime to the room. Morgan pasted a pleasant smile on her face, but when she saw the reddish bronze Svesti opening the door, her eyes widened slightly. *Holy shit, he's huge.*

The Svesti smiled gently revealing his white fangs.

"Lady Morgan. My name is Prixo Naxxar, and this is my colleague, Boriv Ristan. We thank you for attending this evening." Prixo motioned for them to enter. Morgan stepped over the threshold hoping she looked more confident than she felt. A drop of sweat trickled down her spine.

Tarqel held his position and stared at the Svesti males.

"I will be nearby. The female is not to be harmed."

Boriv, a golden bronze male with lavender eyes, bristled.

"We do not harm females. Ever."

"See that you don't." Tarqel dipped his chin at Morgan. "I will pick you up at first light."

"I'll be ready, Tarqel," Morgan said softly as the door closed.

"Please, Lady Morgan, have a seat. Would you like some refreshment?" Boriv gestured to a small table with four chairs. A variety of fruits and pastries, along with pitchers of juice and water, sat in the center.

She sat and dropped her bag on the table. The males took seats across from her. Prixo picked up a pitcher and poured liquid into a glass before holding it out to her.

"Water? Or would you prefer something else?"

Morgan took the glass and sniffed. *Smells fine.*

"I assure you, Lady Morgan, it is only water." Prixo poured himself some and drank.

She nodded and took a sip. Inhaling deeply, she decided to find out their expectations early.

"How is this going to work? One at a time? Both together? If so, how?'

Brown and lavender eyes widened in shock.

"No, no. We do not want to have sex, Lady Morgan." Boriv sat back and sighed. "We should have clarified that immediately."

"You don't? Then why am I here?" Her hand shook slightly.

"Prixo? Perhaps you can begin."

"What do you know about Svesti?"

"Only that you worship a Goddess, and I have never seen any of your kind in Slovis' establishments."

"We dislike slavery, and the thought of females being forced to attend to us sexually is deeply abhorrent. While we may meet our physical needs in erotica establishments, we only visit those where females choose the profession."

Morgan tilted her head.

"Then why me?"

Prixo sighed heavily.

"Almost three decades ago, the Zuvgran released a deadly virus on Costonia, our home world. It killed eighty percent of our females and those who survived are infertile. Our race will die out if we do not find a solution."

"I'm sorry to hear about your troubles."

Boriv leaned forward, resting his clasped hands together.

"Prixo and I are scientists. We have been visiting brothels all over Delizas gathering data in the hopes of finding compatible species. While we were aware humans existed, we had never met any and had limited data available to us. We heard Slovis owned human slaves and that led us to you."

"What do you want with me?" Silently, her foot tapped on the carpeting.

Prixo's cheeks darkened.

"At this point, mostly asking questions. Then, if the answers suggest further research, request blood and other samples."

She frowned and grabbed a pastry before relaxing.

"Ask your questions, but I reserve the right to refuse to respond."

Boriv withdrew a tablet from his pocket and began asking increasingly uncomfortable questions. Prixo took notes on his tablet. Morgan tried to be as honest as possible while she ate the food they provided. *Hell, they paid for the time, and as weird as this is, it's better than having to have sex on demand.*

When they finished, the males looked at each other. Prixo left the room briefly and returned with a small device.

"Would you be willing to provide a small DNA sample for us to test? It is painless."

"What are you looking for?"

"Several DNA strands that may indicate species compatibility. If it comes back negative, then we will know more comprehensive testing would be futile."

Morgan nodded and followed his instructions. The three of them sat in silence as they waited for the device to provide results. Again, their eyes widened and Boriv took out his comm.

A hologram of an older Svesti female with long silver hair appeared above the table.

"Naxxar. Ristan. How is your research coming along?"

"Lady Narilla, please allow us to introduce Lady Morgan of Earth. Lady Morgan, this is Lady Narilla Rivezt of House Yula."

"Lady Morgan, it is a pleasure to meet you."

"Uh, you as well, Lady Narilla." Morgan shifted in her chair.

"Lady Narilla is the Main Medical Advisor to the throne on Costonia."

The Svesti female looked down.

"I see the initial DNA results you transmitted. Interesting." She looked up her blue eyes lighting with excitement. "Lady Morgan, how would you like to visit Costonia?"

Morgan snorted. "I somehow doubt my owner will allow me a vacation."

"I will be honest. Your initial results are the most hopeful we've seen. If you would agree to further testing, it could be just the break we need."

"Again, my owner is unlikely to let me leave."

"If we purchased your contract, we could arrange for your transport."

"So, I would be your slave, and you could experiment on me as you like? I don't think so."

Lady Narilla shook her head, her hair glinting in the light.

"No, you misunderstand me. Svesti don't own slaves, and no testing would occur without your permission. Once you've left Delizas, we would register the paperwork to free you. In return, you help us with our research. Once it's complete, you may remain on Costonia, or you can choose to go to a colony elsewhere. We would give you enough credits to begin a new life of your choosing."

"How long are we talking about?"

"It's difficult to say, as we have not reached such a point before. I estimate a minimum of six *lunars* and hope we would have our answers within two *solars*."

"What if you discover humans are compatible? Will you be invading Earth and taking women?" Morgan crossed her arms.

"I've known King Sovex all his life. While I can't guarantee what he would ultimately decide, historically his preferred method of addressing issues is negotiation and consensus, not force and might."

"I need time to think about it."

"Of course. Naxxar, please provide Lady Morgan with a tablet with Svesti history for the past century, as well as general information, such as Costonian geography, customs, food, and similar things that she might find helpful in her determination."

"As you wish."

"Lady Morgan, I look forward to your decision."

"Wait. Could you purchase my other human friends, too?"

A sad look crossed the female's faded bronze features.

"Unfortunately, we cannot at this time. If we discover humans are compatible, then I can make the case to the King and Council that we should make efforts to retrieve any humans in danger, but without such assurances, I doubt I would be authorized the credits to do so."

"I understand." *I don't like it, but I get it.*

Chapter 4

Six weeks earlier
April 2, 2037 *(Earth calendar)*
Invictus *(Svesti space cruiser)*

Eating his morning meal in the dining area, Grulen enjoyed his *brellia*, a pastry filled with ground *maxiem* meat—*rumik*. Small bits of *lobile* with chopped spicy vegetables accompanied the *brellia*. The warriors around him spoke excitedly about the human females who boarded from Earth yesterday. Speculation about their species had been the main topic of conversation for lunars as the *Invictus* gathered data on the planet and the species from orbit. Commander Durek negotiated for six human females to accompany them back to Costonia for a Choosing at the King's Court.

Naroons. If there's going to be a Choosing for breeding or troth contracts, then that means it will be nobles, not lowly warriors who have a chance for young with these females.

He looked up when Lieutenant Brauvix, a bridge communications officer, escorted them into the dining area. He noted most seemed to be dressed in what he now knew to be pants called jeans and comfortable footwear and shirts. Part of him was amazed at the variety of shapes and sizes of the females. None of their skin tones were exactly the same and their hair and eyes were different. *I wonder if any would be interested in pleasure mating during the two lunars it will take us to return home.*

When Brauvix left them to gather food, Grulen stood and put the remains of his meal in the recycler. When they sat in the Svesti-sized chairs and laughed with each other. He smiled in amusement. *None of their feet can reach the floor. They're so small.*

"Females, may I introduce myself? My name is Grulen Jevax of House Midnar. Welcome aboard the *Invictus*. Your presence honors our warriors."

"Oh, my," said a female with darker skin, brown curly hair, and dark eyes. "It's nice to meet you, Mr. Jevax." She pointed to herself and each of the other females as she spoke. "I'm Emmy Norton. This is Talia Sullivan, Rachel Llewellyn, Lin Chang, Natasha Petrov, and Ava Taylor."

"Jevax," Brauvix growled as he approached with a large tray of foods. "Do not bother the females."

"Lieutenant Brauvix, I only introduced myself." Grulen widened his brown eyes. "I was unaware that I should not do so."

"Nothing untoward happened, Lieutenant. Mr. Jevax was just being friendly," Lady Talia said. She was an older female with pale skin, reddish-brown hair and brown eyes. She appeared more rounded than Lady Emmy who seemed wired with energy.

Brauvix nodded. "There are many nuances to Svesti behavior, Ambassador. It would be best to limit your interactions with the crew until you have been briefed or received an educational pack via the med bay." *Ambassador? So she's in charge?*

"Hmm," said the tall blond female with blue eyes. "Interesting. Have we accidentally agreed to something by exchanging names?" *That female has the alert readiness of a warrior about her.*

"Hardly, Lady Rachel," Grulen said. "I offer my services to teach any of you whatever you would like to know about Svesti males." He spread his arms, palms open, and grinned widely.

Lady Rachel looked at Lady Talia. "Did he just...?"

"Certainly sounded like it, but then, who knows?" Lady Talia shrugged.

"Jevax, enough! Do you not have duties this morning?" Brauvix stared at the other male.

"I am on my way, Lieutenant. Females, it was a pleasure to meet you." Grulen nodded and left, his tail swaying. He looked forward to learning more about the new females.

A couple days later, Grulen walked with Lady Rachel from the training area to the dining area. They saw the tiny one with short dark hair and eyes ahead of them in the corridor.

Lady Rachel called, "Lin. Wait up."

Lady Lin pivoted and waited for them.

Grulen grinned.

"Good day, Lady Lin. May we escort you to the dining area?"

"Thank you, Jevax. Hi, Rachel." Lady Lin gave them a small smile, but he scented her fear.

Grulen leveled a hard look at the other males. "Rovex, Sproid, Mantoor. You were not bothering Lady Lin, were you?"

Lerix Sproid met Grulen's stare.

"We just wanted to talk to her."

"About what?"

Klero Rovex growled. "None of your business."

Grulen crossed his arms.

"Do not pester the females." His nose twitched when Lady Lin's scent became even more acrid.

"We just wanted to ask if her small stature was common on her planet for grown females," Nerid Mantoor said placatingly. He nodded to Lady Lin. "Truly, we meant no harm."

Lady Rachel looked at the males.

"There are grown females even shorter than Lin, while there are others taller than me. Human females are all sorts of shapes and sizes."

Mantoor nodded. "Thank you."

Lady Rachel's eyes narrowed.

"Perhaps you should come to me if you have any questions in the future."

"As you wish," said Sproid, unsmiling. "Enjoy your midday meal." He and his friends continued.

Grulen gestured to the women to precede him.

"After you, ladies. Let's go see what culinary delights Previv has made for us this day." He lowered his voice and tilted his head downward. "I'm sorry you were uncomfortable, Lady Lin."

Lady Lin smiled and bobbed her head.

"I know I get frightened easily, Jevax. Unfortunately, I'm used to it."

Grulen frowned and his tail began to move in agitation.

"A female should never feel scared."

"Relax," said Lady Rachel with a smile. "There's no threat here."

"Let's just go eat, please," said Lady Lin.

Once they got their food, Grulen left them to sit with other Svesti, while Ladies Lin and Rachel headed to the table where Ladies Ava and Emmy were sitting.

After midday meal a couple days later, Grulen saw Ladies Talia and Emmy ahead of him in the corridor. His brow wrinkled when he realized they appeared inebriated. Concerned, he approached them.

"Ladies, are you okay?"

"No, we need to get to…" Lady Emmy looked at Lady Talia in confusion. "I forgot."

"Doctor." Lady Talia said. "My heart's beating too fasht."

"Your eyes look almost black, and your skin is pale and wet." Grulen put an arm around each female's waist. "Hold on to me. I'll get you to med bay."

The humans clumsily wrapped their arms around his neck as he lifted them off the floor and began running to the healers.

"Gonna be shtick," Lady Talia mumbled against his shoulder.

"Me, too." Lady Emmy's eyes closed, and her head bounced as she lost consciousness.

"Oh, Goddess, stay with me, ladies," Grulen said. Commander Durek strode toward them. *Thank the Goddess.*

"What is going on, Jevax?" Durek growled.

"I don't know. I'm trying to get them to the med bay."

"Vared." Lady Talia reached for the commander. "I think Emmy pashed out."

Durek grabbed her gently. "I'll help. Let's go, Jevax."

Grulen couldn't hear what she mumbled to the other male. *Vared? She calls him by his first name?*

They ran into the med bay, and the commander yelled, "Rivezt!" Lady Talia winced.

Rivezt and Lady Natasha rushed from the office. Lady Natasha spoke with Lady Talia as Durek settled the female on the bed. Grulen placed Lady Emmy on another med bed and Healer Rivezt began examining her.

Grulen said, "The ladies were stumbling in the corridor when I found them."

Rivezt and Lady Natasha spoke quietly. She said, "We'll need bloodwork, but it looks like they've been poisoned."

"Poisoned? How?" Durek said as he held Lady Talia's hand, and she closed her eyes.

"I don't know. But from their symptoms and our examinations, they appear to have anticholinergic syndrome. There's a plant on Earth that can induce it. It's called belladonna or nightshade. Maybe there's something onboard that has the same properties. It's rare. I wish I had access to the internet. I would like to look up successful treatment strategies."

Rivezt said, "We do have a copy of Earth's internet from when we left your world."

Lady Natasha's voice rose. "Really? Let me see." She tapped hurriedly on the tablet. "Here. These are the active components and various treatments."

"Let's start with this one." Rivezt pointed to something on the tablet. "As soon as we know the females are stable, I can cross check the plant's components against Svesti flora and see if we have something similar."

"How were they poisoned?" Durek growled.

"I don't know," Lady Natasha said. "As hard and as fast as they seem to be experiencing multiple symptoms would suggest they ingested it."

"Jevax. Locate the other females and bring them here. They may have eaten the same thing."

"As you will, Commander."

Following Durek's instructions, Grulen rushed to the aquiponics area.

"Lady Lin, are you alright?"

"Yes, Jevax. Why?" She stood from where she'd been kneeling.

"The Commander wishes all the human women to report to med bay."

Lady Lin dusted off her knees and gathered her belongings.

"What's wrong?"

"Something happened to Ladies Talia and Emmy. Both are very ill." Grulen's tail twitched.

"Not again. Let's go."

They stopped by the training area to get Lady Rachel. Then they found Lady Ava in the kitchen with Talen Previv, the head cook. When they arrived at the med bay, Durek and Tolvex were already there. Durek sent Grulen back to work.

Is some of our food toxic to humans? No Svesti would knowingly poison females, would they? Not after so many of ours died so painfully.

Present Day
April 15, 2037 *(Earth calendar)*
Invictus *(Svesti space cruiser)*

Grulen was pleased to see all the human females looking healthy and hearty after the poisoning a week ago. He boarded the shuttle after them and stopped by the cockpit to greet Gal'n Kalix and Brestov Xoriv, two security team pilots. As the *Invictus* needed to resupply at Theron, a space station, before continuing on its way to Costonia, Commander Durek assigned a group of warriors to provide protection for the females so they could shop and see more than the space cruiser. *It is an honor to be part of this detail.*

Lieutenant Devik Tolvex, the head security officer, along with Durek, Wurvez, Rivezt, and Brauvix were already onboard. Previv and their supply master, Leriv Volax, joined them to purchase the needed supplies.

At Theron, Grulen bit the inside of his cheek to keep from grinning at the females' wonder and awe as they took in their first alien space station. He almost laughed at Lady Rachel's unfettered joy in the weapons shop. *Watching her train the others daily in self-defense has been illuminating. She is a true warrior at heart.*

His tail swayed as he watched Durek and Lady Talia interact. Earlier Grulen noted traces of the commander's scent on Lady Talia. *They appear to be bonding over a hair comb. I wonder if they are becoming closer than others realize.*

Then they entered a spice shop and Lady Ava chattered with the four-armed purple owner. She and Previv ordered a lot of items to be delivered to the shuttle. The fabric shop interested all the humans, but Lady Natasha ordered additional items beyond cloth. Lady Emmy had much to ask in the tech shop.

While Grulen liked all of the females, none of them ignited any emotion beyond friendship and camaraderie within him. Listening to them as they debated pros and cons of different items or laughed at each other's observations reminded him of his sisters. He rubbed his chest. *It's been too long since I've felt this type of contentment.*

Lady Lin asked if they could look at stalls for a bit. Observing Tolvex's discreet hand gestures, Grulen remained with him, Rivezt, and Ladies Lin, Emmy, and Natasha as the group split up to wander. Their group stopped at a fabric stall, while everyone else except Durek and Lady Talia discussed food at another stall. Those two looked at jewelry. *Hmm. More adornments. And Tolvex seems very protective of Lady Emmy. Interesting. Are the senior officers pairing off with the females?*

Grulen's head whipped up and his hand went to one of his knives when he heard Lady Talia scream. A Durelian had her over his shoulder and she was pounding on his back with her fist. Five additional Durelians trailed the pair.

Then more of the orange aliens attacked their group. He yelled for the females to get behind the warriors. When one grabbed Lady Emmy's wrist, he struck the male and knocked him out. He and the other warriors continued to fight off their assailants to keep the humans safe.

When it was quiet again, Wurvez ordered them to the shuttle. He joined the other males in surrounding the females while they rushed back to the docking area. On the shuttle's lowered ramp, Xoriv was standing with a blaster. Loaded maglevs were at the bottom.

As they approached, Xoriv said, "Kalix has the shuttle started. I stopped loading the supplies when I heard the Commander's orders."

Wurvez said, "Ladies, please go in and get ready to leave. Rivezt, go with them and heal the females. Tolvex and Jevax, keep watch with Xoriv. The rest of us will load the shuttle quickly." He looked at Xoriv. "Are we expecting any more deliveries?"

Drawing his blaster from its holster, Grulen took a ready stance at the bottom of the loading ramp and scanned the area. Tolvex did the same.

Shaking his head, shaved except for a center strip of braided hair, Xoriv said, "Not that I'm aware. Previv and Volax would know better."

"I'll go check what's already loaded for food stores," Previv said.

Volax was running toward the shuttle. "I got here as fast as I could, Lieutenant."

"Determine whether all the deliveries were made. If not, arrange for them to be delivered in an hour and a half. I'll have the *Invictus* send another shuttle to pick anything up, so we can get the females back to the cruiser now." Karid nodded at Volax.

"As you will, Lieutenant." Volax jogged toward the cargo bay.

Wurvez ordered them into the shuttle as soon as he received confirmation that anything purchased had been delivered or rescheduled. Grulen's nostrils flared when the acrid scent of the females' residual fear surrounded him.

"It was us or them, Emmy. It was necessary," Lady Rachel said.

"I know, but it doesn't make the feelings go away."

"At least you did something. I was terrified and useless."

"Lady Lin, you did as we instructed, even if you were scared. That helped," Grulen said gently.

The tiny female scoffed.

"Jevax tells the truth. And you warned us when there were more Durelians behind us," Rivezt said with a smile.

"How does me following instructions help you?"

Rachel said, "Because they knew where you were at all times, Lin. They did not have to worry about inadvertently hurting you as they fought. They did not have to split their focus. And they had confidence that if they needed you to move, run or whatever else, they could expect you to do so. When you are guarding someone, being able to predict their movements is gold."

All the Svesti nodded.

"Lady Rachel explains it well," said Grulen. He leaned back and closed his eyes. He listened to the conversations and the updates that Durek was following Lady Talia. *I almost feel sorry for those Durelians. When the commander catches up with them, his anger will know no bounds.*

Chapter 5

Present Day
April 15, 2037 *(Earth calendar)*
Secret Zuvgran lab on XB9428B

"It didn't work."

The two Zuvgran scientists conferred as they reviewed the latest test results. The older male, whom Morgan designated Primo Asshole in her thoughts, pounded his gray fist on the table.

"We're close, but we can't use this specimen any longer. What we've already given her will interfere with the updated version."

His younger colleague, Buttlicker, said, "You're brilliant."

"Of course I am."

Morgan rolled her eyes at Primo Asshole's conceit. Wearing a thin dingy tunic, she was currently restrained on a medical exam table, unable to even move her head. *Another day, another freezing room, another injection, another day as a goddamn lab rat. Fuck my life.*

While the two Zuvgran ignored her, she dove into her memories of leaving the Svesti home world almost six months ago. *I think it was the last time I was truly warm.*

"Are you sure you won't remain on Costonia?"

Morgan smiled and shook her head at Lady Narilla's question.

"No, although I may return. I can't believe it's been almost a year to the day since I first met you." She hugged the older Svesti female who had become her friend. "Now that you know humans and Svesti are compatible, it wouldn't be fair to stay around your males when I'm not ready for any type of commitment. I need time to determine what I want for my future."

"Now that we know, Lady Morgan, I want to contact Earth and begin negotiations to bring human females here. And I will convince the Council to purchase what human slaves we can and relocate them here or to the same colony you travel to." King Traxen Sovex's jaw hardened. "They will require time to heal from their captivity."

"I would appreciate that. Just be aware that first contact with Earth might be...contentious."

He tilted his head and narrowed his lavender eyes.

"How do you mean?"

"Humans, especially those in power, tend to have an inflated sense of their own superiority. Many will not believe in alien life, while others will see taking what you have as their due. It's not all humans. Most will be shocked but give you a chance. But others might try to capture your people and not treat them kindly. They might even experiment on them."

Sovex's tail flicked sharply.

"Like the Zuvgran do?"

"As much as I hate to admit it, the possibility exists."

He inclined his head.

"I thank you for your warning."

She shook his hand and took one last look around the spaceport outside of Trezoura, Costonia's capital city.

"You have a beautiful planet. I really enjoyed my time here."

"We cannot thank you enough for all your help with our research." Lady Narilla's tail swayed. "I will miss you and our daily conversations."

"You will always be welcome here, Lady Morgan. You have given us hope for our future." The king bowed to her.

Morgan's face flushed.

"I'm nobody special, King Sovex. I just did what I thought was right for beings who earned my trust."

"We are honored." He paused as a male approached. "It looks like your shuttle is here and ready for you. It will take you to meet the transport going to the colony on Bralia."

She hugged Lady Narilla again and picked up her bag.

"Wish me luck."

"Good luck, Lady Morgan. You have your comm. Please stay in touch and let us know if you need anything."

"I will."

As her shuttle rose from the planet, Morgan watched as Costonia grew smaller in the viewer. The blues of the leaves and grass interspersed with the colorful tree trunks and flora gradually became a blur of land masses under a periwinkle sky.

She sighed and closed her eyes. *Once the Svesti make first contact, I could probably return to Earth. I'm not sure I should after everything that's happened. I'm not even close to the same person I was now that I know all this is out here. Even if I don't go back, I'll find a way to let Sophia know I'm safe.*

Four days after she boarded the colony transport, the Zuvgran attacked. Survivors were taken as slaves, while Morgan and the two other human women, Kiki and Colleen, became fodder for the scientists' testing of viruses to kill their fertility. The only positive so far is that the scientists told the warriors the humans were off limits for sex since they didn't want them broken. *We're wasting away from being pincushions and lack of decent food.*

Morgan's attention snapped back to Primo Asshole when he said, "The human females are of no use to us now. Another is arriving soon for testing. Tomorrow, we'll move the three we've got to the barracks and the warriors can have them."

Fuck. This is not good.

Morgan's breath caught in her chest when the Zuvgran threw her onto the cot, and she scrambled not to collapse. The guard turned and left her without a word. She hung her head in relief.

"Are you okay?" Kiki whispered raggedly, raising a tired hand as if to reach for Morgan. Blue veins visible under her too pale skin pulsed weakly.

"Yes, but the scientists plan on giving us to the warriors tomorrow."

Colleen whimpered from her cot. She limply turned her head away.

"I almost look forward to it. A quick painful death fighting, rather than this excruciatingly slow one." Morgan wrapped her arms around her knees.

"We're almost dead as it is. I guess it doesn't matter anymore." Kiki coughed uncontrollably, blood spattering her hand.

Morgan rose, her muscles aching, and retrieved water pouches for the other women and a piece of cloth for Kiki. She dampened the fabric and carefully cleaned up the evidence of internal bleeding. Then she held Kiki up to sip the water. After smoothing Kiki's greasy hair back from her brow, Morgan hobbled to Colleen to give her fluids as well. She held the terrified woman's hand, feeling the bones too close to the surface. *They're dying. I wish I had the courage to end it for them before the warriors come for us. I should have stayed on Costonia.*

"Tell us a story, Morgan." Kiki's voice drifted in the air.

"What kind of story?"

"Doesn't matter. You choose."

Morgan sat on the floor between the two women, holding a hand of each one. Quietly, she told tales of her mother before the cancer took her and the little ways she made life fun without a lot of extra money. Like the time they went to a petting zoo and a camel gnawed at her mom's hair. Instead of screeching, her mom made funny faces and had Morgan take pictures of her hair being stretched by the animal's mouth. Labored giggles from Kiki and Colleen turned to restless sleep the longer Morgan talked until eventually, both women became still and cold.

Morgan cried silent tears and sent prayers into the universe that Kiki and Colleen's souls truly went to a better place where they could be happy and whole. Sniffling, she stiffened when she heard a noise outside their cell. She wiped her forearm across her nose and shakily stood. Rustling, then an electronic noise preceded the door opening. Her eyes widened as she looked at two Jalaxians, both with dark hair. The one with a ponytail knelt to check on Kiki and Colleen. He closed his eyes and bowed his head before looking at the other and shaking his head sadly. He was larger than the one kneeling and held two fingers to his ear.

"Human female, I am sorry about your companions. I am Makai. My team is here to rescue you. Do you know if you are infected with the virus?"

Morgan shook her head.

"They were upset it didn't work on me. They said another human female was coming and they would test on her."

Makai grunted. "We found three human women, but two are already dead. The other says the scientists were angry that whatever they injected her with didn't work. Let me ask her what she wants to do."

"Who are you talking to?"

"A Svesti who came to rescue the most recent female. He says she's been injected with the new virus, and they will quarantine until they know it's safe. They have offered to take you with them. Or you may come with us. Either way, you will receive medical care and food until you decide where you wish to go."

"I won't be a slave? Or expected to service any of you sexually?"

"Absolutely not." Makai and the other Jalaxian growled, their tails whipping behind them. "There are other human women on our ship."

Morgan chewed her lip.

"What do they do?"

"One is a tech wizard, another helps in medical, while the third is a pilot," the ponytail one said. "I'm Tren. We try to help human females whenever we can."

"I'll want to earn my keep." *Geez, Morgan, really? Just get the hell out of here while you can. Almost anything is better than being a plaything for the Zuvgran.*

"We can discuss that after you're safe," Makai said.

Taking a deep breath, she said, "I'll go with you."

Makai nodded. "Durek, the human wishes to go with us for now." He listened, then said, "Rain, hover close enough for us to get to you with the jetpacks. Wing Raiders, meet back at our ship. Durek, let me know when you're clear of the planet. Kara, has Grolo attempted contact with the base yet?"

Tren gently grasped one of her arms.

"We need to go...now."

Morgan stepped forward with them, ready to move on...and survive.

"Check for previous exchanges between the two. I have a plan, but everyone needs to be out of here first." Makai gestured for them to follow him.

In her bare feet, she did her best to keep up with the males, but after the months of Zuvgran experimentation and treatment, her stamina suffered.

"May I carry you, human?" Tren asked respectfully.

Her shoulders tightened, but common sense reared its head.

"Okay. My name is Morgan." She let out a gasp as he scooped her up in a bridal carry and the Jalaxians ran. *Obviously, I was holding them back.*

Tren cocked his head listening to someone in his ear, then said, "It should, but I haven't tested it yet."

Makai veered to the right. He stopped in front of a ventilation shaft and looked at Tren.

"You have something that will keep them asleep?"

"Of course I do." Tren put Morgan down. "Just a moment while I take care of this."

Makai's lips tipped up. Tren grabbed some canisters from his pockets and tapped several buttons before placing them in the shaft. He picked up Morgan again and they ran.

"How long?"

"Six minutes before the gas releases."

They caught up with two other Jalaxians—one with dreadlocks, the other with braids.

"Yaz and Lezon." Tren tilted his head at the two new ones. They reached a huge hangar bay. "Hold on, Morgan."

Morgan almost screamed as they rose into the air without warning. Tren weaved a bit before straightening out.

"Sorry about that. First time using the hover jetpack carrying someone. It threw off my center of gravity."

Morgan held on and nodded. *Holy fuck, this is scary.*

Ahead in the air, a large door opened and the Jalaxians aimed for it. Morgan squinted and noticed a slight disruption in her vision. *It must be a cloaked ship. For a minute, I was reminded of the Cheshire cat's smile surrounded by nothingness.*

A huge, scary-looking Jalaxian with his head partially shaved waited for them. Once they safely landed inside the cargo area, he closed the door.

"Lezon, escort Morgan to the med bay. You and Abby treat her and let me know what she may need. The rest of you on the bridge with me." Makai hustled off, his tail swaying, the others following him.

Morgan walked with Lezon in the other direction. Sleek doors opened and they stepped into a med bay. She looked with critical eyes. After spending so much time with the healers on Costonia, she recognized quality equipment. *Whoever these Jalaxians are, they didn't stint on their med bay.*

"Welcome to the *Fortitude*, home of the Wing Raiders. I'm Abby Quinlan. I was a nurse practitioner on Earth and Lezon here is our medical officer." A brunette with soft brown eyes held out her hand.

Exchanging handshakes, Morgan smiled.

"Morgan Calloway. Teacher, former exotic dancer, slave, and test subject."

"Wow, definitely some stories there I bet. Let's get you checked out. Then you can clean up and eat."

"Could I shower first? The Zuvgran weren't very hygienic when it came to their prisoners."

Abby looked at Lezon who smiled and nodded.

"Why don't you see if you can find something for Morgan to wear after she cleans up. I'll stay with her," Abby said.

"I'll check the stores and return soon."

Abby led her to the bathroom in a corner of the med bay. She ensured Morgan knew how to operate the sonic shower and gave her some towels.

"I'll be in the office. If you need any help, just yell. I'll knock to let you know when the clothing is here."

"Thanks."

After the door closed behind Abby, Morgan peeled off the tunic and tossed it aside. *I'm never wearing that again.*

In the shower, the sonic vibrations tingled. Morgan moaned at the sensation of dirt and grime leaving her hair and body. *It's been so long since I've felt clean. I wish it was hot water, but I'll take what I can get. Beggars can't be choosers.*

She hiccupped back a sob and rested her head on the wall, taking measured breaths. *Poor Kiki and Colleen. I wish they could have held on long enough to be rescued, too.*

Hearing a knock, she watched warily when the door opened, and a pile of clothing slid into the room. The door closed and she was alone again. *Get it together, Morgan. Figure out what's going on and make a plan. Survive.*

Eventually, she stepped out of the shower and picked up the clothes. She grimaced when she saw the bandeau bra and panties knowing Lezon had picked them out. *Another male choosing my clothes.*

Realizing she was being petty, and she really didn't want to wear a medical gown, she sighed and pulled on a soft T-shirt, leggings, socks, and slippers. She found a comb and worked to get the snarls out of her long hair. Braiding it, she used a string in the same compartment as the comb. Popping a tooth-cleansing tablet onto her tongue, she savored the minty taste and the sensation of a pristine mouth once again. *Damn, I almost feel like a human being.*

She inhaled deeply, then squared her shoulders before leaving the bathroom. Both Abby and Lezon smiled when they saw her.

"You look like you feel better," the brunette said.

"It's amazing what feeling clean can do for you."

"Hop onto the med bed and let's see if you need anything specific." Lezon gestured to a table.

Morgan ignored the internal wince at the thought of an examination. Her breathing sped up.

"No one is going to hurt you or do anything you don't want, Morgan." Lezon's sky blue eyes showed compassion. "We just want to make sure the Zuvgran didn't do any permanent harm."

Abby patted Morgan's arm.

"Just lie down and let the med bed scan you. There is no invasive portion of the exam and it's painless."

"No restraints?" The hesitancy in her voice shamed Morgan.

Abby's nose wrinkled in disgust. A low growl emanated from Lezon's chest, and his tail flicked.

"No, no restraints. If you move too quickly, it might interrupt the scanner and skew the readings, but that's the worst that can happen." Lezon's tail slowed.

Morgan let Abby help her into position. A soft green light shimmered around her. Lezon tapped a control at the side of the bed and a hologram appeared above her, but she couldn't read it from her position. Several minutes passed, then the light winked out.

"You can sit up now." Abby raised the head of the med bed.

"It looks like you're malnourished and dehydrated. Several contusions, but no breaks. With your permission, I'd like Abby to draw some blood and obtain some DNA so we can run some other tests to see what any potential long-term effects of the Zuvgran's experimentation might mean for you," Lezon said.

"Okay."

"After Abby is finished taking the samples, she'll take you to the cafeteria to eat. I'm going to prescribe a daily nutritional supplement and a salve to help your body heal. We'll scan you weekly in case we need to adjust the supplement until everything is balanced as it should be. Hopefully, the samples won't indicate any other necessary treatment for you." Lezon's fangs peeked out as he smiled at her.

"Is there anyone we should contact to let them know you are here?" Abby tilted her head and gently rubbed the top of Morgan's hand.

"I need time to process before anything else. Is that okay?"

"Whatever you want, Morgan. I believe Captain Makai will offer you options to stay with us or take you to a settlement or colony if you would prefer that. Right now, I see no reason for you to rush to a decision."

"What are Wing Raiders? Abby said something about that when we met."

"We're mercenaries."

Morgan's lips pulled tightly together. Abby interrupted.

"They're the good kind. They rescue beings, provide security, although admittedly sometimes they also spy."

"Nothing illegal or immoral?"

"Immoral, no. Sometimes we skirt the boundaries of legal." Lezon chuckled.

"Okay."

"Let's get you something to eat, then we'll set you up in your own quarters. If they're done on the bridge, maybe you can meet everyone else before you rest." Abby lowered the med bed and Morgan hopped off.

"Food sounds wonderful." *Anything has to be better than the slop the Zuvgran gave us.*

Chapter 6

The next evening, Grulen approached the females in the dining area.

"Ladies, I understand Commander Durek rescued Lady Talia earlier." He looked at their group. "How is she feeling? Is she resting in her quarters?"

"Jevax," Lady Rachel said. "Sit with us."

"Talia isn't onboard," said Lady Lin with a trembling lip. "She's recuperating on a shuttle with the Commander."

"Recuperating? Was she hurt?"

"We're not sure what happened," Lady Emmy said. "I think she's suffering from PTSD."

"PTSD?"

"Post-Traumatic Stress Disorder," said Lady Natasha. "It's common for humans to suffer heightened stress responses after traumatic events. Nightmares, anxiety, moodiness, depression, and an inability to sleep are several possible symptoms."

Lady Rachel added, "Right now, it sounds like Talia is experiencing increased anxiety near crowds, especially after being poisoned on the ship."

"Is there anything we can do to help her?" A growl left his chest.

Lady Ava shook her head. "She needs to cope in her own way for now, Jevax. Everyone deals with trauma differently."

"Would you pass along my well wishes for her recovery?"

"Of course," Lady Lin said with a small smile.

Grulen stepped back as others approached and helped move furniture so that Lady Emmy could take a picture of the warriors for something called a get well card for Lady Talia. Afterwards, he slowly walked back to his quarters with a frown. *I hope Lady Talia heals soon.*

A few weeks later, Grulen found it difficult to concentrate on his training forms. Despite the peaceful scents, sounds, and sights of the aquiponics area, his mind spun about the recent attack against Commander Durek while on the *Intrepid* where he had been staying with Lady Talia.

He saw Lady Lin kneeling in one area working on some plants. Due to her Earth job as a botanist, she spent much of her time studying Costonian flora and comparing them to those of her planet. Lady Emmy jogged along the gravel path circling the aquiponics area several time. His tail stiffened when he heard a shrill screech of distress from a female, and he ran toward the sound. He found Lady Emmy on the ground and squatted next to her.

"Lady Emmy, I heard you scream. Are you okay?" He gestured to the metal sticking out of her legs. "What are those?"

"I don't know, but don't touch them. I already comm'd Tolvex to come with a healer."

"Stay still, Lady Emmy. There are more on your back." *Where did these come from?*

"Emmy? What happened?" Lady Lin approached from the opposite direction.

"Stop, Lin! I think there's a tripwire on the path. Be careful where you step," Lady Emmy said.

"What?" Lady Lin's footsteps slowed.

Grulen's eyes traced the wire. His thighs bunched as he stood and carefully placed his feet as he searched for the trap. He squatted again and pushed aside some leaves before finding the end.

"I see one side. Some of the needles are still embedded in the source."

Pounding boots on gravel sounded behind Lady Lin.

"Slowly. There's a tripwire that shoots something from it," Grulen said to Tolvex, who immediately checked his speed.

"I see it," said Tolvex angrily. Moments later, he knelt next to Lady Emmy. "Are you alright, *milara*?" His chest rumbled and his tail swished.

Grulen's nose twitched as he caught their combined scent. *Ah, those two are pleasure mating.*

"I might've twisted my ankle, but I've got these things sticking out of me," she said quickly.

Rivezt crouched on her other side and pulled an instrument from his pouch.

"Don't move. Let me scan you first and get these out of you."

"Good plan." Lady Emmy grimaced.

"Do they hurt?"

"They sting like paper cuts...a whole crapload of them."

"I need a sterile container to collect these to ensure they weren't coated with anything." Rivezt looked up at them. Grulen's nostrils flared. *Hmm, he and Lady Lin as well?*

"I'll be right back with my bag." Lady Lin ran off quickly.

"Your right ankle is sprained, but not broken," Rivezt said after he scanned her body. He pulled something that looked like long curved tweezers out of his med kit.

"Here. I have collection bottles in different sizes. Which do you need?" Lady Lin asked breathlessly.

Rivezt used the tweezers to pull out a needle and hold it up.

"Do you have one that can hold something this long?"

"Yes." Lady Lin rustled in her bag and held out a bottle. Rivezt dropped a bloody needle tipped in blood into it with a tinny clink.

"Lady Lin, if you could hold the bottle while I remove the remainder, it would help."

"Of course." Lady Lin knelt next to Lady Emmy and gently touched her hand. "How are you doing?"

"Fine. Just uncomfortable."

"This shouldn't take long." Rivezt continued to remove the needles with the forceps.

"Lieutenant," Grulen said from where he was still crouched. "Assuming the configuration was the same as what is left on this, twenty-seven needles were released from here."

Tolvex checked out what Grulen had found and took images before moving to the other side of the path. He growled when he found a similar thing there.

"We're looking for a total of fifty-four needles."

"I've removed fifteen so far," said Rivezt. "I do not think all of them impacted Lady Emmy."

"I see some on the gravel." Lady Lin pointed.

"Don't touch them with your bare hands. We don't know if they're safe to touch," Tolvex warned.

"Was it a tripwire?" Lady Emmy asked.

"Yes."

After Rivezt finished removing a total of thirty-three needles from Lady Emmy, Grulen helped Tolvex and Lady Lin find the remaining ones either on the gravel or embedded in nearby plants. Lady Lin put on gloves and gently removed impacted plants and placed them in other collection containers. She took off her gloves, leaving them inside out, and put them in her bag.

Lady Emmy sat up and Rivezt treated her scrapes and ankle. Tolvex used some of Rivezt's sealant on his hands, then detached the tripwire at both ends and put it in another container.

"Tolvex, does it seem to you that there have been too many incidents involving the human females? I think someone is trying to harm them." Grulen's tail flicked in short movements.

Tolvex nodded. "It appears that way. We're investigating." He leveled a stare at the male. "Do not speak of this to anyone, Jevax. We have our reasons for not making it widely known."

"As you command, Lieutenant. If you need any assistance, I am happy to volunteer. I do not like knowing someone is trying to hurt females." An angry rumble emanated from Grulen's chest.

"I'll inform the commander," said Tolvex.

"Uh, about that. I'd rather Talia didn't know about this, Devik," Lady Emmy said.

"Why not?"

"She and the commander have had a couple of rough days, and he was just released from the med bay. I really don't want to cause her any more stress right now." Lady Emmy frowned. "They've been through a lot recently."

"I'll brief Wurvez and let him know your concerns."

"Let's get you back to the med bay, Lady Emmy, so I can treat you properly," Rivezt said.

"I'm not sure I can walk."

"Hold on to me," Tolvex said as he picked her up. "Jevax, check the remainder of the path to ensure there aren't any more traps."

"If I find anything, I will notify you." Grulen appreciated the task to ensure the females' safety. He began searching as the others departed for the med bay. *It doesn't make sense to me that someone, especially a Svesti, would hurt the humans.*

"Jevax!"

Grulen lifted his head and turned toward his team lead.

"Yes, sir."

"Grab your go bag and meet Lieutenant Tolvex in Hangar Bay Alpha. You are on special assignment for the foreseeable future."

"What is my assignment?"

"I don't know. I assume the Lieutenant will brief you. You are expected there within the hour."

"On my way."

Grulen met Lieutenant Wurvez, who also had a bag, leaving the lift. They strode in silence to the hangar bay where Tolvex awaited them. *An assignment with our head tactical officer. This might be fun. But there's only two of us.*

"Here's a list of what I put onboard the *Tenacity* in addition to what is normally stocked," Tolvex said as he forwarded the info to their comms. "The commander has also ordered emergency trackers for each of you." He held up two syringes.

Wurvez frowned. "We can inject them when we're on our way."

"No, not taking the chance you'll disobey orders." Tolvex shook his head.

Wurvez grunted. He opened his mouth wide and Tolvex injected the tracker underneath his tongue. Wurvez looked disgusted and moved his jaw in exaggerated circular motions.

"I hate these things. They make me feel like I've got a pebble in my mouth."

Grulen's laugh mixed with Tolvex's, and he opened his mouth without comment for his tracker. *Wurvez is right; the sensation of something hard under the tongue is uncomfortable.*

"These are the upgraded trackers. We received a lot of complaints about the heat from the old ones as well as the fact that it was too easy to inadvertently activate them with the shorter codes. The activation code for these is clicking your teeth in a three-two-two pattern or tapping it directly with a claw in the same pattern. You should feel a minute of cold under your tongue to let you know the activation was successful. Inactivated, they should pass any frequency scan for trackers," Tolvex explained.

"With the Goddess' favor, we won't need them," said Grulen.

Tolvex nodded and stepped back. "Let me know when you finish your preflight checks and I'll open the bay doors. The engine signature you're following is already loaded in the *Tenacity's* computer. Stay safe and good hunting."

Grulen and Wurvez boarded the shuttle, stowed their bags, and headed to the cockpit. The lieutenant motioned for Grulen to take the pilot's seat. Grulen ran his preflight checks, then requested clearance to depart. Once the *Tenacity* left the *Invictus*, Grulen entered a course to the last known location of the engine signature and sat back.

"Lieutenant Tolvex said you would brief me on our mission."

"There is at least one traitor onboard the *Invictus* working with a noble from the home world to sabotage the king's efforts of a treaty with the humans. Healer Rivezt needed to put Lady Talia into an induced coma when someone switched out one of the uploads for the females. You know about Lady Talia and Lady Emmy being poisoned and Lady Emmy's experience with the tripwire. When they kidnapped Lady Talia on Theron, they injected her with a virus that kills human female and Svesti male fertility."

"So that's why she and the Commander sequestered themselves on the *Intrepid*. Not PTSD like we were told." Grulen's jaw hardened.

"Yes. While they were there, the traitor attempted to port Lady Talia to the *Invictus*, then the other human females to the *Intrepid*, as well as used mind control on Mantoor to have him attack Commander Durek. We believe the traitor wanted to infect the other human females. Fortunately, Rivezt developed a vaccine with the aid of Ladies Natasha and Lin and inoculated everyone onboard."

"The one we were told was for a flu virus." Grulen's forehead furrowed. "But why would the traitors work to kill Svesti male fertility?"

"We believe the traitors are unaware of that aspect of the virus. It seems the noble made some sort of deal with the Zuvgran for the virus."

"Have there been other incidents?"

"Yes. Lady Lin almost fell from a sabotaged ladder in aquiponics and was also gassed in her lab. We suspect the oven explosion was meant for Lady Ava. Fortunately, she wasn't in the kitchen at the time."

"How can any Svesti try to harm females?" Grulen growled and his tail whipped furiously behind him. "Or work with the Zuvgran?"

"I don't know, Jevax." Wurvez sighed. "The engine signature is for a Frezzian freighter we believe has been visiting Zuvgran labs with supplies."

"Do we think the Frezzians are working with the traitors?"

Wurvez's ponytail brushed his shoulders as he shook his head.

"It's possible, but I doubt it. It's more likely the Frezzians are just dropping off food for the Zuvgran."

"I'm not sure I see the connection between the freighter and the traitors."

"We suspected these Frezzians supplied the lab on XB9428B before the Durelians delivered Lady Talia to the Zuvgran lab there. The scientists who injected her made comments about a Svesti noble working with them. The freighter may only lead us to other labs, but we can't discount the possibility we may find additional information about the traitors. Either way, we increase our knowledge."

"What are our orders when we find the Frezzians?"

"Follow them discreetly and attempt to get into their computers. If we aren't able to gather sufficient intel that way, then we can always capture one of them and interrogate them."

Grulen nodded, then tapped the console. "We're automatically scanning for the engine signature, and I've set it to alert us throughout the ship if we find it before we reach its last known position."

"How long until we get there?"

"Seven hours."

Wurvez released his safety restraints and stood.

"Let's go check where Devik stowed everything."

"As you command."

Grulen looked out into space from his cockpit seat during his twelve-hour shift. *Wurvez should be showing up soon for our four-hour overlap. Speak of the irrepressible male. Here he is.*

Wurvez dropped snacks and water pouches on the console. Grulen grabbed a water pouch and some green crackers.

"Thanks. I can always count on you to have food." Grulen grinned.

"We're growing males. Need to keep us fueled." Wurvez waggled his eyebrows. "Anything new?"

"It's taken us five days, but we are finally receiving a constant signal from the freighter's engine signature." Grulen tapped the console, and a holographic image appeared above it. "See?"

Wurvez perused the map and the location of the freighter.

"It appears it's going to Praxis. How long until we catch up?"

"I'd say less than a day and we'll be in a good position to follow it cloaked."

"Excellent. I was afraid I'd have an eternity with only you for company."

"That would've been a fate worse than death." Grulen leered.

"Not quite that bad." Wurvez sat back and nibbled on a cracker. "Why have you never moved up in the ranks? You're more than capable of leading your own team, Jevax."

"I'm happy as I am."

"Perhaps a change to security would suit you. You have an excellent cross-section of skills that would work to your advantage. Devik mentioned he may need to form additional teams to protect the females."

"Why the interest in my career?"

"You're a good male with a great deal of the competence and experience preferred in the higher ranks." Wurvez laughed. "Besides, I'm bored, and you're the only one here to annoy."

"Perhaps I should channel the Commander and spar with you to make my case."

Wurvez slapped Grulen's shoulder.

"See? That's what I mean. If Durek can become commander of our flagship, you certainly can aspire higher."

"Respectfully, sir, you are a *naroon*." Grulen laughed and tossed a water pouch at Karid.

"Honesty—another admirable trait for an officer to have. You just keep proving me right."

Chapter 7

The next day, the *Tenacity* entered a cloaked high orbit over the Zuvgran-controlled planet Praxis. Their scans indicated the freighter, the *Sept Reserve*, kept loading supply crates of some sort. Wurvez attempted to hack into the freighter's computer, but eventually he growled, leaned back, then huffed. His tail flicked in short, fast movements.

"We could use Lady Emmy right about now. According to Tolvex, her skills would have that database wide open for us already."

"I apologize that I am unable to assist. I can't even code a synthesizer. I usually ask Volax to do it," Grulen said.

"We'll add some computer courses to your training."

"Please don't do me any favors." Grulen shuddered.

Wurvez chuckled.

"I'll keep trying, but for now, let's just follow them and see where they lead us."

"As you command. I'm trying to determine the number of beings on the ship, but even on the ground, they are using a dampening field."

"Of course they are. Well, we wouldn't want it to be too easy, would we?"

"Easy would work for me. We could get back to the *Invictus* sooner. Synthesizer food and rations are poor imitations for Previv and Lady Ava's cooking." Grulen pouted.

With a grin, Wurvez slapped Grulen's shoulder. "A male whose stomach agrees with mine." *Crekkin' male loves to hit my shoulder.*

Sometime later, Wurvez tapped the console and waited.

"Opening an encrypted comm to the *Invictus*."

Durek and Tolvex appeared holographically.

"Report," said the commander.

"We found the freighter and should be close enough in another hour or so to begin following it. We believe they will be landing on Praxis to take on more supplies."

Durek's fangs gleamed against his golden bronze skin.

"Excellent. You may be able to determine the sites of numerous labs."

"From your lips to the Goddess' ears." Wurvez paused. "Anything new about the traitor onboard?"

"He appears to be taking a break from harassing the females. They've been spending most of their days in the War Room while we deal with Earth's nonsense," Tolvex answered.

"Yesterday, the *Defiant* broadcast Talia's videos and released the proposed draft treaty as well as the medical information about the virus." Durek's smile widened. "The initial responses on Earth's social media have been voluminous and show no signs of ending soon."

"Well, that's one way to open up discussions." Wurvez's lips turned up.

Tolvex's braids brushed his shoulder as he shook his head.

"Already there are groups gathering with signs asking us to 'beam them up.' Emmy said we might have to consider psychological testing before allowing any of them on a ship." He shrugged. "I'm not entirely certain she was joking."

Grulen snorted. "My interactions with Lady Emmy would suggest she probably meant exactly what she said."

"I concur," said Tolvex who turned to look at Wurvez. "We're still working to pare down our list of suspects to identify the traitor. It's going slowly."

"How is Nerid Mantoor?"

"Ash'n has been keeping him sedated. The traitor using an implant to brainwash Mantoor made his mind delicate. He has no recollection of attacking me." Durek's growl rumbled low. "We hope the mind healers on Costonia will be able to help him recover."

"Brainwash?" Grulen asked.

"I'll explain later," said Wurvez.

"Anything else?" Durek said.

"No. Only that we may not check in when we're close to Praxis, depending on how long the freighter remains there. I'm not sure what capabilities the Zuvgran have to catch transmissions near one of their worlds." Wurvez's eyes hardened. "We're too close to potential answers, and I don't want to inadvertently give away our position."

Durek's facial scar whitened.

"I don't like you going dark."

"It probably won't be for long."

"Report no later than three days from now, even if you have to break off from your surveillance temporarily."

Wurvez sighed. "As you command."

Hopefully, we'll have something good to report soon.

"The fourth stripped world in three days. Why wouldn't the Zuvgran have their labs on the worlds where they live? Wouldn't it be easier to keep them safe and supplied?" Grulen listened to Wurvez grumble as they watched the Frezzian freighter skim low over the planet's surface and drop crates. Grulen made notations in their computer for the coordinates and everything they observed.

"I don't know. It doesn't make sense."

Wurvez sat back, and his tail swayed slowly. He extended his claws and lightly tapped the console.

"Secret labs. Stripped worlds. No outside contact." His eyes widened. "I think it's because they're working with biologics. If the scientists make an error and a virus gets loose, an unoccupied planet is easier to contain or destroy. Zuvgran deaths would be limited to those already on the surface."

Nodding, Grulen said, "Now that makes sense to me." *I can see why he is such a good tactical officer.*

"Looks like they're changing direction. I wish I could get into their database."

Grulen tapped the console and entered a heading to follow the freighter. Frowning, he looked at the projected course.

"They appear to be flying toward the asteroid field near Millus."

An angry rumble emanated from Wurvez's chest, and his jaw hardened.

"That's much too close to Costonia." The tails of both males flicked in hard movements. His jaw hardened. "Send an encrypted message to the *Invictus* with everything we've discovered so far and our heading. We'll wait until we know exactly where the next lab is before we check in."

Grulen grunted. "There are solar flares in the Lestanus system. The message may not make it through intact or at all."

"*Crek*. We'll have to try again later. Increase speed to get closer to the freighter. I don't want to lose them in the asteroid field. We need to know if there's a lab close to the home world."

"As you command."

After maneuvering through the asteroid field the next day, Grulen and Wurvez watched as the *Sept Reserve* conducted their low altitude run and dropped crates in the ruins of an ancient gladiator pit on Millus. Numerous Zuvgran appeared as soon as the freighter left the atmosphere.

"Scans show a Svesti speedster approaching the planet."

"How far out is it?" Wurvez asked.

"A little over two hours at their present speed."

Wurvez's fingers drummed on the armrest. He turned to Grulen.

"Feel like hunting?"

"What are you thinking?" *I'd like to get off this shuttle for a bit and do more than observe.*

"We know a Svesti noble has been working with the Zuvgran. This might be our chance to discover who he is."

"I like the idea of identifying a traitor. What is your plan?" Grulen's tail sped up.

"Land on the leeward side of the pit. Less chance blowing sand will reveal the ship and it's in the shadows of the walls. We'll leave the ship cloaked and get to high ground with our surveillance equipment so we can watch and if we're lucky, we'll be able to hear. We should still be able to track the freighter when we're done here."

Grulen tapped the console.

"I'm not seeing any planetary defenses or active scans. There is a chance of passive scanning potentially revealing our presence."

"I believe it's worth the risk. Take us down. I'm going to gear up and gather the equipment. When I return, you can get ready."

"I'll try to send another encrypted comm to the *Invictus* with the latest update. Hopefully, it will get through."

"Good thinking." After he stood, Wurvez slapped Grulen's shoulder. "I'm looking forward to this." *Again with the crekkin' shoulder.*

The yellow moon provided minimal light as Grulen and Wurvez swiftly and silently made their way to the top of the seating surrounding the pit. Layers of brown dust stirred briefly as they lay prone and set up their surveillance equipment. Centuries ago, the Zuvgran invaded Millus, but the Svesti joined the fight and pushed them out of the solar system. But they couldn't save Millus itself—it was now another lifeless world.

They watched as the speedster landed in the center of the pit. Three Svesti disembarked. One stepped forward to meet the Zuvgran waiting. Wurvez's chest rumbled with a silent growl. Grulen took the magnifying equipment Wurvez handed to him. When he looked and saw the noble, his tail flicked hard once before stilling.

The long-range microphone did not catch everything discussed in the pit, but they heard enough to confirm that the noble informed the Zuvgran of the human females being on Theron the intent to infect them with the virus. Another Zuvgran approached the males and they heard, "We are not alone. Did you send others?" *Crek.*

"You recognized the noble?" Wurvez whispered. He quickly gathered the equipment and handed the packed bag to Grulen.

"Yes." Grulen's response was barely audible.

"Go back to the ship and depart. Hide in the asteroid field if you need to. Relay everything to Commander Durek or King Sovex—no one else."

"What are you going to do?"

"Be a distraction long enough for you to escape. This information must make it to the king."

Grulen shook his head. "Come with me."

"No." Wurvez's voice was firm. "The odds are better if we split up. Once you know they receive the intel, you can request additional warriors to return for me."

"I do not like this plan."

"Go now. There's little time. That's an order." Wurvez made his way in the opposite direction of the cloaked *Tenacity*.

Grulen silenced his unhappy growl at having to leave Wurvez behind. *We are supposed to be a team. He'll be unprotected.*

Grulen powered up the *Tenacity*, checked the cloaking device, and took off for the asteroid field. He ran a low-level scan of the surface. *Crek! It looks like Wurvez was captured.*

He debated disobeying orders and returning, but the odds of a lone warrior rescuing the male were slim. His tail flicked as he growled. An alert sounded. He cursed as two Zuvgran fighters left Millus and headed toward him. *Do they see me?*

Grabbing the bag of surveillance equipment, he stuffed some water pouches and snacks inside while he kept an eye on the fighters. *Crek. I need to go.*

He threw the bag into an escape pod and fastened the safety restraints. Tapping the console, he plotted a course toward the backside of a midsize asteroid. *Maybe I can wait them out and return to the Tenacity once they're gone.*

The pod slid silently from the ship using minimal thrusters. Dodging asteroids, he piloted the shuttle manually when he saw one with a large indentation where he could hide. He cut off the thrusters and drifted to remain off the fighters' sensors. A blast of orange light flashed behind him. His body shook from the forces acting on the pod as it sped up from the explosion. Hurtling toward the asteroid at a speed and attitude he couldn't control, the surface grew larger in the viewscreen. Mere seconds passed as he braced himself for impact and pain. Simultaneously, straps bit into his shoulders, debris and loose items sliced and shredded his skin, compression on his chest stopped his breath, and he saw no more.

Blaring alarms and flashing lights interrupted the darkness. Lifting his heavy head, he groggily noticed the blood and debris on his lap. He winced at the noises piercing his eardrums and smacked a clumsy hand to the console. Squinting through foggy eyes, he read the reports of damage. *Crek. Gotta seal some of those hairline cracks in the hull. It's getting cold in here.*

Head aching, it took him three tries before he successfully removed the restraints and relieved pressure on his chest. Reaching below his seat, he pulled out a spare nanosuit enhanced for space operations and pulled it over his legs, grunting with the effort. Standing unsteadily, he wobbled, and his breath wheezed when he tugged it over his chest and arms. He pressed the control on the collar. Gloves encased his hands, and a helmet formed over his head. Inserting his feet into oversized maglev boots, he tapped the wrist control, and a hiss signified the protection against open space was complete. *Where am I?*

Shaking his head gingerly, he attempted to focus on what needed to be done. He grabbed a tube from a nearby compartment and connected one end to his suit and the other to an atmospheric output in the pod which tied into a synthesizer. Inhaling the clean air, his vision cleared a little. *Crek. I think I have broken ribs.*

The compartment also held a laser tool. Using his helmet's heads-up display, he found the closest damage to the hull and gingerly avoided debris in the crumpled pod as he maneuvered. He carefully sealed what he could. Sweat rolled from his forehead and mixed with the blood on his face.

His cheeks burned with pain and his muscles ached. Plopping into the seat, he checked the console readouts. Now that the immediate problems were contained, he realized he didn't know what happened, where he was, or what he was doing in a damaged pod. His head throbbed when he tried to force the memories. *I don't even know my name.*

Breathing rapidly, darkness encroached on the edges of his vision, and he slumped over the console. Before he passed out, his hand bumped the oxygen mixture control, but he never saw the numbers decrease.

"The Svesti is lucky he survived."

"He suffered a lot of injuries. I couldn't heal the scarring on his face. Did you learn anything from his escape pod?"

"From what we can tell from the onboard telemetry, two weeks ago, the pod rocketed forward from an outside force and impacted the asteroid. Somehow, he sealed most of the fractures in the hull which kept the pod from completely freezing. Decreasing the oxygen flow gave him a longer period of air. A risky call, but it kept him alive until our scanners noticed something unusual. The power for the synthesizer was decreasing rapidly."

"The colder temps with the lower oxygen put him a mini stasis. I'm not sure what the long-term effects may be, Captain."

"Will he awaken soon?"

The deep voices flowed over him as he regained consciousness. Keeping his eyes closed, he conducted a mental inventory of his body while he listened to the males talk about him. *Two weeks?*

"I think he might be joining us now."

Crek. I might as well figure out what's going on.

He opened his eyes to two Ladortans looking down at him. The smaller one, who appeared to be a similar height to himself, glanced at the med bed readings before smiling. Tusks peeked out from his cream-colored fur.

"Hello. I am Healer Creet. This is Captain Ordan of the *Morning Star*."

He grunted at both.

"We found you in a damaged pod on an asteroid three days ago. Can you tell us what happened?" The captain's fur was longer and darker than the healer's. He wore a weapons harness and long brown pants tucked into sturdy boots.

He shrugged his shoulders.

"I remember nothing except waking up to alarms in the pod and trying to repair hull fractures. I must have lost consciousness."

"What is your name?"

"My name is..." His face scrunched, and his head began to ache. "I don't know my name."

The Ladortans exchanged a glance. The captain's green eyes narrowed.

"Do you remember why you were in an asteroid belt or where you were when the crash happened?"

His breath quickened as he tried to sit up. Muted alarms sounded.

"Take deep breaths, Svesti. It's not unusual to not remember with a head injury like yours." The healer pressed him back onto the med bed. "You shouldn't be moving just yet. Your body needs time to recover."

"I don't understand why I can't remember. I know you are Ladortans. I know this is a med bay. I knew enough to get into a nanosuit and fix hull fractures. I feel like there's something urgent I'm supposed to do, but I don't remember what it is." His voice grew louder.

"It's okay. It sounds like you've retained some long-term memories. That's promising. With time and healing, it is likely you will recall more short term memories."

"Where am I?" His fingers gripped the sheet covering him.

"The *Morning Star* is a mining vessel. During our scan of some asteroids, we noticed unusual readings and investigated. That's when we found you." The captain crossed his arms, his fur rippling. "We're en route to Nulorn to sell our cargo and resupply."

His brows furrowed, and the end of his tail flicked sharply.

"What if I don't remember?"

The healer squeezed his arm.

"Let's take your recovery one day at a time, Svesti. You just woke up, but you still need rest. Stress will only make it more difficult to remember."

"For now, Svesti, listen to the healer. No decisions need to be made yet." The light glinted off the captain's dagger handle tucked in a sheath. He recognized the iridescence as coveted *pyrix* bone but did not know how he knew the information. Trying to think so much created a pulsing beat behind his eyes. *This is crekkin' frustrating. Why can't I remember?*

Chapter 8

Morgan pushed her plate away, sat back, and groaned. Rubbing her stomach, she said, "I'm stuffed."

"It's good to see you finally have an appetite." Abby took a bite of her meal.

"I think that's the first time that I actually wanted to eat instead of forcing myself in the two months I've been here."

"Whatever the Zuvgran did to your body really messed it up." Abby's frown changed to a smile. "At least your fertility doesn't seem to be affected. I'm glad Svesti sent us the information on the vaccine to counteract the final version."

"Well, since I'm not interested in becoming pregnant any time soon, I'm not sure it matters." She thought about the human women Makai told her were with the Svesti going to Costonia when she was rescued. *They must be there by now. King Sovex didn't waste any time contacting Earth. I wonder how it's going and if the women feel overwhelmed by all the males. They have so few females now.*

"Too many have taken your choices away already. I say don't let the assholes take any more from you."

Morgan grinned at Kara Brinkman's ferocious statement interrupting her ruminations. Shoulder-length pink hair, curvy human body, and fuck-you attitude belied her incredible intelligence. *Damn, the woman makes me laugh.*

"Kara's right." Rain Oakhurst nodded her blonde head. Green eyes narrowed. "It sucks that as difficult as it is for human women on Earth with our own misogynistic men, there are even worse places in the universe for us."

"I want to junk punch the Frezzians that took Rain and me, but if they hadn't, I never would've met my male." Kara's blue eyes went from pissed to blissful. "He's the best."

Rain swallowed her food before agreeing.

"Yeah, I'm happier than I've ever been."

Morgan considered the three women friends, but sometimes she fought down feelings of jealousy. While each went through their own shit, the Jalaxians rescued and protected them before they ended up raped, beaten, or experimented upon. And they found their mates among the Wing Raiders crew. Whereas, if bad things could happen, they happened to Morgan. *I'm such a petty bitch. I wouldn't wish my experiences on anyone, let alone friends.*

She also really liked all of the Jalaxians onboard—Makai, Lezon, Tren, Yaz, and Crax. The only ones unmated were Tren and Makai. As hot as the captain was, she got big brother vibes from him, whereas Tren was fun but exhausting. Sighing, she leaned forward. *I'm just feeling like a fifth wheel. I don't think I really want to be mated right now anyway.*

"Now that I'm feeling better, do you think Makai will let me set up some silks in the cargo bay? Yoga is fine, but I really enjoy the aerial stuff."

Kara tilted her head.

"I don't see why he wouldn't. Can you teach me some moves?"

"Sure."

"I'd like to learn, too," said Rain.

"Count me in." Abby stabbed another piece of meat. "I'll need to keep active."

Every head turned to her.

"Why?"

Her face flushed and she murmured, "Shit."

"Spill, girl." Rain pointed her fork at Abby.

"We haven't told anyone yet, but I'm pregnant."

Shrieks erupted and the women jumped up to surround the brunette and hug her.

"Congratulations." Morgan placed her hands on Abby's shoulders and studied her. "Yeah, I think I see a glow about you."

Abby slapped Morgan's forearm.

"Stop teasing me. It's too early for a pregnancy glow."

"No, she's right. You look serene." Rain smirked.

"Fuck off." Abby stuck up her middle finger.

"Are you going to teach your kid such language?" Kara arched an eyebrow and crossed her arms. "That's my job as auntie."

Laughing, the women pestered Abby about her due date and if she wanted to know the gender beforehand. Kara's expression turned serious.

"Will you guys be leaving the Wing Raiders and settling on a planet?"

Abby shook her head.

"Not in our plans right now. You guys are family. We're happy here."

"But don't you think you'll be safer somewhere else?" Morgan bit her lip. "Space is dangerous and living on a ship with a kid, is that fair to him or her?" She spread her arms out. "I'm not judging. Just trying to understand."

Abby's lips firmed.

"First, everywhere is dangerous. Even if I were still on Earth—a planet—I'd have to worry about safety. Second, every single person on this ship would fight to the death to protect us. I'm not saying we won't ever decide that a planet is better overall for our family, but for now, this is where we want and need to be."

Rain and Kara nodded in agreement.

"She's right."

Morgan chewed slowly and let the chatter flow over her as she digested everyone's thoughts. *I think I'd want to be on a planet if I were pregnant. I'm starting to believe all those alien romance writers might have had it right—humans are universal breeders. Svesti, and now Jalaxians. I wonder if King Sovex would let the Wing Raiders settle on Costonia if they asked.*

Wiping the sweat from her brow, Morgan smiled at the women.

"How'd that feel?"

"Shit, my core fucking hurts," Kara moaned.

"Wuss. That was a great workout." Feet apart, Rain laced her fingers and stretched her arms over her head before arching her back. "I'm amazed at how much my muscles burn just from doing the exercises on silks."

Abby sucked down a water pouch.

"I'm with Kara on this one. I thought I was in shape, but now I'm not so sure."

Morgan laughed.

"You said you performed on Earth and on Delizas. Can you show us what that looked like?" Abby pushed her hair back from her forehead.

"Sure. I'm out of practice, though."

"Didn't seem like it," Kara griped while she grabbed her tablet. "Did you need music? I swiped some from the Svesti when we rescued you. They had Earth's internet in their files."

"Got *Immigrant Song*?"

"Coming right up."

Morgan grabbed her silks and waited until the hard-driving beat filled the cargo bay. Quickly she climbed the fabric lengths sliding them through her feet and pulling with her arms. Wrapping her right wrist and grasping the cloth above, she began a series of movements that looked extremely difficult but relied on strong core muscles and balance. She twisted and turned occasionally billowing the fabric below her for visual effect while maneuvering to wrap each ankle in a silk and pausing in a midair split.

Something small flew by her face. Startled, she snapped her legs together and slid down before she fell.

"What the fuck was that?"

"Oops. Sorry about that, Morgan." Tren stood at the entrance with a remote control. "I'm just testing my newest invention. A mini drone that looks like an insect. The targeting still seems off."

"She could've been hurt, moron." Kara stalked toward the sheepish male.

"It was an accident."

"Why would you test it while we're using the space? Did you learn nothing from the weapons spinner incident?" Hands on her hips, Rain shot him an angry look. "Lezon almost lost his head with that one."

"My apologies." Tren's blue cheeks darkened. "I truly didn't mean any harm." He tilted his head. "Those were some cool moves, Morgan. I got most of it on the drone."

Exasperated, she shook her head.

"Thanks, Tren."

"Makai said there's a meeting on the bridge in an hour."

"Let's shower and change. We'll beat up Tren later." Kara smirked.

Morgan picked up her towel and followed the women out.

She changed into clean cargo pants and a black T-shirt after her sonic shower. She pulled her hair back into a ponytail and shoved her feet into black low-heeled boots. *I really miss Svesti bathrooms and their huge tubs.*

Arriving at the bridge at the same time as Abby, she stopped in the doorway. She saw herself on the viewscreen conducting the silks routine. She groaned.

Yaz grinned.

"Interesting performance, Morgan."

She flipped him the bird. Everyone laughed except Crax who merely lifted his lips slightly. *Wow, grumpy pants enjoyed my reaction. Will wonders never cease?*

Makai raised a hand, and everyone quieted.

"We're heading to Nulorn to resupply and see what's available for jobs. We should be there in…?"

"About two weeks," supplied Yaz.

"We'll plan a week or two on Nulorn with staggering leave days. We've been on the ship quite a while now and need some planetside time."

"What can I do?" Morgan asked.

"Enjoy yourself."

She crossed her arms, and her spine stiffened.

"I'm feeling more like myself now, and I'd like to contribute. I've always worked and paid my own way."

"You're welcome here for as long as you like, Morgan. You fit in well with the crew."

"But I don't have a job." She gestured to the women. "Rain pilots, Abby helps in medical, and Kara is a tech and science genius. I barely cook. I need to do something, or I feel like a charity case."

Makai narrowed his blue eyes.

"What would you like to do?"

"I'm a teacher, but there aren't any children on the ship. I don't know what I'm qualified for here. Grunt work?" She internally winced at the thought of crawling in maintenance ducts or something similar, but she had her pride.

"She could do her thing on Nulorn for a few nights. Entertain the masses and get paid for it." Tren pointed at the frozen image on the viewscreen where she suspended midair between the silks.

"Too dangerous. Humans are a hot commodity out here. The risk of kidnapping is too high." Makai frowned.

Morgan chewed the inside of her cheek and squinted at the viewscreen.

"Actually, Tren's idea is a good one. If you know a place that hires entertainers and has the right sort of space for the silks, we could offer a three-night gig. A couple of the guys could go with me to protect me, and I can add the pay to the ship's coffers."

"There's no need for your credits." Makai's lips thinned, and his jaw hardened.

"At least it would offset some of the cost of my food and clothing." Her chin thrust forward.

"I volunteer to protect her." Crax's rumbly voice interrupted their standoff.

"As do I," said Lezon.

"Any of us would be happy to protect her," Tren said.

Makai's braids swirled across his shoulders as he shook his head.

"I'm going to regret this." Sighing, he pointed at her. "Three nights only. I'll arrange it."

She grinned and barely refrained from pumping her fist in victory.

"Thank you, Makai. Four sets per night, fifteen minutes each—max. Let me know what is decided, and I'll work with Kara for costumes and music."

Makai grunted and said, "That's it. Everyone that doesn't need to be here, get off my bridge."

Chapter 9

Despite his best efforts and numerous headaches, he still didn't remember his name or anything specific about his life. Over the past several weeks on the *Morning Star*, his flesh healed, and he became friendly with the crew of Ladortans and Ermipas. An odd mixture of beings—the Ladortans ranging from two to three heads taller than himself and the Ermipas much shorter. Both species had fur-covered bodies but the Ermipas darker in color. While the Ladortans looked ferocious most of the time, the Ermipas appeared adorable with their round heads and oval eyes. Both races were strong and hardy.

The crew members took to calling him Stalad. When he asked why, they told him it was the tempered version of an ore found on some rare asteroids. The name sat uncomfortably on him like an ill-fitting shirt, but until he could recall more about himself, it was better than nothing. Underneath it all, he had a sense of urgency—something he should be doing but wasn't. Unless he sparred with the crew members or trained solo, the feeling gnawed at him.

The *Morning Star* landed on Nulorn a week ago. Captain Ordan searched for someone who could take him to Costonia in the hopes Stalad could regain his memories there. So far, no one seemed to be traveling in that direction or wanted him on their ship.

"Come, Stalad. Rumor has it that tonight is the last time for an unusual performer at *Diversions*. I expect a number of mercenaries will be there." Ordan's meaty hand slapped him on his shoulder. "Although I will miss sparring with you."

Stalad followed the Ladortan to a unmanned Nulorian flitter and they seated themselves. The captain entered the destination and swiped his credit chip. The vehicle rose and moved forward.

"What is *Diversions*?"

"It's a well-known entertainment establishment in the heart of the capital."

Less than an hour later, a huge semi-circular building with scalloped outer edges appeared. The flitter landed and Ordan's fur waved in the breeze when they disembarked.

After Ordan paid for their entry, he pointed to the far end of the room.

"Come. Let's find a place to sit."

Stalad peered curiously around them as he followed the Ladortan. The upper levels of the scallops seemed to be separate viewing areas with privacy glass overlooking the establishment, while tables and chairs provided seating in the dark areas below. A large stage formed the other side of the room with bars serving drinks on either side. Tall rectangular tables surrounded the big dance floor in front of the raised stage. Other seating and tables dotted the outside edges.

Waitstaff of a number of species moved fluidly among the tables with drinks and food while a Praxite band played loudly on stage. Flashing lights and smoke highlighted the performers. As Stalad and Ordan got closer to one of the bars, he saw two Wrestikan females busily moving their multiple arms mixing drinks for the patrons. Ordan's face lit up when he noticed a small empty table in one of the lower scallops near the left side of the stage. He hustled toward it and sat.

Following more slowly, Stalad's ears rang from the loud music and his nose twitched from the smoke. His tail jerked slightly as he sat with his back toward the wall. From his position, he could see most of the venue as well as the opposite backstage.

Stalad placed an order for drinks and glanced around.

"Hmm, Jalaxians. I wonder if they're the Wing Raiders. They might be able to get you home." Ordan peered backstage where a surly-looking Jalaxian stood with a pink-haired female tapping on a tablet. "I don't recognize that species."

"Odd to see a human here," Stalad said, wrinkling his nose.

"Human? Is that what she is? You know that?"

His brows knitted, and his tail flicked.

"I don't know how I know it, but I know humans shouldn't be here. *Crek*, this is frustrating." He rubbed his temples.

"Stop trying to force the memories, Stalad. You know it only causes you pain." Ordan's tusks gleamed as the lights brightened. A male Pellotian, his colorful wings shining brightly and contrasting with his green skin, strode onto the stage as the

Praxite band packed up and an opaque shield formed to hide their actions.

"Show your appreciation for Stellar Sounds, everyone!" Claps, foot stomping, and various sounds erupted at the Pellotian's words. "Our next act is on her last evening with us, and she's been a rousing hit with our patrons. If you haven't seen her before, prepare to be amazed at her agility, especially as a species without wings." Grunts and chuckles from the audience burst out at the male's joke. "After this set, she'll return one more time in two hours, and she assures us that her finale will be something you haven't seen before. Let's welcome Ariel, the aerial performer!"

The deafening noise silenced when the lights dimmed. A single spotlight shone on the shield which dissolved into colorful sparkles leaving an empty stage. Soft, sensual music piped through hidden speakers grew louder in volume, then a female dropped from the ceiling rolling out from two long vertical lengths of shiny fabric. Her body halted face-up and perpendicular to the floor. Her head tipped back and her long dark hair brushed the stage as she arched her lean body. The crowd gasped.

She wore a burgundy body suit that hugged her curves. Gracefully, she unraveled herself from the cloth and stood with one foot pointed toward the ceiling. Grasping the fabric, she tucked her bare feet around both lengths and shimmied higher in time to the music. She wrapped the fabric around her right wrist and straightened her body. With nothing more than her wrist supporting her, she rotated her body to face the audience, then slowly maneuvered to a horizontal position. *Her muscular control is impressive.*

She continued to turn until she was upside down, her hair waving and red highlights glittering as she twisted each ankle into the separate pieces of fabric. Releasing her wrist with a subtle movement, her fingers pointed toward the floor before she curled her stomach and caught the cloth above her feet. The audience oohed and aahed when she spread her legs and hung in a split in the air.

Entranced by her agility and beauty, Stalad leaned forward and watched as she continued her graceful movements—some reminiscent of his training moves. Several times his heart stuttered when it appeared she courted death if she fell. The accompanying music changed several times. Her actions kept a perfect counterpoint to the beat, whether fast or slow. Lights of varying colors highlighted her from different angles and intensities during her show.

He growled and his tail flicked when he heard males around him yelling what they'd like to do with such a flexible female in the hopes that she'd hear. *Crekkin' naroons. She's an artist, not a pleasure worker.*

Her hair and fabric, both glinting under the lights, flew about when she spun vertically in the cloth. When the music slowed, she did as well. As the light faded into nothingness, she hung with the fabric wrapped around her waist as if she were unconscious.

The crowd went wild with excitement. A spotlight came on and she stood still on the stage with a large smile before conducting a sweeping curtsy. She stepped back and the opaque shield formed once again.

"If she plans on something better than that for her finale, I think we should stay to watch." Ordan lifted his drink and tipped it at Stalad before taking a sip.

"I agree. Her performance was worth the price of admission."

"Especially since I paid." Ordan chuckled and stood. "I think I see some mercenary captains here. Let me check if any are headed in the vicinity of Costonia."

"I'll wait here."

Over the next couple hours, Stalad's eyes drifted over the crowd repeatedly. He watched Ordan stop and speak to various beings. Loud music played and the dance floor filled with all manner of beings. The strobing lights made his eyeballs ache, but to see the human perform again, he was willing to deal with the discomfort. Moving his seat aside, he made room for some of the *Morning Star*'s crew when they showed up later. Sipping his drink, his attention flitted to another human female with a Jalaxian who peeked out from backstage, waved at someone, then disappeared. *That makes three. One with pink hair, one with blonde, and Ariel with her dark tresses with red highlights.*

His shoulders drew up and his tail straightened when he noticed a large number of Durelians pushing patrons away from the tall tables and taking their places on both sides of the dance floor closest to the stage. Growling, he watched them closely. His nose wrinkled when their scent began permeating the space. *I don't trust the Durelians not to harm the females.*

In a repeat from earlier, the overhead lights grew brighter, the music stopped, and the Pellotian introduced Ariel for her last performance of the night. This time, when the opaque shield dropped, an uplight focused on the fabric and a tune began to play. The crowd collectively drew in a breath when the human slipped down the cloth via large clear lighted hoops. Wearing a blue bodysuit this time, with irregular holes cut out on her arms, legs, and torso, she bent when she reached the floor and disentangled the hoops. Some of the lights changed colors as she spun, threw them, and caught them.

The hoops created a visual buffet as she conducted a new routine on the fabric with the hoops in time with the music. Stalad reluctantly pulled his attention from her mesmerizing display to check on the Durelians. Most continued to move closer to the backstage area while the audience watched spellbound. He stood abruptly and made his way closer to the stage. During the finale, he followed the Durelians on his side of the room and extended his claws when they attempted to take the blonde human female. The Jalaxian with her fought the group as they approached, while Stalad knocked one unconscious from behind. Two of the orange aliens turned when they heard their comrade drop and began to fight him.

From the corner of his eyes, he saw the other Jalaxian across the stage fighting to keep the pink-haired female safe. He drew his claws across the neck of one Durelian and kicked the front of the other's knee simultaneously. They both went down. He heard a scream from above, tilted his head back, and saw Ariel being thrown over the shoulder of one of the attackers. Members of the *Morning Star* crew had followed him and fought the remaining Durelians.

"Help the Jalaxians keep the females safe. I'm going after Ariel," he shouted to Ordan as he ran around the fighting to keep the female in sight. His heart pounded, and he used his tail to push people from his path as he stayed below the kidnapped human. The Durelian stopped at a metal ladder and using the vertical rails slid down using his feet and only one hand as the other attempted to keep Ariel's struggling body from escaping. The pair left through a door to the outside and Stalad rushed to keep up.

He caught a glimpse of the Durelian ducking into the next alley. When he turned the corner, he stopped when he saw Ariel awkwardly kneeing her kidnapper in the face. The Durelian yelped and swung her body down. He held her in front of him facing Stalad with an arm around her neck. Her fingers dug into his skin and her unshorn feet flailed while she cursed the Durelian.

"Let the female go." Stalad slowly stepped forward.

"Leave, Svesti, this doesn't concern you. We're just having a friendly disagreement." The Durelian snarled when Ariel bit his arm.

"Do you want to be with this male, Lady Ariel?"

"I want this smelly Durelian to get his fucking mitts off me." She let out a frustrated scream. "I'm sick and tired of being kidnapped." Blue eyes met his angrily. "A little help would be nice."

"As you command." Stalad's tail whipped up and smacked the Durelian's face which caused the kidnapper to stagger and loosen his hold on Ariel. She immediately reached low behind her, grasped the male's balls, and squeezed. The Durelian howled and released her. She scurried away behind Stalad who leapt and kicked the attacker in the head. Doublechecking that the male was unconscious, he stood and turned to Ariel. "Are you alright? Do you require medical attention?"

"I'm fine." She briskly rubbed her hands on her arms, then straightened. "I'm going back inside."

"We may wish to wait out here until it calms down. He wasn't the only kidnapper. His companions attempted to take the other human females as well."

Her eyes narrowed before she headed back toward the door.

"Then we need to help them."

"I believe the Jalaxians are taking care of it with help from some Ladortans and Ermipas."

She huffed, then tilted her head.

"How did you recognize us as human?"

"I don't know."

Her lips firmed.

"That is not an acceptable answer and doesn't inspire trust, Svesti."

"Lady Ariel, I suffer amnesia from an accident. I don't know how I know many things. I don't even know my own name."

"Morgan." Her expression softened.

"Excuse me?"

"My real name is Morgan. What should I call you?"

"The crew that rescued me calls me Stalad."

"Thank you, Stalad, for helping me. I appreciate it."

He nodded. The door opened and Ordan's furry face looked out.

"Oh, good, you found her. It's settling down in here, and the Wing Raiders are pissed. Come back in before Makai destroys the place with his glares."

Lady Morgan laughed.

"I guess that's our cue."

Chapter 10

Hiding her shaking hands, Morgan preceded Stalad into *Diversions*. Her soles disliked the rough pavement outside. She took care to avoid stepping on debris from the fight. *I can't believe I was almost kidnapped again.*

The relief when she saw the Svesti in the alley surprised her. After a year on Costonia, she expected a Svesti male to be protective, but something in her recognized him on some level. Even when she was spitting nails at him, she knew in her bones it wouldn't make him turn away. His cinnamon and caramel scent gave her the warm fuzzies, the likes she hadn't felt since she before her mother got sick. He felt like home and safety.

As good-looking as most Svesti were, Stalad outdid them all. His reddish bronze skin with its fur-like appearance, warm brown eyes, shoulder-length dark hair, as well as his muscular shoulders, biceps, and thighs, caused pleasant tingles in her lady parts—something else that she hadn't experienced since she left Earth. When they entered the lighted area, she noted the small scars dotting his attractive face. *From the accident he mentioned?*

Even his scars couldn't detract from his handsomeness. His body heat seared her back as he followed her closely. Squaring her shoulders, she walked toward the Wing Raiders. Makai, Crax, Lezon, Tren, Rain, and Kara stood in a cluster with the Ladortan that told them to return. Internally, she winced. *Makai is never going to let me perform to help the Wing Raiders in the future after this debacle.*

"Morgan, thank god you're okay," Kara said.

"Thanks to Stalad here." Morgan jerked a thumb at the male.

"Our thanks, Svesti," Makai said with a tight smile. His eyes traveled over Morgan looking for injuries.

"I'm fine, Makai. Just shaken up."

"Lezon can check you out when we return to the *Fortitude.*"

A low growl sounded from Stalad. Knitting her brows, she glanced at him with surprise.

"Were you hurt?"

"No, Lady Morgan."

"Just Morgan, please."

His lips quirked.

"As you wish."

"Captain Ordan, is this the Svesti we spoke of?" Makai asked.

"Yes, Captain Makai. We found Stalad in an escape pod, and while his body has healed, his memories still haven't returned. We've been looking for a way to return him to Costonia in the hopes they can help him."

"Unfortunately, we're not heading in that direction at this time."

"I understand. I appreciate you considering it." Stalad's tail straightened, then relaxed.

"I'm curious, why did you intervene?"

"I knew the Durelians presented a risk, so I kept watch when I saw them gathering near the stage. Human females are to be protected at all times. "

"Why is that?"

"Uh, I don't know. My instincts tell me it is the right thing to do." Stalad's brows pinched together as if he were in pain. Morgan's fingers twitched.

The Jalaxians shared a look. She knew they were silently communicating in the way of men who have fought together a long time. Crax stepped away.

"If you're willing to work in the meantime, we can take you with us now and we'll get you home when we can. I can give priority to jobs that will take us in that direction."

"I'm not sure." Stalad glanced at the Ladortan.

"Captain Makai and his crew have an excellent reputation. I also think you're a better fit with a ship of warriors than a ship of miners." Captain Ordan's tusks peeked out from his long facial fur when he grinned. "We've enjoyed having you, but I believe the Wing Raiders are the best and safest option to continue your healing process."

Stalad met Makai's eyes. His tail rested on her lower spine. *Is he considering it? Do I want him to? Yes, I think I want to know more about him.*

"Are you certain? I can't even tell you what my experience is."

"Captain Ordan assures me you have sufficient fighting skills, your instincts are to protect females, and you need help. We have the room and are indebted to you for saving Morgan."

"Then I will be happy to join you until I can find a way to Costonia." Stalad's face lit up when he grinned. His fangs glinted against his skin. *I like the laugh lines around his eyes.*

"Gather your things and meet us at the *Fortitude* as soon as you can. I don't want to remain on Nulorn longer than necessary after tonight's events."

"I have nothing on the *Morning Star.*"

"Actually, there was a bag in the pod with you. I can have it delivered to Captain Makai's vessel." Captain Ordan tapped his comm unit.

"There was?" Stalad looked at the Ladortan with crinkled brows. "I didn't know that."

"It contains surveillance equipment, food, and water. Nothing to identify you."

"Surveillance equipment?" Makai's eyes lit up. "What were you investigating?"

Stalad pressed his temples and closed his eyes.

"I have no idea."

"Do you often have pain when you attempt to remember?" Lezon asked quietly.

"Yes. It's frustrating. I have a feeling of urgency that there is something I'm supposed to be doing, but I have no recollection of what it could be."

"Don't push it. The mind can close itself off for any number of reasons. You'll remember when you're ready." Lezon turned to Captain Ordan. "Can you send me a copy of his medical records?"

"Of course."

"If that's all, let's get back to the *Fortitude*." Makai nodded at the males, who surrounded the women. Outside, Crax stood by a large flitter. They hustled the humans into the vehicle and stood waiting.

Stalad spoke briefly with Captain Ordan. They exchanged warrior's clasps, gripping the other's forearm. Then the Svesti slid into the vehicle with the Jalaxians and ended up across from her.

Morgan intertwined her frozen fingers to keep them still as they rode back to the *Fortitude* and listened as everyone chatted around her. From their conversation, she learned that the *Morning Star* rescued Stalad almost a month ago and their investigation determined he had been injured about two weeks prior to that. When Lezon asked how he survived those two weeks, she internally winced and closed her eyes when he said he'd somehow ended up in a quasi-stasis with lower oxygen levels and the cold of space.

Shivers racked her body. The scent of cinnamon and caramel wafted over her. She opened her eyes to see Stalad offering her his shirt.

"I think you're going into shock. Please take this to keep warm." Liquid brown eyes showed concern. His tail tentatively wound around her ankle and rubbed gently over her leotard.

"Thank you." His body heat emanated from the cloth as she pulled it over her head, and she sighed. She shifted so it covered her thighs. Tension leaked from her body, and she relaxed against the seat.

"I think they deliberately planned their kidnapping for the last performance."

Makai nodded at Crax's grumbled observation.

"I agree. They knew there were three human females and how many of us protected them."

"I'm sorry. I just wanted to help fill the coffers." Morgan blinked rapidly.

"It is not your fault. If we do this again, it will be one night only."

Her eyes widened, and she leaned forward.

"You're not stopping me?"

"I negotiated a part of the entrance fee and drinks profit if a higher-than-normal crowd showed up. People waited in line last night and tonight in hopes of seeing you perform. Word got around after your first performances." Makai smiled. "You made quite a few credits."

"Keep them."

He grunted.

"No. I'll take a small percentage which will more than cover the small pittance you eat and transfer the rest to an account for you. You earned it."

"But…"

"No arguments." Makai mock glared at her.

Dropping back against the seat, she nodded tiredly.

"I don't have the energy to argue with you right now." Stalad's tail moved to her other ankle and continued to soothe her for the rest of the trip back.

On the *Fortitude*, her feet protested walking on the cold metal. She yelped when Stalad lifted her in a bridal carry without warning.

"I can walk. And I'm too heavy." *Damn, he smells good. And he's so warm.*

"Your feet are injured."

"Follow me," Lezon said. "I'll heal her feet."

Grumpily, she crossed her arms and tried not to lean on the Svesti. He jostled her slightly, and she fell against his chest. She huffed when she realized he was grinning at her discomfort.

"You're just a little thing, *ciebala*."

Her nose wrinkled.

"*Ciebala?*"

"Sky dancer." *Oh, I like that.*

"Whatever."

He put her on a med bed and stood nearby as Lezon ran a healing wand over her abused feet. Abby came in as the healer scanned the rest of her body.

"Hey, girl, are you okay? And who's this?"

"I'm fine. And this is Stalad."

Lezon put down the scanner and turned to the brunette.

"Stalad is traveling with us for a while until we can get him to his home planet."

"Nice to meet you, Stalad. I'm Abby and this is Lezon. Welcome." Abby smiled, and Stalad dipped his head.

"Lady Abby, it is a pleasure."

"Lady? No, just call me Abby." Confusion crossed her face.

"The Svesti usually use Lady in front of female first names," Morgan said.

"You know this?" Stalad glanced at her.

"I spent close to a year on Costonia."

His eyes lit up.

"You did? Are there other humans there? For some reason, I feel like humans aren't usual in this part of space."

"You are correct, we aren't usually around here, unless we're kidnapped and brought here against our will."

His tail whipped behind him, and his claws extracted.

"Did a Svesti kidnap you?"

She placed a hand on his tense forearm and shook her head.

"No, that was Frezzians and Durelians. The Svesti treated me well."

His tail slowed, his claws retracted, and his muscles loosened.

"I'm sorry you were taken in the first place, but I am glad the Svesti made your stay on Costonia comfortable." His head tilted. "Why were you there?"

Her lips tipped up.

"They found me on Delizas, and after some questioning and DNA tests realized I might be able to help them test our races' compatibility to recover from the Zuvgran virus that decimated your female population. They invited me to Costonia for more testing. Unfortunately, when I left there, I was kidnapped by the

Zuvgran who experimented on me with a new virus. The Wing Raiders saved me and another human woman."

His face scrunched, and he lifted a hand to his temple. He swayed on his feet. Alarmed, she said, "Are you alright?"

Lezon moved to stabilize Stalad and had him sit down on the med bed next to her. He began scanning the Svesti.

"A memory?"

"Something about her words triggered it, as if I should know what she was speaking of. But I don't know what." His fist impacted his thigh. "It's so *crekkin'* frustrating."

"Healer Creet sent me your medical records, and I reviewed them on the way here. You're lucky you survived and are doing as well as you are, Stalad. The memories may or may not come back on their own soon. Like I said earlier, and as I'm sure Healer Creet told you, attempting to force them will only cause you more pain."

"I know, but it's difficult."

She took Stalad's hand and squeezed.

"Listen to Lezon. He and Abby helped me return to full health. I trust them."

"I just hate having holes in my memories."

"Understandable, but give yourself some grace."

Lezon put down the scanner.

"Both of you can go. It's late and we all need rest. Makai said Stalad can have the quarters across from yours, Morgan, if you'd like to show him the way."

She hopped down.

"I can do that. Oomph." She shook her head when Stalad picked her up again. "I can still walk."

"You're barefoot on cold floors, and we're going the same way."

"Fine. Have it your way. Take a left when we leave the med bay." She tried to keep from sinking into his strong, warm chest.

"As you wish."

She directed him to her quarters.

"We're here. You can put me down now." She pointed to the door opposite them. "Those are your quarters. There's a comm system if you need anything."

His arm under her knees dropped and the one around her back tightened as she regained her footing.

"Thank you, Morgan. Sleep well."

"You, too. Thanks for saving me." She grinned. "And I guess for being my ride here."

His brown eyes caressed her face.

"My pleasure."

Watching to ensure he was able to open the door, she closed hers when he was out of sight. *He looks as good from the back as he does the front. Firm ass and that tail, whew.*

Changing into a nightshirt she purchased on Nulorn the first day they arrived, she smoothed the soft fabric along the front. Padding to the bathroom, she washed her face, used a tooth cleaning tab, and brushed her hair after using the facilities. Her reflection in the viewer showed her face flushed and her eyes bright. She made a face and laughed at herself before heading to bed.

She clutched her pillow and snuggled under the blanket. *What is it about Stalad that makes him so appealing to me? I met lots of Svesti on Costonia. Hell, King Sovex was fucking gorgeous and a nice male, but he didn't make me want to get closer to him.*

Closing her eyes, she drifted off to sleep dreaming of warm brown eyes, a naughty tail, and tasty desserts.

Chapter 11

Stalad roamed the halls to orient himself to what facilities were on the ship. *I'm hungry, and my quarters are too small to practice my forms.*

Turning at the slap on his shoulder, he saw Captain Makai. Except for the two white braids on the side of his head, he had pulled back the remainder of his long hair.

"Good morning. Looking for morning meal?"

"I was hoping to find a dining area."

"Walk with me." Makai moved up next to him. "After we eat, I'll give you a tour."

"I'd appreciate that."

"Thanks for your help yesterday."

"It was the right thing to do."

As they approached their destination, the smells of cooking food greeted them before they arrived.

"Oh, good, it seems Morgan is taking care of morning meal. We all suffer when it's Yaz's turn." Makai's fangs flashed.

Stalad grinned. He took in the crew members as Makai introduced everyone. The primary pilot, Yaz, hadn't been at

Diversions the night before, and he already met Abby in the med bay when Lezon treated Morgan's feet.

Jalaxians were the closest to Svesti in body type, both tall and having retractable claws, fangs, and tails. Although Jalaxian tails tended to be wider than Svesti and their skin was blue. He knew they lost their home world fifty *solars* prior, but once, again, he couldn't tell when or how he learned the information.

He took one of the empty seats next to Crax. The pink-haired female sat on the Jalaxian's left. Makai introduced her as Kara. Rain sat on Kara's left next to Lezon.

Makai sat opposite him in a seat between Tren, the engineer, and Yaz. Abby came out with several platters of food and sat next to Yaz. Morgan followed her with large pitchers of juice and water, then she settled next to Stalad.

"Hi," she said quietly with a small smile.

"Good morning, Morgan. Did you sleep well?"

"Yes, actually I did. You?"

"Mmm, pancakes and bacon." Tren's boisterous voice interrupted them as he grabbed a platter with stacks of circular disks and piled a number of them high on his own plate. Stalad watched him slather butter on each disk before drizzling a dark, thick substance over them. "I love Earth food."

"Make sure you leave some for the rest of us," Crax grumbled.

The dishes with the pancakes circulated around the long table with the females taking much fewer than the males. Another platter of a wonderful smelling meat also was passed around. When one came their way, he offered Morgan first choice before taking some for himself. Surreptitiously, he inhaled her scent. *Fascinating. She smells like grass and trulet in a light rain. Reminds me of growth and hope.*

After preparing the pancakes like everyone around him, his tail swayed as the unusual tastes hit his tastebuds. Chewing slowly, he savored the new flavors, but one familiar one stood out.

"Is there *leringa* in these?"

Morgan nodded.

"Yes, I found some fresh on Nulorn. I enjoyed the berries when I lived on your home world. On Earth, we sometimes use different fruits in our pancakes, as well as other things, like chocolate. I thought it would be a nice change."

"What is this? It's sweet like a fruit sauce, but not."

"Syrup. I tried to find one close to Earth's maple syrup, which is made from the sap of sugar maple trees. The meat is similar to bacon."

"This is delicious. Thank you for cooking us a wonderful morning meal."

Her cheeks flushed.

"It was nothing."

"He's right, Morgan. Accept our compliments." Makai pointed his utensil at her.

Huffing slightly, she said, "Thank you."

Chatter mixed with the tinkling of utensils hitting plates. A relaxed atmosphere and genuine enjoyment in each other's company permeated the morning meal. *What a nice way to begin a day. They act like family with one another.*

When they were finished, everyone placed the remains of their meals in the recycler.

"Okay, I'm off to take my shift at the helm," Rain said.

"I need some sleep. It was a long day yesterday." Yaz yawned and gave a little wave as he and Abby turned toward the quarters corridor.

"Give us a couple hours and we'll meet you for our classes," Abby said as Morgan joined her.

"Sounds good." Their voices trailed off. He watched the sway of Morgan's hips. His fingertips ached to trace the soft, but firm muscles of her behind. *I can't recall ever feeling this way about a female before. But, then again, I guess that's not really a surprise given I can't remember much at all.*

"We'll be on the bridge with Rain," Kara said as she and Crax turned to follow the blonde.

"Come with me, Stalad. Let me show you around."

He matched Makai's strides as they walked the corridors. Makai pointed out the large training area, offering to spar with him in the future. Further along, they came to the med bay, then a break area. As they continued, they passed offshoot hallways. Stalad realized the main corridor ran the length of the ship from front to back.

They took the last offshoot hallway to the left and entered a huge shuttle bay near the uppermost portion of it. Makai gestured for him to enter a lift, and they began descending.

"We keep two transports that can handle atmospheric conditions so we have the option of keeping the *Fortitude* in orbit. One smaller, one larger. We also have four fighters. We have three shuttle bays—two on this side of the ship and one on the other. Occasionally, we'll use one as an additional cargo bay. By using both sides of the ship, we can deploy the fighters quickly in either direction if we need to."

"Impressive. But it seems a lot for the size of your crew."

"True. However, we like to have options. We may add to our complement in the future, but when we liberate a vessel, sometimes we choose to keep it, rather than sell it."

"Who maintains your vessels?"

"All the Jalaxians, although Lezon isn't on a rotation."

Throughout their tour, Stalad noted all the vessels appeared to be well-maintained. In the lower hallway, Makai pointed out storage areas and armories. *Impressive armament stores, both large and small.*

"We have weapons storage areas on all levels coded to only us. It allows us easy access in the event we need them quickly," Makai said as they entered a growing area which appeared to run underneath the main corridor areas. "We call this our green-house. This used to be living quarters meant for a significantly larger crew, but we repurposed the space. Abby started it a few years ago. We now have year-round fresh produce and improved air quality in the ship."

"It seems similar to Svesti aquiponics areas yet not quite the same." Stalad proceeded to mention specifics. Makai's blue eyes lit up.

"Perhaps you could help Abby in here occasionally and share your thoughts for improvement. It sounds like you have quite a bit of knowledge about aquiponics."

"I guess I do." Stalad frowned.

"It'll come back to you eventually." Makai squeezed his shoulder. "Engineering's back here. It's Tren's area of expertise." He paused. "Stay back after I open the door."

Stalad's brows crinkled at the unusual order. The door slid aside, and he heard a strange buzzing.

"Tren! Turn off whatever isn't standard before we come in."

The buzzing ceased, and Makai stepped forward.

"Come on in. I was just testing a new design for a remote-control laser tool."

"Where is it?"

Tren lifted a shoulder in the direction of an open maintenance shaft while tapping on a small tablet. A small drone left the shaft and hovered near the engineer. He gingerly took it and powered it down.

"Are you testing it on the ship's equipment?" Makai's tail slapped the metal floor. "We've talked about this."

"I need to see what it can do."

"Test it in areas where it cannot do harm to our ability to move...or breathe."

"The females are usually in the cargo bay this time of day. You told me not to test near them again."

Makai sighed heavily.

"I do not understand how such an intelligent male can be so lacking when it comes to common sense. Just wait until they're done or set up a separate designated testing space." Makai growled at him. "Stop being so impatient. I know your new designs excite you, but the safety of this ship and crew always come first."

Tren's cheeks darkened to cobalt. His shoulders and tail drooped. Stalad bit back a smile at the Jalaxian's chagrin. *He acts like a big youngling.*

"You're right. I'm sorry."

Another sigh left Makai's chest.

"Have you made progress on the hover jetpack?"

Tren's face brightened.

"Yes, I made some adjustments and added a separate control to improve stability if we're transporting more than one being with it. I haven't had a chance to test it yet."

"Good. We'll do that later in the cargo bay. You can instruct us on your changes."

Stalad enjoyed the tour of engineering and found he understood enough to speak intelligently about the type of engines the *Fortitude* employed, as well as their maintenance. Impressed with the weapons and cloaking abilities of the ship, his tail swayed while he asked a number of questions. Makai dipped his head, and the edges of his lips tipped up.

"When you recall everything, I think you'll discover you are a warrior of some sort that is used to ship duties. Your knowledge encompasses a number of subjects and is solid."

Stalad slowly nodded as he digested the captain's comments.

"That assessment doesn't feel wrong."

"Come, let's check out the cargo bay." Makai led them to the other side of the ship.

When they entered the large bay, Stalad's eyes swept the well-ordered space. Safely secured crates lined one wall. In the center of the high-ceilinged area, long lengths of fabric like Morgan used in her performances hung from above.

"Morgan teaches the other females some exercises on the aerial silks, as she calls them. The females say it is a good way to tone their bodies and create better muscular control than simply using our training gear. They also participate in something called yoga, which involves twisting their bodies into unusual shapes. They tell us they enjoy the increased flexibility."

"Would it be acceptable for me to practice my training forms here or in the greenhouse? There's more room for me to move without interrupting anyone else."

"Of course, unless the females complain, and I don't see why they would." Makai gestured to the wall of crates. "Sometimes we simply transport goods for merchants if they need it or we have it to sell after liberating it from, what is it Kara called them? Oh, bad actors. Sometimes it's sensitive cargo. Other times it's like these tablets and electronics parts we're dropping off at the Orkite home world, Arona."

"How is it you have human females onboard?"

"Those stories are theirs to tell or not. But we consider the *Fortitude* a safe haven for human females in trouble."

Stalad frowned. His tail straightened before whipping once.

"Are they in danger now?"

"Not any longer. Their previous threats were eliminated. Events like the one on Nulorn where others think to kidnap them and make them slaves or worse are what we protect against now."

Stalad's tail relaxed.

"Good. They should be kept safe."

Makai grinned.

"Absolutely."

Going up to the top of the ship, Makai led him to the bridge where Rain sat in the pilot's seat. Kara tapped on a tablet while sitting on Crax's lap. Crax appeared to be reading something on the console.

"Report," Makai said.

"On course for Arona. We should reach there in four days." Rain glanced at them before turning back to the console. "Scans indicate nothing in our immediate vicinity along our heading."

"Good."

"Lezon comm'd. Now that he's had a chance to fully review all Stalad's medical info from the *Morning Star*, he wants Stalad to have the measles vaccine," Kara said.

Stalad frowned.

"Measles?"

"A new variant of Earth's measles disease began showing up on different worlds. About a month ago, the Svesti developed a vaccine that protects most species in this region of space. While they believe Svesti are immune, they recommend all be inoculated just in case. Lezon said you can go to the med bay any time to receive it."

"I'll talk with him more about it."

"Crax, show Stalad the weapons stations and our capabilities." Makai sat in the captain's chair.

Crax lifted Kara as he rose. He kissed her on her forehead after he placed her back on the seat where he had been sitting.

Definitely a lax atmosphere on the bridge, but everyone seems competent. I think I like it here.

Chapter 12

Morgan enjoyed experimenting with alien foods and hummed while she prepared dinner. Tonight, she tried a combination of chopped vegetables with meat in a stew. Using a spoon, she tasted her concoction. *Hmm, needs more salt and something savory. Good thing we're headed to Arona. Our stash of crusty bread rolls is running out. They'll go great with this meal.*

Rummaging in the spice compartment, she found what she needed. She let it all simmer as she rolled out a pastry dough and made mini fruit pies. *I'm really glad that vendor on Nulorn allowed me to taste samples. This drisima from Ladorta tastes like apples.*

Taking liberties with the ingredients and using a sugar found on Pellotia, she added some homemade caramel. Its scent combined with the cinnamon took her thoughts back to Stalad. She only saw him briefly during the day. The Jalaxians kept him busy in the training area discovering what the Svesti remembered. *It's gotta be weird not knowing who you are or remembering how you know things.*

After she put the pies in the oven, she fanned her face as she pictured how he looked while he sparred. Clad only in tight pants that hugged his legs, his muscles tensed and released with his surprisingly graceful maneuvers. His tail fascinated her. He exhibited superior control of his when he sparred. Yet sometimes his emotional state showed itself in his tail's movements. Rivulets of sweat ran down his taut abs and she licked her lips. Her cheeks flushed and she rubbed her thighs together. *Shit. It's been three years since I've truly been horny. I need to think of something else before everyone else shows up.*

"Do you need any help?"

Morgan turned sharply with a hand on her chest at Stalad's question.

"You startled me."

"My apologies." His brown eyes twinkled.

"Dinner, uh, evening meal won't be ready for another half hour or so." She pushed some strands of hair back from her forehead. "How was your day?"

"I'm enjoying the *Fortitude*. Everyone is friendly and I'm discovering how much I have retained from before the accident." He leaned back on the counter.

"Anything in particular stand out?" She wiped her hands on a towel and picked up a water pouch. "Would you like one?"

"Not at this time, thank you." His head tilted slightly, and his eyes grew hazy as he thought. "The sparring feels very familiar. So far, there hasn't been anything specific that I haven't known. Generalized knowledge about species and worlds seems intact, although I'm not sure how I know as much as I do about humans. According to Makai, your race isn't widely known to be in space."

"Makai's correct. Although I have a feeling that will be changing." Morgan sipped some water.

"How so?"

"I'm not sure how much I'm allowed to say." She wrinkled her nose. "I guess no one told me I couldn't talk about it."

His tail swayed.

"If you believe you'll betray a confidence, you don't have to explain."

She smiled at him.

"That's nice of you." Morgan inhaled deeply. "Before the Wing Raiders rescued me from a Zuvgran lab, I spent a year on Costonia."

His tail snapped behind him.

"The Zuvgran experimented on you?"

She placed a hand on his tense forearm.

"I'm fine now."

"It should not have happened."

"No, no one should have to go through what we did."

"We?"

Her vision wavered for a moment.

"There were two other women with me." She glanced away and whispered, "They didn't make it out."

"I'm sorry, Morgan." His tail gently wound around her ankle and stroked softly.

Sighing, she said, "Thank you. But to go back to what I was doing on Costonia. I agreed to medical tests." She patted his arm when his tail tightened on her ankle. She registered the shocked look on his face. "No, nothing like the Zuvgran did. Every exam or test received my consent beforehand."

"But why?"

"To see if humans and Svesti are biologically compatible and can have babies together."

His eyes widened.

"And?"

"Yes, we are and should be able to. I think King Sovex was planning to open up negotiations with Earth to bring humans to Costonia."

"Svesti might be able to have younglings again?" A sheen of tears coated his eyes. "It's been so long. Our females died thirty years ago." He rubbed his chest.

"I know. The virus the Zuvgran released did a lot of damage." Lowering her voice, she asked, "Do you think your mother was one of those lost? I know some females survived."

"Probably. When I think of my mother, all I can recall is a scent. No name or face." His lips twisted. "Talking about the virus makes my heart hurt, but there are no memories to go with the emotion."

"I'm sorry, Stalad. Maybe I shouldn't have mentioned it at all."

"Please, always speak your true thoughts with me." His expression softened.

Oh my, he's a heartbreaker.

"Okay. Want to help me carry everything to the table?"

"As you wish."

"What time do we arrive at Arona tomorrow?" Morgan wiped the sweat from her brow.

"Rain said not long after breakfast." Pink suffused Kara's face from her exertions. "Damn, girl, how can you make me perspire so much with stretches? It's not even hot yoga."

Abby's laugh mixed with Morgan's at Kara's complaint.

"Don't you get sweaty with your mate?"

"Of course, but at least I get orgasms in trade. Yoga's never done that for me." Kara's eyebrows wiggled and she tapped the ashes off an imaginary cigar.

Morgan shook her head with a grin.

"It's official. You're insane." She picked up some water pouches to hand to the women.

"Damn straight."

Loud yelling started from somewhere down the hall. All three of them straightened and their eyes darted to each other in alarm. Morgan still had the water pouches in her hands as they ran out of the cargo bay in the direction of the noise.

They veered into the hangar bay and wrinkled their noses.

"What the fuck is that awful smell?" Kara wheezed as she made a beeline for the open transport.

Running up the ramp, the women headed for the loud cursing. They turned a corner and stopped dead at the sight of three large garbage-covered beings and a wall panel lying on the floor. Abby pinched her nose.

"Eew."

The males looked up from flicking refuse off their bodies and the largest one walked toward them.

"Don't you fuckin' dare." Kara narrowed her eyes and pointed her finger at him. His fangs poked out from the mess on his face when he smiled.

Looking like something from a horror movie, the others approached. Morgan's breath stuttered in her chest and her hands reflexively clenched. Water shot from the pouches in her hands and hit the first two in their faces. Her eyes widened and her mouth opened in a huge O. She stared at the second one as debris slid down his face. Water droplets hung from his long eyelashes and a single one held on tenaciously to the tip of his nose.

"Oops." She dropped the empty pouches and bent over with her hands on her knees while her shoulders shook.

"Are you alright?" Stalad shook his head, and the watery mess spattered the women.

"Stop that," Abby giggled, and her face turned pink.

Morgan couldn't contain her laughter any longer.

"I'm..." Wheeze. "Sorry." She desperately tried to inhale more air. "Oh my god. I can't..." Her face reddened. "Your faces." She gestured. "You look like..." Her hands pushed against her stomach when it began to ache. "Swamp monsters."

"What happened?" Kara held her hand out, palm open, to stop Crax from advancing.

Morgan's laughter slowed.

"We took Stalad out to see how he handled the transport. He noted that it operated sluggishly on one side. The diagnostics all came back as normal, so we returned to physically check it out." Yaz unsuccessfully tried to rub his face clean. He held up a dirty instrument. "Scans showed an unusual mass behind a wall panel. When we removed it, this mess exploded from the interior."

Morgan imagined it and tried to suppress her laughter again. Tears streamed from her eyes.

"What is it? It stinks." Abby's entire face scrunched.

"We'll have to investigate more, but I believe the recycler on the transport hasn't been working properly for a long time. Diagnostics and alerts failed, a line broke when it became full, and the waste ended up in the wall. We don't use this transport regularly, so it went unnoticed," Crax grumbled.

"Swiss cheese theory." Kara nodded.

"Swiss cheese?" Yaz said.

"It's a cheese with holes in it on Earth. Swiss cheese theory is that while many layers of protection exist to prevent accidents, if flaws in each layer line up, that's when incidents occur. If each layer is a slice of cheese with holes in it, the holes are the flaws," Kara explained.

All three males nodded in understanding.

Kara squealed when Crax picked her up and held her against his chest.

"You bastard. Now that crap is on me and I smell, too." Debris squelched when she slapped his shoulder.

"We should take a shower," Crax growled.

"You should clean this shit up." Kara's feet flailed. She protested until he squeezed her ass, then her body went slack in his arms. "Take me to our quarters."

"I'll set up some cleaning bots to take care of the worst of this for now," Yaz yelled after Crax. "I expect you to help with the interior wall and maintenance."

"Allow me to assist," Stalad's brown eyes glinted with humor.

"You guys stay here. We'll get the bots. We won't track nearly as much mess as you two." Abby grabbed Morgan's hand. "Come on."

Morgan's breathing normalized as they walked to a storage compartment.

"That was hilarious."

"I don't know how Kara kept a straight face." Abby pulled out a few cleaning bots and hit the buttons for them to follow them. Morgan grabbed more. They ended up with six bots.

"I think she was more concerned with not getting dirty. Looks like that didn't work out for her."

"Guess she'll be getting sweaty again." Abby winked.

Morgan smiled.

"Sometimes I think this crew is nuts."

"Yep, but you have to admit we're a lot of fun."

"True."

They helped Stalad and Yaz program the bots, then led the way into the hangar bay. The males entered a decontamination unit in the corner.

"I'm not tracking this into the main corridors. Makai will kill us," Yaz said.

"Good plan," Stalad said as the door closed.

"Should we wait for them and go in ourselves?" Morgan looked at Abby.

"I think so. We don't want this odor in the other parts of the ship."

"Do you think Kara and Crax used it?"

"I hope so. Yaz is right. Makai will be pissed if they bring this into the residential quarters."

They chatted while the decontamination cycle ran. Morgan's eyes widened when the males exited naked. Seeing the women, both men covered their genitals with the clothing in their hands.

"Geez, guys." Abby grabbed some towels from a nearby compartment and threw them at the males.

Morgan turned so she wasn't looking directly at the males as they wrapped the towels around their waists. But she couldn't help peeking at them from the corner of her eye. *Wow, both are well-endowed.*

Cinnamon and caramel hit her nose and the wetness in her panties became uncomfortable. Stalad inhaled and his tail straightened momentarily.

"We weren't expecting you to still be out here." Yaz smiled at Abby. "Are you going to use the unit instead of a shower?"

"I'll have a shower afterwards. We didn't want to spread the smell throughout the *Fortitude.*"

Morgan took a couple towels and handed one to Abby.

"Let's get this done."

Juggling a tray laden with food and using her elbow, Morgan tapped a spot on the wall. A small tabletop slid out and she placed the heavy tray on it. The smell of hot food filled the bridge as she opened the containers.

"Please tell me some of that is for me," said Yaz.

"Of course."

"What did you make for midday meal today?" Kara said.

"A chunky soup and the last of the rolls. There's some fruit for dessert."

"Yum." Kara tapped her console. "Uh, Makai, you're going to want to read this."

Sitting in his captain's chair, Makai pressed the armrest. His eyebrows rose as he looked at what Kara mentioned.

"Emperor n'Tuli died."

"Who's that?" Morgan's nose crinkled. "I've never heard of him."

"The Zuvgran emperor." Kara tapped some more and a picture of an old Zuvgran appeared on the viewscreen with a biography. "A royal piece of shit."

Morgan crossed her arms over her torso hugging herself. The sight of a Zuvgran made her shiver in remembered fear. She snorted in disgust. His supposed accomplishments read like a fascist dictator's resume.

"Who's taking his place?" Deliberately, she relaxed herself and inhaled deeply before delivering food to everyone.

"That's the interesting part. He never named a successor." Makai's braids swung when he turned her way. "There are several contenders, but it won't be pretty until they resolve their leadership. I'm not sure any of them will be better than n'Tuli."

"Chaos," said Crax from his spot near Kara.

"Mayhem," Yaz said with a grin.

"Opportunity?" Kara smiled at Morgan in thanks as she took the container from her.

"Monitor communications, Kara. I want to know what's going on and what beings are saying." Makai bit into a roll. "Civil unrest in the Zuvgran empire will affect operations."

"You got it, boss."

Chapter 13

Stalad grinned as he entered his quarters. Morgan's unfettered amusement at the males' misfortune lifted his spirits. Her green eyes sparkled above red cheeks. Her blunt, white teeth surrounded by her pink lips when the water hit their faces made him think of where he'd like her mouth to be. And her scent when she saw him naked had him hiding his instant erection. *I think I'm a lusty male. At least around her, it seems.*

Striding into his shower, his fingers grasped his needy cock. He hissed at how sensitive his flesh felt. Groaning as his fist worked to thoughts of her on her knees with her mouth engulfing him, he imagined her sultry green eyes watching him. Warm water beat down on his chest as he imagined her mouth wet and hot around him as her tongue licked. The image of soft fingers tracing his heavy balls and trailing to his base node sent his seed exploding against the wall. Her name left his lips like a whispered prayer.

His forehead fell forward as he extended his orgasm for as long as possible. The water turned tepid. *Crekkin' timer on the showers to conserve water. A few more minutes would be nice.*

Rapidly cleaning his body, he finished just before the water turned frigid and shut off automatically. He shook his body, then stepped into the dryer. After popping in a mouth cleaning tab, he combed his short hair and stared at himself in the viewer. *I must not think of her this way. I don't know if I have a female waiting for me. It would not be honorable to pursue her.*

Along with Crax and Yaz, Stalad loaded maglevs into the larger transport with the crates being delivered. The *Fortitude* would orbit Arona while they took the smaller ship to the surface. Makai arrived just as they secured the last crate.

"Let's get this done. I have a meeting about another potential job afterwards. It will only be the four of us going to the planet."

In the cockpit, they each took seats and fastened their restraints as Yaz conducted his preflight checks.

"Same place as last time?"

Makai nodded.

"*Fortitude*, we're ready to open Hangar Bay One and depart."

Rain's voice sounded through the comms.

"*Experience*, cleared to depart. Stay in touch."

"Will do."

Stalad watched with interest as they broke atmosphere. Arona appeared to be a world of lush greens, blues, and browns.

Famous for its precious gemstones and ores, the Orkite home world produced some of the finest jewelry in the known galaxy. The Orkites lived in conjunction with nature eschewing tall metal or glass structures. Natural stone or wood dwellings nestled in the smaller villages near water. Larger cities contained the same, but the buildings sprawled around several larger keeps.

They landed near the outskirts of one city, Urzo. Stepping down the ramp, Stalad inhaled deeply. Clean, fresh air, laden with the scents of Arona's nature filled his lungs. He closed his eyes and savored the rich smells. His limbs felt heavy due to the planet's higher gravitational pull. *Must be one reason Orkites grow sturdy.*

"Does any of this look familiar?" Yaz asked quietly.

"No. I don't recognize the specific scents or surroundings."

"Must not have ever visited Arona before," Crax grumbled.

"Dablar, well met this fine day," Makai greeted the approaching older Orkite. The massive dusky green male stood taller than all of them by half a head. A relatively trim waist separated broad shoulders over thick biceps and tree trunk thighs in brown leather pants. A pronounced brow ridge overshadowed his dark eyes as well as his broad, flattened-tipped nose. Tusks yellowed with age framed the lower half of his wide smile. Strands of silver interspersed his black braids. Thick gold chains decorated his neck while numerous scars interrupted the intricate designs in black ink found on his arms and torso. A large green gemstone shaped into a hoop hung from one ear. Daggers hung from sheaths at his hips.

"Makai, welcome to Urzo." A meaty hand grasped the Jalaxian's forearm, the flesh on flesh smacking loudly in a warrior's clasp.

"As promised, your items are here safely." Makai squeezed the male's arm before stepping back.

"No issues?"

"None."

"Good. Let's get it unloaded and settle accounts." Dablar looked at Stalad. "New member of your crew?"

"Stalad is traveling with us for a bit until we get in range of Costonia. Stalad, meet Dablar, the best technology merchant in Urzo."

"Best on Arona," the Orkite corrected with a grin. "Well met, Stalad."

"Well met, Dablar. You have a beautiful home world."

"Thank you, lad."

Several younger Orkites assisted in moving the crates while Makai and Dablar chatted. Stalad noticed that their skin tones ranged from pale to a deep forest green. Some had piercings in one or both nipples, or their noses. *I wonder if the piercings mean anything.*

"Everything looks good. We have a meeting with Lord Heggar to get to," Makai said.

Dablar's expression turned serious.

"I suggest going forward, if you speak to anyone, say you are paying your respects to the Lord, rather attending than a scheduled meeting."

"Oh?" Makai's eyes narrowed.

"It's best if fewer beings know the real reason for your visit."

"Can you elaborate?"

"Not my place. You'll understand after you see Heggar."

"Thank you, Dablar. I'll do as you say."

The Orkite clapped Makai's back.

"I'll let you know when I need another shipment delivered."

"We'll do what we can."

Stalad walked with the Jalaxians toward the largest stone building with appeared to be four stories high. Every Orkite, male or female, wore weapons, be it daggers, swords, or axes. He narrowed his eyes at one huge male carrying a mace. *Someone likes it bloody.*

Two guards stood at the oversized wooden entry doors.

"Captain Makai and crew to pay our respects to Lord Heggar."

"One moment." The guard spoke to a boy behind him. The youngling scampered further inside the building. The boy returned quickly and nodded enthusiastically.

"I'm to escort you to Lord Heggar directly, Captain Makai." He looked at the guards. "The Lord says they do not need to be disarmed."

The first guard grunted.

"Follow the lad."

"Thank you."

The inside of the building took Stalad by surprise. He expected it to be dark, dank, and cold, but instead they traversed along well-lit, clean halls with doors leading to well-appointed, comfortable rooms. They climbed a wide set of stairs to the third floor. The ambient temperature remained constant throughout—just slightly cool.

The young Orkite stopped at a set of doors with another set of guards.

"Captain Makai for Lord Heggar."

"Thank you, lad. Head to the kitchens and see if Cook has a treat for you." The oldest guard said gruffly. "Then back to the front to resume your duties as runner."

"Thanks, Papaw." The young male grinned. "You're the best."

"Go on with you." The guard ruffled the boy's hair then looked at them. "My son's son."

They smiled.

"He seems like a fine youngling," Stalad said.

"Too much energy. Even a busy day running errands and messages can't tire him out." The grizzled male smiled and opened the door. "Lord Heggar is expecting you."

"Thank you," Makai said.

They entered a large study. Lord Heggar sat behind a desk that hid most of his bulk. Weapons hung on the wall behind him. Books lined shelves around the room. Heavy, wooden chairs with thick cushions in front of the desk and the fireplace on the opposite wall looked comfortable. A single window overlooked the grounds of the city.

Lord Heggar stood. The massive male was even larger than Dablar. Unlike the merchant, Heggar wore a sleeveless, brown shirt with open sides belted at his waist.

"Captain Makai. It's good to see you again."

"Lord Heggar. It's my pleasure. Please allow me to introduce members of my crew—Yaz, Crax, and Stalad."

"Well met, warriors." The Orkite cocked his head slightly. "You've added Svesti to your crew?"

"Just the one."

"Would you like something to drink?"

"No, thank you."

"Please have a seat." Heggar gestured with a hand. "Feel free to move chairs as needed."

Stalad and Crax pulled two chairs from the fireplace group to the others in front of the desk and sat. The Orkite frowned, placed a device on his desk, and tapped a button.

"A dampening field to discourage eavesdroppers. I have a sensitive job if you're interested, Captain."

"What does it entail?"

"I need to send an ambassador to Ladorta in secret. No one can know about the negotiations until they are completed."

"How large a contingent will accompany the ambassador?"

"An assistant and two guards. Your crew would transport everyone and be supplemental security for my delegate."

"Are you expecting a long negotiation?"

"I expect no longer than a *lunar*."

"When would they need to leave?"

"They can be ready in tomorrow. The Ladortans are expecting someone within a week."

Stalad observed Heggar as the negotiations proceeded. His tail stilled when he realized the Orkite was withholding information. He tapped the captain's back. When Makai looked sideways at him, Stalad gestured with his hand using an old Jalaxian military code. Makai dipped his chin.

"Have your people meet our ship after morning meal, along with the supplies we've agreed upon."

Heggar appeared uncomfortable.

"We need to formulate a plan to get them to you without anyone noticing."

"Why the secrecy, Heggar? What aren't you telling me?"

An unhappy grumble left the Orkite's lips.

"The ambassador is my daughter, Niksen. Two attempts on her life have occurred in recent weeks. I don't know if the threat is to her personally or because of my position. Publicly, I named another to travel to Ladorta to negotiate in a month. I'm hoping to discover who is behind the attempts on her life while she is under your protection."

"Is she qualified to handle the Ladortan contingent?"

"Absolutely. While she can be headstrong, she knows the intricacies of our position and is well-versed in political maneuvering. There are those who fail to acknowledge her intelligence and worth, but she is my heir and extremely capable."

"Any chance the Ladortans are behind the assassination attempts?"

"Unlikely."

"So we proceed as if she's in danger until you inform us otherwise." Makai paused. "The three accompanying her—do you trust them?"

"Yes. The guards have been with her since birth and conducted most of her warrior training. The assistant is another guard experienced in covert operations."

"How will you explain her absence?"

"We'll have a public fight tonight during last meal about her safety. I'll order her to a secure location immediately. That's where you need to retrieve them."

Crax murmured, "We'll be obvious if we land anywhere else on Arona."

Makai and Heggar looked at him.

"Do you have a better idea?"

Crax leaned forward.

"Yes."

Stalad listened, and his lips lifted slightly as they added important details to Crax's plan. *This should work.*

"How will you let the *Fortitude* know what to expect?" Heggar asked.

"We have secure ways of communicating." Makai's expression bordered on smug. "We need to add items to the cargo list to create confusion. Ideas?"

"Morgan said something about more bread," Yaz said. "I bet she would love to have Orkite spices and foods to work with as well as new recipes."

"You just want to get out of cooking." Crax crossed his arms and smirked. "The females could benefit from additional fabrics."

"Do we need luxury items for your people?" Makai turned to Heggar.

"No."

"We should have larger items that can be sold on Nulorn to account for some of the crates," Stalad added quietly.

A crafty smile rose on Heggar's face.

"Some Orkite furniture should work."

"Let's finalize the list so I can send it to the *Fortitude*." Makai tapped on his tablet. "They'll prepare on their end."

Chapter 14

"Everyone to the bridge. We've got a job."

Morgan's head lifted at Rain's announcement. She dried her hands before leaving the kitchen. *What's going on? I'm not normally involved in the jobs.*

All the women were on the bridge with Lezon. Tren hustled in right after Morgan.

"What's the job?" Tren asked.

"Kara?" Rain glanced at the focused woman.

"Just finishing the decryption. Makai used the program I developed and added the info behind the inventory list they're picking up on Arona. The unsecure part says we're taking the items to Nulorn to a specific vendor, apart from some stuff we're keeping, like food and fabrics." Kara chewed on her lip. "Oh, this is interesting. In four of the crates, there will be Orkites hidden whom we'll transport. He didn't say where they're going."

"That's strange. Orkites are not known for hiding. They tend to be extremely forthright." Tren's brows closed together.

"We're to prepare two sets of quarters next to each other—one for males, the other for females. Expect to provide increased security for about a *lunar* for the HVT's mission."

"HVT?" Morgan said.

"High Value Target." Rain smiled. "Military term."

Morgan nodded.

"Thanks."

"Did he say what the mission is?" Lezon's tail swayed.

"No, I imagine he'll tell us in person. However, he wants us to scan the crates for trackers and listening devices. We're to leave them in place and act as if there are no additional beings. All the crates stay on the transport except the ones marked as our payment."

"Lezon and I will conduct the scans. If there is anything to worry about, I'll let everyone know and set up a dampening field around the transport." Tren grinned.

Kara tapped her console and the main viewscreen filled with both messages. Everyone read Makai's exact words and discussed how to handle different scenarios. *Four Orkites will be returning with the guys tonight.*

Morgan and Abby went to prepare the quarters, grabbing bedding from stores.

"No." Abby shook her head at the stuff Morgan picked and pointed at some softer sheets and pillows. "We'll use these ones here. Makai said to make the females' quarters more comfortable."

"What does that even mean?" Morgan put back the things in her hands and replaced them with the ones Abby suggested.

"It means at least one of them is high born or important. So, they get more amenities in recognition of their status."

"They're hiding in crates. Are they going to have silk cushions in there?"

Abby smirked.

"Maybe. Aliens can act as entitled as some humans."

Morgan laughed.

"Point taken. Is this kind of job normal?"

"I've learned over the years is you never know what to expect."

"Well, let's get the quarters ready. Where are we putting them?"

"Across from you and Stalad. If we're supposed to protect someone, that will place them centrally between all of us."

"Not sure I'll be much help keeping anyone safe."

"I guess your contribution is ensuring they don't eat anything Yaz prepares."

Both women grinned.

"Got it. I'm on kitchen duty." Morgan pursed her lips. "How much do you think Orkites eat?"

"I'd say at least as much as Jalaxians." Abby's eyes brightened.

"Of course they do." Morgan shook her head.

Morgan brought the remainder of breakfast to the dining area before taking an empty seat between Stalad and Kara. The heat from his body seared her thigh and his cinnamon and caramel scent relaxed her. Pouring herself a glass of juice, she glanced at the full table.

The Arona group arrived late the night before, so this was the first time she saw Orkites in the flesh. Like all the other aliens, they were tall and had green skin in varying shades with broad, muscular builds. The tusks seemed to make their jaws look like a big underbite. Each one had horns, most with some type of curve, although the females appeared to run smaller. *They look like the orcs in Earth's stories. I wonder if they visited our planet long ago and that's how the tales originated.*

From what she could gather, Niksen, a beautiful Orkite with shiny, decorated braids was the HVT, with Lollek as her assistant. Lollek's piercing dark eyes watched everything intensely, although she attempted to look disinterested in the rowdy conversation. Two older, scarred guards, Krinir and Fraddar, accompanied the females never moving far from them.

"Lady Niksen's argument with her father was explosive." Yaz gestured wildly. "Dishes, food, and furniture flying." He looked at Tren. "You would've loved it. She stomped out with these three trailing her, looking utterly aggrieved."

"They boarded a large transport. What others didn't see was them leaving through a maintenance conduit on the other side where Crax waited with the crates. By the time the ship departed, they were already onboard *Experience*." Makai spooned a large pile of scrambled eggs onto his plate. "Crax returned to the hall to the chaos left in their wake. No one suspected the switch."

"No one will realize they're missing?" Rain asked as she passed a platter of bacon to Yaz.

"Not for some time. Lord Heggar ordered us to take her to a remote safe house. It takes an additional three-day hike to get to it from the nearest landing area big enough for the transport. It will be a week minimum before anyone realizes Lady Niksen is not there. The four Orkites already on the ship, as well as the pilot, will wear cloaks as they begin their travels to the safe house. Their instructions are to remain there for three weeks." Krinir's gruff voice traveled the length of the table easily. He chewed on the fried meat and poured some more juice for himself.

"I scanned everything and everyone when they arrived. No trackers or surveillance of any kind." Tren scooped up some chopped *lobile* onto his utensil and made a happy noise. "This is good, Morgan. What do you call it?"

"Hash browns. The *lobile* is similar to an Earth vegetable called potato. I added some other vegetables to it to enhance the flavor." Morgan didn't react when Stalad's tail wrapped around her ankle, and he hummed contentedly as he ate.

"It really is close to something we'd find on Earth." Abby smiled. "I'm glad you like to cook."

"When I was on Delizas, the chefs at our establishment were kind enough to teach me about many of the foods out here in the galaxy," Morgan said.

"You worked on a pleasure planet?" Lady Niksen frowned in her direction.

"I had no choice," Morgan answered curtly.

"After morning meal, I will give you all a tour of the *Fortitude* and explain various safety protocols to our guests."

Makai's words interrupted the tense moment. "How long before we arrive at Ladorta?"

"Five days," said Yaz.

"Good. Lady Niksen, you will keep me apprised of where and whom you will be meeting so your guards and I can coordinate resources for your safety."

The Orkite's face twisted with displeasure. Dark green highlighted her high cheekbones.

"I can protect myself."

"Your father hired us to do a job. We will do it to the best of our ability." Makai's eyes narrowed, although his voice remained pleasant.

"Lady Niksen, we will not be taking unnecessary chances with your life, not after the recent attempts on it." Fraddar glared at the female. "You are a skilled warrior. That does not make you invincible."

Morgan suppressed a shiver at the female's angry growl. *Shit. She's intense.*

Lollek pushed her plate forward and sat back.

"Milady, your primary orders are to broker this agreement. Let the guards and the Wing Raiders handle the security."

"I dislike being treated like a pup." Niksen stood abruptly.

Krinir calmly looked at her.

"You are being treated like an important Orkite asset. However, I suggest you stop acting immaturely. It's unbecoming for someone of your status."

"I am your boss."

"You are my charge. If you need a reminder, we'll spar later," Krinir said with a small smile.

"The tour?" Niksen bit out.

"Is everyone ready?" Makai looked at the other Orkites.

Fraddar wiped his face with a napkin.

"Might as well do it now. It will give her time to walk off some of her ire."

Niksen stomped out of the room.

"Please excuse us. Morning meal was delicious. Thank you." Lollek stood and smiled at the group. "We'll have more time to become acquainted during our travels." She and the other Orkites followed Makai.

"Wow. Spoiled much?" Kara snagged some bacon from Crax's plate.

Rain's expression turned thoughtful.

"I'm not sure. We know how difficult it can be to prove we're as capable as men. She may simply be reacting to something cultural."

"Well, I hope she settles down. We don't need to be walking on eggshells for this mission." Abby sipped some water.

"Will you be training later?" Stalad asked.

Morgan nodded.

"We'll be working on the silks. Why?"

"May I join you?"

Her eyebrow raised.

"You want to exercise with the women?"

"If you ladies wouldn't mind. I've discovered I like learning new techniques and skills." Stalad's brown eyes brightened.

"Would you teach us some of your training forms? They look a lot like some martial arts moves from Earth. Those could come in handy." Rain leaned forward.

"Of course."

"Are you guys okay with Stalad joining us? If you'd rather, I can teach him separately." Morgan glanced at each of the humans.

"Doesn't matter to me." Kara shrugged.

"Sure." Abby stood. "I'm going to change, and I'll meet you all there."

Rain and Kara pushed back from their seats.

"We'll clean up first." Rain began stacking dishes.

Morgan smiled at Stalad.

"Let's go. I'll show you how to do the safety checks before everyone else shows up."

"After you."

Morgan fanned herself. Stalad proved to be an attentive student. He asked pertinent questions and took corrective criticism well. And his muscular control impressed the hell out of her. Watching his abs contract and release or his thighs wrap around the fabric caused electric tingles in her girlie parts. *Damn, he's a fine example of manliness. Maleness? Not sure what the proper word is out here in space, but I sure do like watching him.*

When he wound his tail around the silks and hung upside down, the women cracked up. Kara added monkeyish vocalizations. When the women explained why they found it so amusing, he imitated the sounds which they found hilarious. *He's so damned likable. Fun sense of humor and not afraid to be a bit silly.*

His scent grew stronger as he exerted himself. She enjoyed his cinnamon and caramel scent more than she should, especially when she moved closer to correct his grip or position. At one point, she forcibly stopped herself from licking his straining bicep.

Now she stood in line with the other women as he demonstrated basic Svesti training forms. According to him, most of the more advanced forms would build from this small set, and they needed to master these before moving on. Patiently, he walked among them, adjusting their stances as they held the first form. *It feels a little like standing yoga combined with some Bruce Lee.*

"You're too stiff. Relax your neck."

His scent surrounded her when he stepped behind her. She shivered at his breath on her nape. His tail nudged her right knee to move it slightly into the correct position. Palms upright, he ran them on the underside of her upper arms to her hands and adjusted her properly. She bit back a moan, and her panties dampened. *It's not sexual. It's not sexual. Damn, his hands feel so good.*

"There. Much better." His quiet words rumbled low in her belly. He stepped back quickly.

"Good, everyone. Hold that position. Beginning with your scalp, start tensing and relaxing your muscles. Slowly move down your body until you've done all your major muscle groups and the tension has left your body. But keep your position as you do so."

A few minutes later, Kara blew out a breath.

"This is a lot more difficult than it looks."

"I thought Morgan gave us a workout, but just standing here takes a toll." Rain grimaced.

"Whiners." Morgan smirked.

"Bitch." Kara flipped her the bird.

"You moved out of position."

"Tattletale."

All the women started laughing and lost their poses.

Stalad shook his head and grinned.

"I guess we're done for today."

"Sorry. Not sorry," said Kara.

"Go. We'll do this again when you want." He grabbed a towel and wiped his face. The women grabbed their things, chattering and waving as they left.

"Thank you, Stalad. You're a good instructor." Morgan sipped from a water pouch.

"You are as well. I learned a great deal on the silks." He ran the towel over his head, messing up his short hair. *Damn, even with his hair sticking up every which way, he's sexy.*

Inhaling deeply, she stepped closer to him stopping with mere inches between them. She tilted her head back to meet his eyes. *I can do this.*

"I like you, Stalad. A lot. I want to get to know you better."

Chapter 15

Stalad hated himself for it, but he couldn't help but caress Morgan's arms when he adjusted her stance. Her hair with hints of red tickled his skin. Her scent grew heavy and indolent. He had to step away to hide the sudden stiffness of his cock. The banter of the females gave him time to get his unruly body under control. When they were alone and she crowded close, all his efforts seemed a waste as his cock bulged again in his pants. *I can't want her. It's not right.*

"I like you, Stalad. A lot. I want to get to know you better."

At her words, he bent down slightly and gazed into her blue eyes.

"I like you, too." His head tilted, and he lifted a shoulder. "Aren't we already getting to know each other better?" *Maybe she isn't saying what I think she is.*

She bit into her plump lower lip then her pink tongue licked it. Her eyes left his and focused near his neck. *I'd like my tongue on her lips...and on her body.*

"I meant romantically." Her words hung in the air between them.

His tail jerked involuntarily caused her to stumble into his chest. His arms rose to keep her from falling. Her *trulet*, grassy scent filled his nostrils. *Crek. I didn't realize my tail was wrapped around her ankle.*

"I'm sorry. I didn't mean to unsteady you." He lifted his hands away from her back and his feet reluctantly moved backwards. His tail lingered before leaving her ankle.

"Have I misread the signals?" Her cheeks turned red.

"No. Yes." He ran his hand through his damp hair. "I mean, I find you extremely attractive, Morgan. Not just in appearance. Your personality is wonderful. I enjoy spending time with you."

"But…"

Shrugging, he sighed heavily.

"I don't know who I am. I could have a mate or be under a troth contract. It wouldn't be honorable to pursue a romantic relationship with you until I know for certain."

Her eyes flashed upwards to meet his. Red tinged her cheekbones.

"Oh, I hadn't even considered that. I'm so sorry I said anything." She bent to pick up her things. "Please forget this conversation." She swore under her breath when the water pouch slipped from her fingers. His hand covered hers.

"I should, but I don't want to forget it. Please don't be embarrassed. I am honored by your interest, Morgan. You have no idea how much I would love to explore more with you." His voice lowered. "But I can't." His tail flicked in short bursts. "This amnesia is beyond frustrating. I feel like there's something important I need to do. I don't feel like I'm missing someone specifically, but I...don't...know." He slapped his chest needing the sting to punish himself for hurting her.

She murmured, "Integrity is doing the right thing even when no one is watching." Tears filled her compassionate eyes. "I understand, Stalad. And I respect you and your reasons more than you know. If you do have a mate, she is a lucky female." She drew in a shaky breath. "I hope we can remain friends."

He reached a hand toward her, then slowly dropped it by his side without touching her.

"Please. I would like that, *ciebala*."

Giving him a sad smile, she said, "Well, I better go. Training tomorrow?"

"Yes."

He admired the gentle sway of her hips as she walked away. *Why can't I remember? What if there's someone waiting for me that doesn't make me burn like she does? If my memories return, will I still feel the same way about the human?*

For the first few days, the Orkites kept to themselves. Stalad observed them sparring and at meals. Ladies Niksen and Lollek trained with each other and also with Krinir and Fraddar. Even when provoked, Krinir remained measured. Solid fighting skills and exuding calm in every circumstance, his stalwart presence kept the others from escalating irritating behaviors. Fraddar's humor sometimes went too far, but he reminded Stalad of a young male looking for attention, even though he old enough to be Niksen's sire. Lady Lollek appeared subservient and helpful. If he didn't know she operated covertly for Heggar, he might have missed her watchful eyes.

Lady Niksen sported a leaner body than most Orkites. A symmetrically beautiful face and muscular control made for an appealing picture as she fought. He wasn't a fan of her tusks, but that was his personal preference.

In between, he trained with the Jalaxians on Tren's invention called a hover jetpack. The engineer upgraded the controls to account for carrying another being. With practice, all of them became proficient on using the device, but each of them suffered various injuries from impacting the bay walls and ceilings. Lezon spent some time healing each of them. The medic also told the story of how one of Tren's earlier inventions, a weapons spinner, almost took of his head. *Makai's caution on my tour at the engineering door now makes sense. Tren is brilliant, but he lacks restraint.*

All of them discussed the latest updates about the happenings in the Zuvgran empire. Without a successor named, the initial chaos resulted in a military commander, Rufen d'Urfan, taking control. None of them knew much of the male, so they couldn't project whether military rule would continue or if another bid for power would happen. Makai shared that there were a number of Zuvgran who hated n'Tuli's rule and had been escaping for years. Whether that foreshadowed a significant change for the future, no one knew.

Fortunately, he and Morgan settled into their friendship without rancor or hurt feelings. While they continued to teach each other their respective skills, they did so in a group setting. Although he wished for more that he couldn't have, he refrained from flirting or unnecessary physical contact. His tail, however, had a mind of its own and he frequently found it sneaking to hold her ankle gently or resting on the small of her back if they were in close proximity.

He shook off his thoughts of others on the *Fortitude* and concentrated on Crax in front of him. The huge Jalaxian rolled his head and shrugged.

"Are we doing this?" For a big male, Crax moved lightly in the sparring ring.

"Of course." Stalad chose a loose stance and waited for Crax's opening move.

When a blue fist aimed at his face, he pivoted on his right leg. Air displaced near his head creating a false breeze. *Well, I guess we're starting strong.*

Continuing his swivel, he elbowed his opponent in the torso. Internally wincing at the shock up his arm from the hit, he jumped over Crax's tail when it swept toward his legs. Landing in a crouch, he threw an uppercut toward the Jalaxian's armpit. Crax grunted and Stalad resisted the urge to shake his hand. *Crek. The male is a rock.*

For the next several minutes the males didn't speak, although the space was alive with the sounds of flesh meeting flesh, as well as growls and grunts. Neither male gained a significant advantage overall.

"Stalad!"

Makai's interruption distracted the Svesti and Crax took advantage of the moment to punch him in the face. Stalad fell backwards and air rushed from his lungs. Sucking in a breath, he sat up and rested his elbows on his knees. He looked up to see Crax holding out a hand to help him up and Makai's eyes twinkling in amusement.

"You should know better, Svesti. Never take your eyes off your opponent." Makai grinned.

"Did you want to see Crax drop me?" Stalad clasped Crax's hand and allowed himself to be pulled up.

"Not particularly. It was an extra benefit."

"What do you need?" Stalad caught the towel thrown at him and wiped his forehead.

"To talk and get your opinion." Makai's levity ended and a serious expression formed on his face.

"About?"

"I just received a contract offer from Costonia. Before accepting it, I wanted to talk to you."

"Would we need to go there?"

"No. The job involves intel gathering on Rumaska. There's no guarantee that the *Fortitude* would do anything other than report back via comms. However, I can introduce you to my contact and have him investigate who you might be in the meantime."

Stalad's tail swayed, and his teeth clicked together.

"I'm not sure. What if he discovers something that might impact your operations?"

"Like what? You're a wanted male?" Makai chuckled.

"I don't know. Maybe I have to return to Costonia immediately for some reason I cannot remember. I feel like if I'm told who I am, but have no means to learn more, it doesn't truly help me regain my memories. I'm concerned it might frustrate me more." Stalad tossed his towel into the refresher and grabbed a water pouch. "You may need me to help with the Orkites." *I don't think I'm ready to leave the Fortitude yet...or Morgan.*

"We would survive without you." Makai grinned. "However, if you prefer, we can wait until after we complete the Costonian mission before we follow up on your identity."

"That sounds acceptable." A relieved breath left his chest. *Why aren't I using every resource I can to find out who I am as quickly as possible?*

"Consider that our plan, then."

The next day, Stalad entered the cargo bay a little earlier than usual to train with the females. Loud music rang bounced from the metal walls as Morgan performed a routine similar to those on Nulorn. He leaned against a crate and watched spellbound. Even in simple clothes and with no special lighting effects, her fluid movements took his breath away. *So much talent.*

The doors opened and the Orkites, as well as Lezon, Crax, and Makai, followed the human females into the area. Abby placed a forefinger to her lips so the others would not distract Morgan. They observed as she twisted, turned, climbed, slid, spun, and contorted her body into a moving work of art. All of them gasped as she swung to another set of silks floating in midair with her legs split horizontally to the floor as if she were leaping. Once on the second set of silks, her hands gripped the fabric and her body rotated to wrap itself before she released and spread her arms wide with her head bowed, hanging above the floor as the music ceased.

Silence reigned for a moment before he, the humans, and Jalaxians clapped. The Orkites, with the exception of Niksen, slapped their thighs, their version of approval. Morgan's head snapped up and she grasped the silks, untwisted herself, and slid to the floor. She smiled, imitated a curtsy, and smiled. Her flushed face glistened with perspiration. When her scent reached him, he wrapped his tail around his ankle to keep it from wandering.

"I didn't realize you were here. I was just working on a new routine." She caught the towel Kara tossed to her.

"The switching between sets of silks is new," Rain said. "It's impressive."

"I would prefer you didn't conduct such maneuvers alone." Makai crossed his arms. "If you fell, there would be no one to assist."

"I put down mats." Morgan's spine stiffened.

"You could still be injured if you landed wrong." He dipped his chin. "I'm not saying not to do it. I want you to practice safely." Sighing, he added, "Just like I want Tren to test his inventions responsibly."

"Did you compare me to Tren?" Morgan's fists rested on her hips, her jaw lifted, and her blue eyes flashed. *So fiery and passionate in her anger.*

The other humans tried to hide their snickers at her outrage, but the usually stoic Crax guffawed. She included him in her glare.

"Do I need to make it an order?" Makai's eyes twinkled.

"If the human wants to break her neck, let her," Lady Niksen interjected. Everyone turned in disbelief. "I doubt it would be a great loss." Krinir frowned, while Fraddar and Lollek shifted uncomfortably. *Crek. What a petty female. Her attitude dims her outward attractiveness.*

"Why are you even here?" Kara said, her face tight.

"I wanted to see where so many of you disappear to each day."

"You've seen us. You can leave now." Kara gestured toward the door. Stalad bit back a smile at the pink-haired human's contentiousness. *The human females protect each other.*

Rain tapped her lips with a forefinger.

"On Earth, we have fictional beings similar to Orkites in build. We call them orcs. In many of the stories, the females orcs tend to be the leaders and take pride in supporting the other females. Is that not so for Orkites?"

Lollek spoke. "It is similar for our species in that we have female councils that meet regularly and ensure all are treated fairly. They are also responsible for disciplining those few males who are foolish enough to abuse or assault females."

"Hmm, obviously, Niksen won't be leading such a council with her personality."

"I demand satisfaction for the insult to my character." Lady Niksen's lips firmed.

"What does that entail?" Abby chewed on her lower lip.

"For something like this, a sparring match until first blood." Krinir pinned Lady Niksen with a hard glance. "I doubt it's necessary since you insulted one of our hosts first."

"She implied I'm not fit to lead." Lady Niksen's cheeks turned a dark green and a growl rumbled from her chest.

"And you insinuated that Morgan is not fit to live." Rain's lips tightened. "I demand satisfaction for the insult to my friend."

Morgan tugged at Rain's arm.

"That's not necessary. Niksen is a guest onboard. Worse has been said to me."

"You're a puny human. You think you can draw first blood from me with no claws, fangs, or tusks?" The Orkite raised an eyebrow and scoffed.

"I know I can." Rain looked at Makai. "Do you have any issues if I beat the shit out of the entitled mean girl?"

The captain exchanged glances with Krinir who nodded.

"When would you like to do this?" Makai tilted his head.

"Now works, if it's okay with her." Rain shrugged.

"Let's go, then, human." Niksen spun on her heel and strode toward the door.

"Well, you heard princess bitch," Kara said with an evil grin. "Let's go enjoy watching her getting her ass kicked."

Females may look like sweetness, but they are dangerous.

Chapter 16

Morgan followed everyone to the training area. She wiped her palms on her leggings. *I can't believe this is happening. I don't want Rain to get hurt, especially for me.*

She didn't understand why Niksen disliked her so much. *I've been polite. I've tried to serve foods she's familiar with. I've been courteous. Most people like me. Why the hell does she hate me?*

Stalad's quiet presence next to her as she walked calmed her slightly. She peeked up at him from the corner of her eye. *He doesn't look concerned. Does he know something I don't?*

They reached their destination. Crax stood in the center of a sparring area and gestured to Rain and Niksen.

"No weapons other than your bodies."

Niksen huffed, removed several knives hidden on her body, and handed them to Lollek.

"I'll referee. If you step outside the designated area, it'll cost you a point. Three points will be considered first blood."

"What nonsense is this?" Niksen's eyes narrowed.

"This is to ensure the bout proceeds as it should. No going out of bounds to catch your breath or to avoid getting pummeled." Crax crossed his beefy arms. "Is that a problem for you?"

Niksen's long braid swung when she shook her head.

"No. So long as the rules are applied fairly to both of us."

"They will be. If I say 'stop,' you both step away from each other. No exceptions."

Rain nodded and rolled her shoulders.

"Anything else, Crax?"

"Yes. If Rain wins, Niksen ceases to insult all the human females, whether directly or indirectly. If Niksen wins, you all suck it up and smile when she exhibits her superior attitude."

"Fuck her up, Rain," Kara yelled from the sidelines. "You know I have no filter."

Rain rolled her eyes and raised her middle finger at her friend.

Crax looked at Makai and Krinir.

"Do you have anything else for them?"

"I think you've covered it." Makai leaned back against the nearest wall.

Krinir looked at Niksen.

"One more thing. If the Wing Raider wins, Niksen cooks an edible evening meal for everyone each night for a week as an apology to our hosts."

Niksen glared at the older Orkite.

"What?"

"As a representative of our people, your behavior should be better. You'll learn, or your father will hear of it."

"It's a good thing I have no intention of losing."

"Are we agreed?"

Everyone nodded. Morgan shivered slightly as she moved between Abby and Kara.

"I don't like this."

Kara glanced at her and grinned.

"No worries. Rain knows what she's doing."

"But Niksen has at least a foot and a hundred pounds on her."

"Doesn't matter. Remind me to tell you sometime how we met the Wing Raiders."

Morgan's forehead crinkled. Her attention focused on the females as Crax signaled for them to begin.

Niksen immediately threw a punch at Rain who sidled sideways. When the Orkite overbalanced from missing her target, Rain elbowed her in the kidneys. Niksen let out a grunt and regained her balance. She turned to face the human who said, "Missed me."

The green female growled in anger and rushed to tackle Rain. The blonde dropped and dove to the right into a somersault landing on all fours. She then kicked backwards like a mule and her foot impacted Niksen's upper thigh. Rain jumped up and spun with a roundhouse kick that knocked the Orkite female in the nose. Red blood spurted from Niksen's face. Rain stepped back.

"First blood. This puny human looks forward to your improved attitude."

Wow. They barely got started and Rain owned her. Uh, oh.

Niksen growled fiercely as she rose to her feet.

"I'll show you attitude."

Crax stepped forward.

"The bout is over. Rain won. No more fighting."

"She made me bleed."

"It was a fair match. Accept the results and move on," Krinir said as he approached. When the female Orkite continued to growl, he narrowed his eyes and firmed his lips. "I look forward to this evening's meal."

Back rigid, Niksen stomped from the room. Lollek followed. The silence broke when Kara jumped onto Rain wrapping her legs and arms around her.

"Yeah, baby. Good job."

"Get off me, you insane woman." Rain laughed and pushed Kara away.

"What I want to know is if Niksen can cook well or if we should fill our stomachs beforehand like we do when Yaz is in charge of meals." Crax lowered an arm around Kara when she snuggled into his side.

"She doesn't like to cook, but her meals are edible," Fraddar said with a grin. He looked at Krinir. "You do realize we'll be on Ladorta before she can finish the week of discipline."

Krinir dipped his chin.

"Yes. It will make her feel as if she escaped the majority of the discipline, but the end result will be an improved outlook."

Abby said, "Is she always like this?"

Shaking his head, Krinir said, "No. I'm not sure what is going on with her. She's hotheaded, but she usually is much more personable."

"It's possible the assassination attempts upset her more than she is willing to admit," Stalad said. *He's got a point. Knowing someone wants you dead and not knowing who or why has to be unsettling.*

"Possibly. However, taking her moods out on those around her is unacceptable."

"Have you known her long?"

"All her life. Fraddar and I have been her personal guards since birth."

"You seem to have a paternal role," Makai said.

"Despite how ill-mannered she has been recently, I am proud of how accomplished Niksen has grown to be and hope my guidance has helped in some way. She hides it too well at times, but she has a giving heart."

"You'll have to forgive me for not seeing it," Morgan said quietly. "She has been less than kind to us."

"Unfortunately, you have seen her at her worst. Hopefully, that will change now that Rain has illustrated not to underestimate humans. I apologize for her behavior."

"It is not your place to apologize for her. It is hers."

Everyone nodded at Makai's words.

"Are we still working on the silks today?" Abby tilted her head.

"Why don't we forego it today and just stay in here and concentrate on yoga and Stalad's training forms?" Morgan looked at each of the women.

"Sounds good to me," Rain said with a bright smile. "I've already had a short workout."

Laughter filled the space as the women moved to a matted section and Abby led them through a series of yoga stretches. Morgan's mind drifted as she arranged her body in the different positions and held them. *If Krinir is correct about Niksen, why has she been such a bitch? Should I offer to help her with evening meal or leave her alone?*

Stalad joined them after speaking with the males for a while. The Jalaxians and Orkites lifted weights and punched some heavy bags. He had them perform the basic forms, correcting their stances when necessary. *It sorta reminds me of Tai Chi. He always makes it look so elegant and easy, but these moves can be tough.*

Morgan attempted to keep her arousal under wraps, but occasionally Stalad's nostrils flared. Whenever she noticed, she tried to put physical distance between them in the hopes it would get easier for both of them to ignore their attraction. *Damn, that enhanced Svesti sense of smell is inconvenient. I can't help it if he's so hot and just a nice guy. My libido picked the worst time to make a reappearance.*

After their training sessions, she headed back to her quarters to relieve the pressure between her legs. After years of literally no desire for sex, she found herself spending far too much time in the shower pinching her nipples and rubbing her clit to fantasies of Stalad. *Is it the forbidden nature of it all making me even more horny or just him?*

While they trained the next day, Niksen and the other Orkites returned to the cargo bay and observed. Finishing on the silks, Morgan and the other women began the Svesti training forms. Niksen sidled close to Stalad.

"I find myself attracted to you, Svesti. I invite you to my quarters so we can mate."

Holy fuck. Talk about direct.

Stalad's tail jerked before it settled around his ankle. Krinir's eyes narrowed and Fraddar smirked. Lollek shook her head.

"I'm honored by your interest, Lady Niksen. However, I suffer from amnesia from an accident and do not know if I have a female waiting for me. Until I know for certain my status, I do not feel comfortable pursuing sexual relations with anyone."

The Orkite placed a hand on his shoulder and kneaded his flesh before slowly caressing his arm. He stepped back and she followed.

"No one has to know. I'm not looking for commitment, just the hard fuck I think you can provide."

Shaking his head, Stalad said, "I would know. It's dishonorable." He glanced down at her hand on his arm. "Please refrain from touching me."

She drew a claw across his skin marking his flesh.

"Do you know who I am? How important I am on Arona? No one dares to tell me no."

"I just did, and I will continue to do so."

She placed her fists on her hips.

"You will regret your refusal."

Morgan saw red. She dropped her pretense of not listening and stepped between the two. Her forefinger poked at Niksen's chest. She tilted her head back to look the Orkite in the eye.

"Listen, bitch, he said no."

"This is none of your concern."

"It's everyone's business when someone forces another and tries to take away their agency as it pertains to their own body." Morgan's breathing became shallow, and her vision turned black at the edges. Her arms wrapped around her waist. "Male or female, no means no. It does not mean you should convince or coerce another to consent to something they don't want."

"Perhaps our cultures are different in how we approach mating."

"If a being says no and you force someone who is unwilling, it's rape." Sweat beaded on Morgan's face, but chills ran down her spine. She collapsed to the floor, rocking herself. "No means no," she repeated over and over.

"Oh, shit. Someone get Lezon down here," Kara said.

Abby glared at Niksen.

"Everyone step back and give her room." She knelt in front of Morgan. "Morgan, honey, it's Abby. Can you hear me?"

"No means no, otherwise it's rape." Tears ran down Morgan's face.

"You're right. Can you take a deep breath for me? In through your nose and out through your mouth." Abby demonstrated, but Morgan's eyes were blank, then her head fell forward, her auburn hair blocking her face.

"What's wrong with her?" Niksen demanded.

Rain said, "You triggered her PTSD."

"PTSD?"

"Post-Traumatic Stress Disorder," murmured Stalad.

All the human women except Morgan looked at him sharply.

"How do you know that term?" Kara asked.

"I don't know."

"You've obviously had experience with humans if you know that acronym. There's more to you, Stalad, than we realized." Rain gave him an assessing look.

"Why is she like this? Is she insane?" Niksen's eyes clouded. Concerned looks filled the other Orkites eyes as they witnessed Morgan's distress.

"No, you stupid bitch. She was forced to work as a sex slave on Delizas after being kidnapped from Earth. Then later she was captured by the Zuvgran and experimented on." Kara's hard expression softened as she looked at Morgan and her voice lowered. "Honestly, she holds it together really well most of the time. We've never seen her like this."

"I thought pleasure workers wanted the jobs."

Fraddar shook his head.

"There's only one relatively small section on Delizas where the pleasure workers choose to be there. The rest of the planet uses slaves. Orkite males only frequent the establishments without slaves."

Niksen whispered. "I didn't know."

"There is much you don't know, Niksen," Krinir said sadly. "I know you did not mean to harm the human, but your careless attitude towards pleasure mating obviously struck painful memories."

Lezon ran into the cargo bay. He dropped to his knees next to Abby.

"What happened?" He ran a scanner over Morgan as the nurse quietly filled him in.

"Morgan, it's Lezon." When she didn't reply, he said to Abby, "I can sedate her, but I don't want to upset her further."

Morgan heard it all through a distorted tunnel of sound that bounced around her, but the words didn't register. The words "no means no, otherwise it's rape" played over and over like bad soft muzak in her mind. Despite her yearning and panic, she couldn't find a way out of the horror funhouse of her brain.

Chapter 17

"May I try?" Stalad asked quietly. *Goddess, it hurts to see her pain.*

Abby and the Jalaxian exchanged glances. They scooted back and made room for the Svesti.

He sat cross-legged on the floor in front of Morgan. Reaching out slowly, he placed his hands lightly on her knees. His tail slid to embrace her ankle. An acrid note overlaid her usual appealing scent. His nose twitched at the bitter smell.

"Breathe, Morgan. You're safe here." He inhaled deeply and loudly and held his breath for several seconds before exhaling slowly. Repeating the measured breaths, he tentatively moved his hands to cover hers at her waist. "You're safe. No one will hurt you. Come back to us."

Incrementally, Morgan's breathing relaxed. Peering through her hair and raising her red-rimmed eyes, his heart clenched when recognition lit her eyes. She crawled into his lap and burrowed her face against his chest. His arms automatically surrounded her, and he held her close. He bent to whisper in her ear.

"I've got you. You're safe, *ciebala*."

She hiccupped and snuggled closer. His tail stroked her calf, and his hands lightly caressed her back.

"When you can move her, take her to her quarters. She needs peace and quiet right now, but she should not be left alone. One of us can stay with her if she wants." Lezon said quietly.

Her hair tickled his bare skin when she violently shook her head.

"No."

"No what, *ciebala*?"

"I don't want anyone else. Would you please stay with me?" His ears strained to hear her barely audible voice.

"Of course." His answer rumbled low in his chest. "Can you walk, or should I carry you?"

"I don't want to see pity in everyone's eyes." Tears clogged her words.

"There's no pity, but I will carry you anyway. Hold on." Stalad maneuvered so he could stand in a single fluid motion to lift their bodies upright. Adjusting her weight against his torso, he used his arms to support her as he walked while his tail rubbed her back. When he reached the residential corridor, he waited until she noticed the lack of motion.

"I need you to unlock your quarters."

She waved a shaking hand over the security scanner. He instructed the computer to adjust the lighting to fifty percent.

"Where do you want to sit, *ciebala*? The couch or your bed?"

"Couch, please."

He sat on the furniture with her still in his embrace. She sighed. Long moments passed. Her eyes downcast and cheeks pink, she drew back.

"I'm so embarrassed. You can go now, Stalad. I'll be fine."

"You do not need to be embarrassed. If you wish me to leave, I will, but not until I call whomever you want to take my place. Lezon said you shouldn't be alone."

"I don't need anyone."

"Morgan..." His tail tugged on her wrist. "It's either me or someone else."

"So I don't get to say no?" Anger grew in her voice.

"This is about your safety. Your emotional state can worsen if you are left to your own devices right now. None of us want you to suffer more than necessary to get through this." He lifted his hands from her body. "I don't have to touch you to keep you company. Your body remains your own." *I want to be here for her, but I won't push her.*

Her shoulders fell.

"I'm sorry. You're trying to help, and I'm being pissy."

His brows came together as he tried to understand the word 'pissy' from her context.

"You are entitled to feel how you feel, *ciebala*." His voice softened. "It seems you have unresolved emotions from your captivity."

Water clouded her blue eyes making them shimmer in the low light.

"Oh, I know exactly how I feel about it all. I just wasn't expecting those feelings to overwhelm me unexpectedly like they did." She rubbed at her eyes. "It felt like a freight train hit me, and the impact took my ability to breathe, hear, or see. My physical reaction scared me and made it worse."

"Does this happen often?"

She pulled the remainder of her hair from her disheveled ponytail and combed her fingers through the tangles. Her scent settled into her usual pleasant one. When she leaned back into him, his arms rose to hold her.

"No. I've never had an episode like this. Not long after I arrived on Costonia, I experienced smaller ones where I froze in panic. I worked with a mind healer for a while and the panic attacks went away. After the Wing Raiders rescued me from the Zuvgran, I spent most of the first two *lunars* recuperating from the residual effects of the experiments. By the time I felt better, I also felt safe with everyone here."

"This is a good ship and crew."

Her lips lifted. *There she is. She should always be happy.*

"They are. As fierce as they are, they still have huge hearts." She sighed. "If you don't mind babysitting, I would rather have you here than anyone else right now." Her voice lowered. "You make me feel safe."

Stalad consciously kept his chest from inflating with pride. *She feels I can protect her and keep her safe.*

"I'm happy to keep you company."

Resting her cheek against his chest, she fell silent. A low, contented rumble emanated from him. *I hope I don't have a female waiting for me. I can't imagine feeling this close to anyone else.*

After some time, she said quietly, "I hated it."

His tail stilled momentarily, then continued to stroke her back.

"I hated the fact that anyone with credits could do whatever they wanted to my body and I couldn't say no. In some weird way, I was lucky that my owner wouldn't allow us to be beaten, didn't like using pain collars, and took steps to keep us healthy and relatively safe physically. But mentally, I had to go away in my mind to survive each sexual encounter. It's difficult to admit, but each of those instances I consider rape. It sounds crass, but to the males, we were just a series of warm holes."

His rumble morphed into a growl and his fists clenched at the small of her back. He made himself release as much tension as he could to keep from upsetting her.

"No one should have to go through that."

"No. You know, on Earth, there were some men who felt if they bought a woman dinner or a drink, we owed them a sexual favor. Or if they were powerful, they felt entitled to who or what they wanted. It wasn't unusual to have to disabuse them of such notions. But I couldn't do any of that on Delizas if I wanted to live or not be punished with pain. Others technically owned and directed my body without my consent. My self-worth grew smaller and smaller as time went on, despite talking my owner into a different type of establishment that relied on providing sexual fantasies, rather than the sex act itself."

"It sounds like you did the best you could under the circumstances. There is no shame in that, *ciebala*." His fingers played with the silky ends of her long hair.

"I survived."

"I'm glad you did."

"You don't think less of me?" Uncertainty and hesitation laced her voice.

"Of course not. Even if you had chosen to be a pleasure worker, I would not judge you for it. Doing what you hated ensured your survival. I abhor that you had to do it, but you are safe here now." *I want to go to Delizas and maim every male who hurt her, starting with her owner.*

"I think Niksen pulling the same crap on you that some human men do on Earth brought all those complicated feelings up too fast and with too much intensity. The words I said were the words screaming in my mind on Delizas during the worst of it." Her breath hitched. "As time went on, I was afraid of losing my sense of self."

"That makes sense. I wish I could carry your pain for you."

Her cheeks lifted against his chest.

"That's sweet. No one should have to bear this, but too many people do."

"May I ask you a question?" *Time to change the subject to something lighter.*

"Of course."

"Were you a performer on Earth?"

She laughed softly.

"I had to interrupt my schooling when my mother became ill. I cared for her until she died and worked as an exotic dancer. Yes, I did that on the silks. That paid for me to return to college and get my degree. While I was traveling across the country to my new job, I was kidnapped by Durelians."

"What was the new job?"

"Teaching."

"Teaching younglings?"

"Yes, I wanted to teach children." A heavy exhale left her body, and her shoulders sagged. "It's probably no longer possible."

"Don't say that. I'm sure you can find a suitable place to do what you enjoy."

"I know if I stay with the *Fortitude*, it will never happen. However, I feel safe here, especially after the Zuvgran kidnapped me from the transport ship taking me to a colony."

"You don't have to decide today or even this *solar*. You're young and have time."

She sat back to look him in his eyes. He hoped she didn't feel his erection underneath her luscious ass.

"You're incredibly supportive, Stalad. It wouldn't surprise me if there's a nice female waiting for you somewhere."

"If so, I hope she's as wonderful as you, Morgan."

When her hand came up to cup his jaw, he turned into it savoring her touch.

"You're very sweet...and honorable." Her fingers drifted away from his face.

The door chimed. They both looked in that direction.

"I should see who it is."

"No, stay here. I'll check." He lifted her from his lap to the couch and stood. Opening the door, he found Abby waiting with a tray of food.

"May I come in?"

He glanced over his shoulder at Morgan who nodded. He stepped aside and gestured to Abby to enter.

"I brought you something to eat. Don't neglect to rehydrate."

"Thanks. I'm sorry for my meltdown."

Abby waved a hand.

"No need. It's normal after the shit we've been through. Are you feeling better? Can I get you anything?" She placed the tray on the table in front of Morgan.

"I've calmed down a lot thanks to Stalad. He's a good listener." *Only because everything you say is interesting to me, ciebala.*

"If you want to vent to any of us or work through stuff, just comm and we'll be here. Or if you decide you want something to help sleep later, Lezon or I can bring something by for you."

"I appreciate it, but I think I'll be okay. I might even make it to evening meal tonight if I can handle facing Niksen after all that."

"She seemed pretty shaken that her behavior triggered a PTSD response in you. Maybe she's not as big a bitch as we've thought." Abby grinned. "One can only hope."

A small laugh escaped Morgan.

"Thanks, Abby. I don't know what I'd do without you."

"You'd survive, girl, because that's what we do." Abby fist bumped Morgan.

"Maybe."

"Definitely." Abby headed for the door but turned halfway back. "Oh, Yaz says we'll reach Ladorta in the morning. Makai says he'll brief everyone on the plan to split up so we can handle the Svesti mission concurrently. Not sure when he's going to do that, though."

"We'll be ready." Stalad watched the human female leave before locating the cooling unit and pulling out some water pouches. He sat next to Morgan. "Let's see what she brought." He divided the food and between the two of them.

After swallowing a bite, Morgan said, "Thank you for being here with me, Stalad. I feel much better than I did an hour ago."

"Any time you need me, *ciebala*, I will do my best to be there for you." *I only hope I can be there for you after I regain my memories.*

Chapter 18

After eating, Morgan left Stalad on the couch and took a shower. Crying always took a lot out of her, which was one reason she hated to do it. Gazing in the mirror after getting dressed, pink still rimmed her eyes, but it was fading. She brushed her hair and left it down. The weight pulling on her scalp would only exacerbate her residual headache. *I can't believe I had such a massive panic attack.*

When she returned to the living area, Stalad looked up as he closed his comm.

"You look refreshed. Do you feel better?"

"Yes, thank you."

"I just spoke with Makai. There's a meeting on the bridge in an hour. Should I call Abby to sit with you?"

"No, I'm good to attend."

His brown eyes softened.

"Are you sure?"

"Yes. I'll be fine." She spied a deck of cards Kara synthesized for her during her recuperation. "Do you know any card games?"

"Earth ones? I don't think so."

"Why don't I teach you a couple before the meeting? We can pass the time without any more of my drama."

He frowned.

"Don't do that."

"Do what?"

"Make it sound like there's something wrong with you when there isn't."

Her eyes widened.

"Did you miss the part where I completely lost my shit?'

His nose wrinkled.

"I don't recall you losing any excretions."

She stared at his serious face while she tried to decipher what he saying. Then she clamped her hands to her stomach when she laughed so hard more tears formed in her eyes. Bringing herself under control, she gasped, "Earth Euphemism. Means Meltdown. Or Anger."

His confusion morphed into humor, and he chuckled.

"That makes much more sense."

Wiping the dampness from her eyes, she smiled at him.

"Thanks. I needed that." *Amazing how hilarity can relieve stress.*

"I'm glad my words inadvertently helped." His smile faded. "I meant it, *ciebala*. There is nothing wrong with you. You're still dealing with a past that was not under your control. There is no shame in that."

Her gaze traced his face. *He really has no idea how wonderful he is.*

"You are a good male."

He dipped his chin then pointed at the cards on the table. "What am I learning first?"

Morgan explained the four suits and explained card values sometimes changed depending on the game. She showed him how to play Go Fish, then War.

"I much prefer this version of war. Much less bloody than others." His eyebrow arched.

"That's a good point. Maybe we should have leaders play cards instead of sending warriors into battle." Morgan gathered up the pile and tapped the edges to straighten out the cards. "It's almost time to head to the bridge. I'll show you more games another time. Earth has a lot of them." She slipped her feet into her shoes, and they left her quarters.

She squared her shoulders before entering the bridge. Everyone smiled at them before turning in Makai's direction. The Jalaxian's blue eyes scanned her, then nodded once with his lips rising slightly. A long exhale left her. *Good. No one is fussing over me.*

"We reach Ladorta tomorrow. We'll be providing security for Niksen. I also accepted a job from the Svesti that requires a small team to go to Rumaska and gather contact information for bremmite suppliers. However, they do not want the Rumaskans to know that is their primary interest."

"Rumaska?" Morgan's nose wrinkled. "They're a bit extreme. You'll have to send a couple."

"What do you know about them?" Makai lifted an eyebrow.

"Not a whole lot. A few came into the club on Delizas. The females dominate the males and honestly, dressed trashier than the sex slaves. My friend Faith questioned them as research to see if we needed to add anything to *Fantasia*. The males are called body servants. Faith said she thought it was just fancy name for slavery because of the way the females treated them." She bit her lip. "Uh, the males were in collars, and their cocks were on display."

"That tracks with my research." Kara tapped her tablet. Several holographic images popped up. "Were they dressed like this?" Skin tones from pink to magenta, cat-like ears, and gray eyes with yellow pupils in deep orbital sockets were common among all the beings. The females wore outfits with exposing their breasts and genitals or translucent gowns, while the males wore pants cut out in the crotch to reveal their erect penises.

Morgan nodded.

"Very similarly. I know one of the males had his cock in a locked cage to keep him from obtaining an erection. According to Faith, in public, the body servants had to display themselves one way or another according to the whim their mistresses." Disgust laced her voice. "I know Slovis spoke to the Rumaskan females about refraining from blatant sexual activities or using their pain collars at the club. He suggested they relocate to one of his brothels—for a fee—to continue. One of the females became strident and super bitchy about it."

"I can easily synthesize similar outfits and a fake slave collar." Kara looked at Makai. "I just need to know who I'm dressing for the mission."

The captain frowned.

"This job is more complicated than I expected. I'm assuming I can't send a pair of males alone."

"They'd never be allowed planetside. According to what I've found, males are considered unintelligent, and their sole purpose to is keep the females happy." Kara blew out a breath that stirred her pink hair. "Crax and I went over all my research to see what might be required and are willing to do it."

"I'm not sure I like this." Makai crossed his arms. He looked at his fellow Jalaxian. "Are you willing to act subservient for the mission and have Kara dressed like the Rumaskans?"

Crax grunted.

"I will do whatever is necessary to keep Kara safe. Of all the human females, she is best suited for the mission."

"Hey." Rain smirked. "Are you saying I wouldn't be able to handle it?"

"Abby would be too uncomfortable being on display. Morgan isn't mated to anyone and shouldn't be put in a position to have to perform sexually in front of a crowd with anyone, especially after this morning." Crax sent an understanding glance at her. "And you are more likely to choke information from someone than talk it out of them."

Rain lifted the middle finger of her right hand at the huge blue male and grinned.

"I hate to admit it, but your thought process is sound." Makai pinned Kara with a hard look. "Can you handle being on display?"

"I'm not crazy about the idea, but as long as Crax is with me, I can pretend it's just elaborate sex play for us." Kara leered at her mate.

I might have been able to do it several months ago, but Crax is right—I'm too emotionally fragile right now. As much as I'd like to contribute, I just can't do this.

"Then you two gather what you need and take the smaller transport to Rumaska. We'll continue to Ladorta where the human females will remain on the *Fortitude* in orbit, while the rest of us escort the Orkites to the surface with the larger transport. Morgan, would you be willing to learn more about the weapons systems before we get there?"

"I would, but I'm not certain if I'd be accurate with them." Morgan chewed her lower lip.

"I can remain with the females," Stalad said. "If needed, I can operate the weapons and repair most of the equipment if something breaks."

Makai's lips firmed.

"Rain would be in charge. Can you accept that?"

"Absolutely." Stalad bowed slightly in Rain's direction. "She's a competent pilot and has been with you a long time. It's logical she make any final decisions."

"Then we have a plan. Do not tell the Orkites about the Rumaskan mission. It's none of their business."

"Do we know what the Svesti need the bremmite for?" Rain tapped her upper lip with a forefinger.

"What is bremmite?" Morgan said.

"It's an ore used in a variety of applications. The Svesti did not indicate what they wanted it for." Makai glanced at everyone. "Those going to the surface, pack your gear and be ready. I'll coordinate with Krinir and get a better idea of what will be required of us. We'll probably be on shifts to ensure adequate coverage of Niksen. Hopefully, her negotiations won't take long."

Everyone nodded.

"Lezon, Tren. Double check that everyone's trackers are working satisfactorily. Especially Kara's. Crax and Kara, I want daily reports. Stalad, begin teaching Morgan about the weapons systems, just in case."

A chorus of "yes, sirs" sounded on the bridge as most of them left. Rain remained at the helm, while Makai took a seat in his captain's chair. Stalad gestured for Morgan to follow him to the weapons console.

She spent the next couple hours learning the various controls and weapons available. Throbbing behind her eyes finally made her ask Stalad to take a break.

"You look stressed."

"Cramming all this information into my brain is giving me a headache." She rubbed her temples. "I'm afraid to get it wrong because our lives might depend on me."

"Hopefully, this is nothing more than a precaution. Let's go see Lezon and get you a pain reducer."

She nodded gingerly.

As they walked to the med bay, he said, "I'm sorry I didn't notice your discomfort sooner."

"Don't worry about it. I should've spoken up, but we're on a deadline."

"You can still learn while we're in orbit. You don't have to know it all before we arrive." His tail rested on her back.

She stopped momentarily then continued.

"You're right. I kept thinking I needed to learn it all by tomorrow."

Within moments of Lezon injecting her, her shoulders relaxed. She stretched her neck and groaned with relief.

"That's so much better. Thanks."

"Not a problem. How are you feeling from earlier? Should we make time to talk?"

"I think I'm okay. Stalad is a good listener."

"If you change your mind, comm me. I'll be happy to help." Lezon patted her forearm.

"I'll keep that in mind." *Thankfully, no one is looking at me with pity in their eyes. I'd hate that.*

Morgan took a deep breath before entering the kitchen. Niksen stood stirring soup in a large pot. The scent of cooking meat filled the room.

"Do you need any help?"

Niksen glanced at her briefly and shrugged.

"You can assemble the salad. I've already cut the vegetables." She gestured toward the large cooling unit.

"Okay." Morgan pulled out the containers and two large bowls. Dividing the vegetables between the bowls, she quietly said, "I want to apologize for earlier. I did not mean to make you feel uncomfortable."

The Orkite stilled.

"I am the one who should apologize. My words and actions caused you significant distress."

Surprised, Morgan looked at Niksen.

"Why are you being nice to me? Because you think I'm weak?"

Niksen's braid swung as she shook her head.

"I've been nasty when all of you have been welcoming and helpful. I acted poorly. Your reaction reminded me others have problems, too, not just me." A darker green spread along her cheekbones. "I have been taking my bad mood out on everyone around me."

"Is there anything I can do to help? I'm willing to listen." Morgan tossed the vegetables. "We've hypothesized that the assassination attempts may have upset you."

"Not the attempts themselves. Just everyone's reaction to them." Niksen snorted. "My father and guards act like I am weak and unable to defend myself."

"There's no shame in having extra protection when it's clear that you're in danger from someone unknown."

"It's not being consulted beforehand with the plans. I dislike being treated like a child." Niksen left the soup, picked up potholders, and removed the meat from the heating unit. "You were correct. No means no. I shouldn't have pushed with the

Svesti." After she transferred the meat to serving platters, her shoulders rolled inward as she leaned on the counter. "Truth is, it wasn't that I wanted him that badly. I just wanted to be seen as a grown female."

"Krinir?" Morgan said quietly.

Niksen's head whipped around, and panic lit her dark eyes.

"Is it obvious?"

"I don't think so. I noticed you push back against him more than you do anyone else." Morgan hesitated. "Would either of you get in trouble with your father if you got together?"

"I don't know that my father would like it, but it's not his place to choose who I mate."

"How does Krinir feel?"

"I'm afraid he still sees me as a youngling." Niksen's dark eyes watered. "But the age difference doesn't bother me. In fact, I prefer a mature male. Most Orkites my age are too immature to settle down."

Morgan tentatively reached over to squeeze the Orkite's hand. Niksen squeezed back. *Her behavior makes a little bit of sense now. Still not right, but she's floundering. I can relate.*

"I'm sorry you're going through this. I'm not sure how to help since I'll be staying on the ship while you're on Ladorta."

"Please keep my secret. No one else knows."

"Of course. It's your private business. I do think you should tell him how you feel, though."

"He's not taking my hints. But sometimes I catch him looking at me as if he might be really seeing me."

"Maybe be direct? If there's no chance, he'll tell you. He seems like that type of guy."

"I'm not sure I'm ready for him to completely shatter my hopes." Niksen sat on a stool.

"I'm no expert, but I think you should concentrate on being yourself and doing your duties. Let him see you as a female with something to offer." Morgan bit her lower lip. "No offense, but the way you've been acting doesn't really present yourself in the best light."

Niksen laughed heartily.

"What a polite way to say I've been acting like dung."

A smile lifted Morgan's lips.

"I have to say, I like this version of you much better, Niksen."

"Me, too." Niksen's humor faded. "I thought you worked on Delizas voluntarily. I didn't realize that was the case. I'm sorry you went through that, and I apologize that my actions caused you pain."

"How about we start over?"

"I'd like that."

That went much better than I expected. Too bad she's leaving tomorrow. I might actually end up liking her.

Chapter 19

Stalad watched the large transporter leave the hangar bay. After he ensured all systems operated as they should, he headed to the bridge. Crax and Kara left hours earlier for Rumaska.

As he walked, he thought about the night before. At evening meal, Morgan and Niksen talked as if they were friends. He, the Jalaxians, and the Orkites exchanged raised eyebrows, but the humans acted as if the behavior was expected. *Females. I don't think I'll ever really understand them. Although knowing that neither female seemed upset about earlier relieved me. I would hate if Morgan continued to berate herself for her reaction.*

Rain and Abby sat on the bridge quietly talking. The pilot glanced at him when he arrived. He sat at a console and checked the scans.

"We're in orbit. Ladorta's defensive systems are ignoring us."

"I'm going to set an alert to notify us if that changes." Stalad tapped the console.

"Good idea. You and I are going to have to take shifts at the helm, since neither Abby or Morgan can pilot. I'm thinking twelve-hour shifts with a four-hour overlap midday when we're expecting comms from everyone."

"Sounds good to me."

They looked up as Morgan entered with a tray of food.

"Breakfast." Morgan placed the tray on an unused console and handed out cups of a hot beverage. She went back to the tray and scooped out servings of breakfast casserole onto plates before distributing them to everyone.

"Thanks, Morgan." Abby sipped at her cup. "I really wish we could find an acceptable substitute for coffee. I really miss it."

"This is the closest I've been able to find so far," Morgan said. "It's some sort of blend of seeds from Praxis. Not easy to obtain."

"It's more tea-like than coffee-ish," Rain complained. "But at least it has a caffeine hit to it."

"Thank you, Morgan." Stalad bit into the egg and meat concoction and hummed. "This is good." *She's a good cook.*

"I figured I'd make sure everyone stayed fed unless something else takes priority. I'm not very useful up here otherwise."

"Why don't we take the opportunity to train you on various positions so you have some working knowledge? It'll kill some time, and you'll feel more confident up here afterwards." Rain's eyes scanned her console and out the window as she ate.

"Just don't expect great things from me. Working on the bridge is a far cry from teaching children or exotic dancing." Morgan's eyes twinkled.

"You'll be fine."

Stalad coordinated with Rain on when she wanted him to return for his shift, then helped Morgan collect the used dishes. He carried the tray for her back to the kitchen.

"Are you going to take a nap before your shift?" Morgan placed the dirty items in the recycler.

"Yes. I'll get up a little earlier to do my training forms and take a shower before I have to relieve Rain. You're welcome to join me."

"In the shower?" Morgan giggled.

Heat filled his face. *Crek. Now I can't get the vision of her wet and slippery out of my mind.*

"I meant on the bridge during my shift. I can teach you about the different systems."

She gently pat his back.

"I knew what you meant, but the look on your face was priceless." Her eyes sparkled.

"Very funny. If I knew I were free, I would take the other offer." His nostrils flared as her scent deepened.

"I believe I might say yes to such an offer...if you were free."

His hands gently squeezed her upper arms, and he rested his forehead on hers.

"You are far too tempting, *ciebala*. We shouldn't talk like this."

Her eyelids dropped to hide her blue eyes.

"I know. I couldn't resist teasing you. Forgive me?"

"I think I could forgive you anything."

She inhaled deeply then pulled back. She made a shooing motion with her hands.

"Go get some sleep. I'll have a meal waiting for you when you're ready."

He stepped away slowly. When she turned to the sink to wash the tray, he left with his tail swaying quickly.

I want her. I only wish I knew if I could pursue our attraction fully.

With the reduced ship's complement gone, the next few weeks tested Stalad's resolve. Morgan spent a great deal of time on the bridge with him alone. He taught her how to read the various scans and consoles, as well as how to operate the weapons system. She taught him how to program the small synthesizer on the bridge for snacks. She found it strange he didn't know how to do it when he capably handled every other ship operation.

His tail found ways to hold her, usually around her ankle. Most times he didn't even know it had moved. Her wonderful scent clung to him, even if they hadn't touched. *Trulet*, grass, and rain smells followed him into his dreams. He began waking a little earlier so he could spend extra time in the shower, fisting himself to thoughts of Morgan. But he resolutely kept his hands to himself when they were together.

He looked forward to their times alone. Morgan spoke of her mother with a great deal of love and shared her memories of the female who birthed her. His need to hold her when she spoke with sadness about her mother's cancer battle almost over-whelmed him, but he resisted. His claws bit into his palms, but the pain reminded him he shouldn't give either of them false hope for a future together.

Crax and Kara reached Rumaska and waited almost two weeks before they received clearance to land because of some planetwide celebration where outsiders were not invited. On Ladorta, Makai reported that negotiations appeared to be progressing well. Then Niksen disappeared for two days. Krinir barely slept while she was missing. Triumphantly, she resurfaced unharmed with two Orkites trussed up.

Last he heard, Krinir threw her over his shoulder and spanked her ass when she protested. Tren gleefully reported that it was another two days before Krinir let her out of her quarters to resume negotiations which were almost completed. When Morgan heard about it, a secretive smile grace her plump lips and she only said, "Good for her."

The Ladortans transported the perpetrators to Arona, so at least the *Fortitude* didn't have to put them in their brig. Now they waited for the team on Ladorta to return after the signing of the treaty.

He met the larger transport in the hangar bay and exchanged warrior clasps with the Jalaxians. Krinir tugged on Niksen's braid to pull her to his side, looked at everyone, then said, "We'll be busy for the foreseeable future." He lifted her over his shoulder, and she pummeled his back.

"I can walk."

"You're too slow. I want you now." He slapped her ass. "No sass or I'll teach you a lesson." Her furious retort was lost in the laughter that filled the hangar bay.

Now that the bulk of their personnel was onboard, they traveled to meet the smaller transport to pick up Crax and Kara who already contacted Costonia with the results of their investigation before returning the Orkites home.

At evening meal, everyone except Krinir and Niksen sat and shared stories of their time apart.

"Oh, I can't wait until Heggar finds out about our newest mated pair." Fraddar grinned. "He owes me a bottle of Estalan liquor."

"He knew about them?" Morgan stabbed some meat on the platter and transferred it to her plate.

"A lot of us have been placing bets on when she'd wear him down. It's taken years. Krinir's one stubborn Orkite." Fraddar scooped up some roasted vegetables. "I told Heggar this was the trip where he'd finally realize how he felt about her."

"The sexual tension between the two has been unbearable." Lollek smirked and fanned her face with a hand. "I had to work it off with a pair of Ladortan guards numerous times."

Everyone laughed at the female Orkite's antics.

"I'm glad they figured it out," Morgan said quietly. "I know she was very unhappy."

"You're very kind to say so, especially after how she treated you." Fraddar's normally cheerful face became solemn. "It hurt to watch her take her pain out on all of you, but he needed to witness it. I apologize that I couldn't step in sooner."

"It's okay. Everything worked out." Morgan popped a vegetable into her mouth.

She's such a caring female. And forgiving. Goddess, is there nothing unattractive about the human?

"We'll meet up with Crax and Kara in three days. Once they're back with us, we'll take you home," Makai said. "That should take another week."

"Such a shame I couldn't bring those guards with me. They were very inventive," Lollek said.

"If you're in the market for another pleasure mating, feel free to knock on my door. I'm certain Krinir won't be there." Fraddar wiggled his eyebrows.

"You're much too old for me." Lollek pointed her utensil at him. "I'd hate for you to keel over dead from pleasure."

"You wound me." Fraddar clutched at his chest. "I wouldn't mind testing your theory."

"Another lifetime, perhaps."

Stalad shook his head at their banter. *Everyone is much more relaxed. I wonder what's next for us.*

Stalad chewed on his fruit and glanced around the dining area. Except for Yaz, everyone onboard sat enjoying morning meal. Grouped together at one end of the table, the females chattered, while the males concentrated on their food. Crax and Kara returned four days ago and from her gestures and the laughter around her, she must've been telling another story about Rumaska. Even Niksen and Lollek participated happily.

Closing his eyes, he couldn't quite hear the details of the conversation, but the rise and fall of female voices soothed him before an ache in his chest began. A sensation of a memory flittered in his brain, but when he tried to grasp it, pain throbbed at his temples. Ceasing his efforts, he reverted to listening and entered a meditative state similar to when he conducted his training forms. The sensation returned, although he didn't try to force any memories. He simply enjoyed the warmth the voices provided him.

"Stalad?"

With his peace interrupted, he opened his eyes to see Lezon peering at him with concern.

"Are you okay? I called your name several times."

"Yes, just thinking."

"We're going to spar later with the Orkites. Did you want to join us?"

"I'll be there." Stalad sipped his juice. "Does Makai have another mission for us?"

"Not that I've heard. Come by for a checkup after we spar. I want to see if there have been any changes."

"Of course."

Morgan's peal of laughter drew his gaze. Her bright eyes and pink cheeks highlighted her beauty, while the slight jiggle of her pert breasts as her shoulders shook intrigued his cock. His tail rose slightly before he wrangled it around his chair leg. *Goddess, I'd love to see her riding me, her flesh all dewy and pink, those luscious globes free of confinement and in my hands. Despite my best efforts, I want her now more than ever.*

To give his hard cock a chance to settle, he offered to clean up. He remained seated after everyone left to hide the bulge. Standing, he snorted in disgust at himself as he picked up the dirty dishes and put them in the recycler.

I think it's time to seriously consider going to Costonia. I'm not sure I can continue to resist her.

Chapter 20

The time to travel to Arona passed quickly now that Niksen and Lollek spent time with the women. With Niksen's relationship with Krinir resolved to her satisfaction, Morgan realized she liked the Orkite's true personality. Funny, kind, and a good head on her shoulders made her beautiful inside and out. *I almost wish I could still hate her. When she was queen bitch, I didn't feel jealous at all of her stunning looks. But now, I wonder if Stalad regrets turning her down.*

The females trained with the humans and taught the women defensive moves. The Orkites also asked Rain and Kara to teach them some of their human fighting techniques. Each learned more about each other's species and cultural beliefs.

Sitting on the floor in the cargo bay on the mats, they drank from water pouches and talked.

"What is going on with you and Stalad? Have you taken him to your bed yet?"

Morgan's eyes flew up to meet Lollek's.

"Nothing. No. It's as he said to Niksen. He doesn't know if there is someone waiting for him, so he doesn't want to pursue anything."

"You know the male wants to do wonderfully dirty things with you, don't you?" Niksen sighed. "If you're lucky, he'll be as talented as Krinir."

"Stop." Morgan tossed an empty water pouch at the Orkite. "It's not like that."

"Of course it is. As soon as he knows he's single and free, he'll be all over you like white on rice." Kara waggled her eyebrows. "When that time comes, if you want to borrow some of the outfits I made for Rumaska, just let me know. I kept them for my own private time with Crax."

"There's definitely heat between you two." Rain stretched her legs out in front of her and leaned back on her hands. "You have to respect the guy being honorable. What a difference from a lot of Earth men."

Morgan picked at non-existent lint on her pants.

"I'm sure it's just sexual attraction. He won't want me long term. They never do. It's worse now that I was a sex slave."

"The right man won't care about your past beyond how it affects you now. You had no choice but to survive any way you could." Abby pinned her with a sharp look. "Stalad does not strike me as a male who would make you feel less because of it."

"No, he never has. I just feel like we're in limbo until he regains his memories. I care for him enough that I'm willing to risk that nothing will ever happen, but I just want to know one way or another." *I'm still not sure I'm worthy of him.*

"What are you going to do about it?" Rain brought her knees to her chest and sat forward with her elbows resting on them.

"What can I do?"

"Push the issue." Niksen's tusks jutted out. "It worked for me...eventually."

The ladies giggled.

"How?"

"Talk to Makai about heading to Costonia sooner rather than later. We reach Arona tomorrow, and we have no jobs waiting. Sounds like a good time to take the detour." Kara's pink hair stood up after she combed her fingers through it.

"I agree with Kara. Time to rip the bandage off." Abby finished her water pouch and folded into a small square.

"We'll back you." Rain's forehead wrinkled. "Would you stay on Costonia with him while he figures it out? I'm not sure how long the *Fortitude* could remain there, especially if someone hires us."

"Probably. Although I'd miss you guys a lot." Morgan rubbed her palms on her thighs and sniffed. "The last few years I've had to say goodbye to too many friends." *I miss Sophia and Faith. I'll miss these women, too.*

"Hey, we'd stay in touch." Kara held up her tablet. "As much as I enjoy having you around, I think if you could use your degree and teach, you'd feel more fulfilled. At the very least, you deserve the chance to find out if it's right for you."

"You're our friend and we want you to find what makes you happiest," Abby said with a gentle smile.

"This reminds me of the best female circles on Arona," Niksen said. "Direct and supportive. Our species have more in common than I originally thought."

Morgan grabbed the hanging silk next to her and twisted in her hands as she considered her options. The other females left her alone and talked quietly about other unimportant things. Finally, she huffed and released the fabric.

"I'll go see Makai now."

"Good for you," Kara said. "Do you want backup?"

"Thanks, but no. I should do this on my own." Morgan stood and dusted her hands off. "I can do this."

"Of course you can. You're a strong, independent female." Niksen's tusks jutted from her lower jaw as she grinned. "We have faith in you."

"Thanks, everyone. Hopefully, this works out." Morgan gave the ladies a smile before she left.

Words of encouragement followed her as she made her way to the bridge.

"Can I speak to you privately?"

Makai narrowed his eyes briefly then jerked his head toward his attached office. She kept her spine straight as they entered the room, and he sat in his chair. He motioned to another seat for her.

"What do you need to talk about, Morgan?"

"What are your plans for after Arona?"

"Why?"

"If we don't have another mission, I think we should go to Costonia and help Stalad discover who he is and get his memories back."

He leaned back and rubbed his chin between his thumb and forefinger.

"You think that is an effective usage of our time and resources? It'll take us close to a week to reach Costonia."

"I believe it's the right thing to do."

"If he's willing, we could drop him off on Arona and he could find passage from there."

"No! I mean, I don't think that's fair to him. He's been an asset to the ship." She hesitated. "However, if that's what you think is best, then I'd like to disembark at Arona and go with him so he has a friendly face during his recovery."

Makai stared at her before chuckling.

"I'm teasing, Morgan. I asked Stalad this morning if he felt it was time to go. He said yes. I instructed Yaz to calculate the shortest route." He hesitated. "What are your plans once we're there?"

"I'll stay until he knows who he is. After that, I don't know."

"I'm not sure how long the *Fortitude* can remain at Costonia."

"I understand you might have to leave without me. I expect I will be welcome back there. I did spend a year on the planet."

"What if he has a mate? Are you prepared for that?" Kind blue eyes watched her closely.

Inhaling deeply, she said, "If that's the situation, I'll deal with it." Her eyes watered. "I just need to know one way or another, Makai. Even if there's no one, it still might not work out between us. Until we know who he is and what his life is, everything is in flux."

"You'll always be welcome to join us, Morgan." He reached across the desk and covered her hand with his.

"Thank you. I think we both knew I would leave eventually. My training doesn't really fit with what the Wing Raiders can use."

"You've become family. We take care of our own." His fingers squeezed once before he drew his hand back.

Sniffing, she said, "I'm going to miss all of you."

"We'll miss you, too." Humor lit his blue eyes. "Especially your cooking."

A surprised laugh escaped her.

"Thanks. You're all heart."

He's a really good male. I hope he finds his mate soon. He deserves it. Now if only things go the way I hope on Costonia.

Morgan said her goodbyes to the Orkites, hugging Niksen and Lollek tightly. They promised to stay in touch. She watched them board the transport with Lezon and Tren operating a maglev carrying their belongings. Makai accompanied the Orkites to receive final payment for the mission.

Stalad stood close to her.

"Could I ask a favor of you?"

She looked into his serious brown eyes.

"Yes."

"Makai plans on contacting Costonia with me when he returns. Would you be there to support me? I admit I'm nervous."

"I'd be happy to." She rested her hand on his arm. "Whatever I can do to help."

"Thank you."

They waited on the bridge for Makai. Stalad's tail occasionally snapped, then swayed. Hoping to calm him, she grasped it and held on. His eyes heated as she absently caressed it. *Oops. Didn't mean to do that.*

"We're ready to go. Once we leave orbit, open a secure channel to King Sovex," Makai said as he entered.

Both Yaz and Kara nodded at his orders.

"Comm link established," Kara announced not long afterwards.

"I'll take it in my office. Stalad, with me."

Morgan followed the males.

Makai tapped his desk console and an older Svesti appeared.

"Captain Makai, it is good to see you. I hope all is well with the Wing Raiders."

"Xeliv, thank you for your kind welcome. You also look well. I am hoping to speak with King Sovex. I believe it is important."

"Please wait while I see if he can take your comm now."

Morgan almost giggled when a digital representation of a waterfall, complete with sound, replaced Xeliv's image. *Alien visual muzak. Who knew? Glad I emptied my bladder earlier. All that running water...*

The hologram of King Sovex with a blonde human woman on his lap abruptly appeared.

"How may I help you today?" *King Sovex looks happier than when I left. Good for him.*

"I think I have something of yours," Makai said.

"I'm sorry, what are you talking about?"

Stalad moved to stand next to Makai. The blonde gasped and leaned forward.

"Jevax? Is that you?"

Stalad looked at the human female as if trying to figure out who she was.

"Is that my name?"

The blonde's eyebrows raised, but King Sovex responded.

"Your name is Grulen Jevax, and you are a warrior in the Svesti military. We have been looking for you." *Grulen Jevax. His name is Grulen. It's a strong name.*

Grulen stared at the couple on Costonia.

"I don't know you. I don't even know who I am."

Morgan snuck under his arm. Grulen rested it over her her shoulders and pulled her closer. She peered at the blonde suspiciously.

"How do you know him?"

"He's my friend."

"Is that all?"

The woman smiled.

"Yes, that's all. I'm with him." She motioned to King Sovex with her thumb.

"Good. Can you help Jevax?" *Glad I remembered Svesti use last names in general company.*

"Of course. Bring him home to Costonia," said King Sovex. "By the way, it's nice to see you again, Lady Morgan."

"Thank you, King Sovex. We'll be there shortly." She reached across Makai and disconnected the comm.

"Don't you think it was a bit rude to disconnect so abruptly from the King of Costonia?" Makai raised his eyebrows.

"I didn't like the way she looked at Stalad...I mean Grulen." Both males chuckled.

"It appeared she was quite happy on the king's lap." Grulen tucked her hair behind her ear.

"Maybe so, but it's already done." Morgan shrugged and felt her cheeks heat up. *God, I can't believe I was jealous that she knows him. I'm a mess.*

"Well, he's sending an encrypted message asking where we are and when we'll be planetside." Makai looked up from his comm and shook his head, his braids brushing his shoulders. "Go on. Get out and I'll answer him."

They walked side by side down the corridor to the kitchen.

"Does your real name jog any memories for you?" Morgan glanced up at him.

"No. And before you ask, the human didn't seem familiar other than I immediately thought 'warrior' but without any context or memories."

"Hmm. Okay."

In the kitchen, Morgan pulled out a *leringa* pie and sliced servings for each of them.

"Are you ready to find out who you really are?"

"Yes and no. According to the king, I'm a warrior."

"We kinda figured that out already."

"You probably have family and friends waiting for you. King Sovex said they'd been looking for you."

"That's what I'm worried about. What if I don't remember anything?"

"Costonia has great mind healers. I'm sure they'll help." She chewed a bite of pie, swallowed, then said, "If you want, I'll be with you as you figure it all out."

He frowned, and his tail stiffened.

"Until the *Fortitude* leaves and who knows when that will be."

"No, I'm staying on Costonia for a while unless you have a mate who can be there for you." Her teeth dug into her lip. "Unless you don't want me around."

"*Ciebala*, I hope you stay." His eyebrows drew together, and his lips hid his fangs. "Although if I have a mate, then perhaps it's best if you leave. It would be too painful for both of us."

"No sense worrying too much about it yet."

His hand cupped her jaw, and he rested his forehead on hers.

"Whatever happens, please know how much I've enjoyed every moment with you."

Her eyes teared up.

"Don't say it like that. Like you're already saying goodbye."

Their breaths mixed. His scent enveloped her, and she shivered.

"No goodbyes, *ciebala*."

Chapter 21

In the greenhouse, Grulen read the information on his tablet for the thousandth time. His tail swept in the small patch of grass where he sat cross-legged. When Makai responded to King Sovex, he sent everything the Wing Raiders knew about his amnesia and injuries. The next day, under the advice of mind healers, King Sovex relayed a redacted file about Grulen in the hopes it might ease his transition. The healers warned Grulen might not recognize himself in the file yet, but until they had a chance to examine him in person, they were unwilling to give more details.

Name: Grulen Jevax of House Midnar. Father: Nurin Jevax. Mother and sisters: deceased. Age: Forty-one. Born in the village of Nestune. Status: Unmated and under no contracts. Children: None. Identifying marks: None. Graduated the Warrior Academy with no specialization. Current ship assignment: Warrior on the *Invictus*, flagship of the Svesti military, serving under Commander Vared Durek. Duration of assignment: Over five years. Previous ship assignment: Warrior on the *Diligence*, science vessel. Included were several commendations as well as ratings from superior officers. Last assignment: Classified.

Images of a younger him accompanied the file. Two from the Warrior Academy—one from when he arrived and the other taken the day of his successful completion. Then others from the *Diligence* and *Invictus.*

"Hey," Morgan said softly as she approached. "Anything ring a bell?"

Frustrated, he tossed the tablet aside and watched as she sat next to him.

"No. Bare facts. Nothing more. I don't recognize myself in any of it." His hair stirred from the harsh breath he blew.

"We arrive at Costonia tomorrow. Maybe being back on your world will help." She clasped his tail as it slid toward her. "At least you know your name and age."

"They're just words on a screen, *ciebala.*" He removed her hand from his tail and held it instead. Her fingers entwined with his.

"What can I do to help?"

"You've been doing it for days. Listening to me complain and whine." He rested his forehead on hers. "Not pushing me for more while I work through this even though we know I have no mate."

"Knock it off."

"What?"

"Being so hard on yourself. Not long ago, you told me I was allowed to feel what I feel. That goes for you as well." She glanced down at their hands. "Even if I could magically forget all the bad things that happened to me, I'm not sure I would. Would I still be me if I didn't remember? We're a sum of our experiences. Take them away and would my current strength be less?"

"I think that's part of it. The way I'm feeling and behaving now…is it the same as I would have before the accident? Am I the same male?"

She pursed her lips.

"Does that mean you aren't sure about your feelings about me?"

"You misunderstand me, Morgan. I don't doubt us at all. I doubt me." He slapped his chest with his free hand.

"Well, stop it. You've behaved honorably. You're kind, considerate, and patient with everyone but yourself. I imagine the core of who you are is the same, whether you remember or not."

"Have you changed your mind about us? It's been days since I received the file, yet we haven't done more than talk."

"Grulen, you've been dealing with a lot. I didn't want to push you. I can wait."

His tail wrapped around her waist, and he tugged her onto his lap.

"I don't think I want to wait any longer unless you do." He searched her blue eyes for a hint of her feelings. Her scent deepened.

"Then kiss me." Her fingers traced his cheek.

He lowered his head and savored the moment. Long dark lashes framed her blue eyes with hints of green and gold which held affection and anticipation. Her scent deepened and mixed with the natural odors of the greenhouse. The warmth and silkiness of her flesh under his fingertips sent tingles down his arm. Her breath hitched, and her eyelids drooped as his mouth neared hers.

I've waited so long to hold her like this. I want to sear it into my memory so deeply it can't ever be dislodged.

His lips delicately met hers. Pressing gently, he explored and licked her plump flesh. When her lips parted in invitation, his tongue danced with hers. His eyes closed as the taste of her exploded inside his mouth. *Goddess, the softness of her lips under mine is divine.*

Her hands clutched at his shoulders and her chest rubbed against his. A low rumble emanated from his chest as he gathered her closer. Delving deeper with his tongue, their passion increased. Caresses became firmer and needier. His tail snuck under her shirt hem and caressed her back. Her fingers moved to burrow into his hair and pull him closer.

"Yes, *ciebala*, take what you need."

His hands roamed down her spine until her ass cheeks filled his palms. He kneaded and squeezed. Her small moans peppered the air. His heart pounded and blood rushed to his cock leaving him slightly dizzy. She pulled away from his lips with a gasp then buried her face in his neck. He groaned when she licked his pulse.

"Jesus. You should come with a warning label." Affection and humor laced her words. Her fingers restlessly moved over his chest. Her warm, slightly rough, palms flattened against him seeking more contact.

"You as well." He nuzzled her ear. Her satiny hair tickled his skin sending electric sparks through his veins.

"Where do we go from here?" She tilted back to brush hair from his eyes.

"I want to give you pleasure. I've imagined numerous ways since I met you."

Her fingers spasmed against his forehead.

"As have I, but are we moving too fast? You just found out your name."

"I know I'm not mated or under contract."

"That doesn't mean there isn't someone waiting for you." Her gaze lowered to his collarbone. "I don't want you to have any regrets. A few kisses is entirely different than getting naked together."

Using his forefinger, he raised her chin and saw the concern in her eyes.

"If you're not ready, I'm willing to wait, *ciebala*."

"I'm worried you might have been dating someone. You'll feel guilty if that's the case."

"*Crek.*" He dropped her forehead to hers. "I hadn't considered that."

A reluctant smile tipped her lips upwards.

"So we wait for more?" The pulse in her neck thrummed against his hand.

He closed his eyes and silently prayed for patience.

"I find out tomorrow. If there's no one I need to consider, we spend some quality time alone as soon as we can."

Her hands cupped his face, and she kissed him softly. She maneuvered off his lap leaving him chilled.

"Agreed. I'm going to go now and make it easier for us to resist temptation."

His tail wound about her wrist, and she paused.

"I don't deserve you or your understanding."

Morgan smiled sadly and rubbed his tail before unwrapping it.

"You're one of the few beings I've met out here who does, Grulen. I'll see you at mealtimes."

Her firm ass swayed as she left. His head fell into his hands, and he tugged on his hair.

This is so crekkin' difficult. Goddess, please let me be free and remember everything.

"Ready?"

Grulen inhaled deeply and squared his shoulders. Nodding sharply at Makai, he took the first step down the ramp to set foot on his home world. Morgan joined them at the head of the line, while the remaining Wing Raiders followed, each carrying bags. The *Fortitude* received special permission to dock planetside and a flitter waited for them.

Taking in the area, he saw only military vessels. *Makes sense due to the size of the Wing Raiders' ship. The Fortitude would take up too much room at one of the civilian spaceports.*

Two royal guards approached.

"Captain Makai, I am Wexan Yanz and this is Jespan Kragen. King Sovex asked that we escort your party." He dipped his chin. "Lady Morgan, it is a pleasure to see you again."

"Yanz. Kragen. It is good to see familiar faces."

Grulen's tail began flicking at Morgan's genuine delight at seeing the males. He suppressed the unbidden growl in his chest.

"King Sovex believed sending guards you knew would alleviate any concerns Jevax or the Wing Raiders might have."

"That was thoughtful." Morgan introduced everyone as they walked to the large flitter.

"We'll be taking all of you to a cabin in the King's Forest."

Morgan frowned.

"Why is that?"

Yanz looked at Grulen.

"The mind healers suggested we house you in a place where you would have privacy as your memories return. They felt it would be counterproductive to require you to participate in unstructured interactions with Court members where you might not recall their names or any prior history with them."

Grulen's anger at not being consulted surprised him. He glanced down at Morgan's hand patting his forearm. Taking a deep breath, he realized the mind healers had a legitimate point.

"That may be best."

"If you like, the Wing Raiders may stay with you as additional security for your safety and familiar faces, but you may find the accommodations crowded."

"Do we need to make the decision now?" Makai frowned.

"No."

The group stowed their gear and took seats in the flitter while Kragen and Yanz sat in the cockpit. Once airborne, one of them activated the outside viewer. Like everyone else, Grulen took in the greenery below once they left the spaceport. Pink gravel paths weaved in the more populated areas. Buildings merged with native flora to keep a natural look to Svesti-made structures. Occasionally, they saw other flitters in the air. The quiet chatter of the human females and the Jalaxians registered only as background noise.

This feels familiar, almost like a dream.

He recognized Trezoura, the capital city, and the palace, although he had no memory of being in either. Not long afterwards, they landed in a clearing outside a large structure.

"We're here," said Kragen. "Someone will get your bags. I believe the King and Lady Rachel await your arrival."

Crek. I'm meeting the King? Now?

Morgan sidled closer to him, and his tail rested on her lower back. She gave him an encouraging nod. Familiar odors tickled his nostrils—the trees, flowers, and soil.

Silently, he entered the building as everyone but the guards followed. In the large living area, King Sovex stood with two other Svesti and two human females. One of the Svesti males had golden bronze skin and lavender eyes suggesting kinship with the Costonian ruler. The other had deep bronze skin and blue eyes. While the king and blue-eyed male wore their hair long, the other sported short hair. One of the females was the tall, lithe blonde from the comm. The shorter female was curvier, and her hair color was a duller shade than Morgan's.

Behind him, Kara squealed, then whispered loudly, "It's her. She wrote the dragon shifter books."

"Not the time, Kara," Rain hissed.

"Kara, it's nice to finally meet you in person." The dark-haired female moved closer with a wide smile. She looked at each of the Wing Raiders. "I'm glad to have the opportunity to thank you all in person for your assistance when I was kidnapped."

"We were happy to help Commander Durek." Makai grinned. "I hear congratulations are in order."

The short-haired Svesti stepped forward and clasped Makai's forearm enthusiastically.

"Makai. It is good to see you. Yes, Talia and I are fated mates." *That must be the commander. I should know him, but I don't.*

"Human females are sparking fated mate bonds with the Svesti, too?" Lezon's eyes narrowed.

"Yes, we're seeing fated mate bonds again after almost a century of none," the blue-eyed Svesti said. "I'm Healer Ash'n Rivezt."

"Lezon. Medic."

"I would like to speak with you afterwards and compare observations."

"I would be happy to."

"Rivezt? Are you Lady Narilla's grandson?" Morgan asked. At the Svesti's nod, she continued, "She is very proud of you. She used to tell me stories about your childhood."

Rivezt smiled.

"She also mentioned you with affection, Lady Morgan. I'm glad I finally get to meet you."

Tren moved his way forward.

"Morgan was the human female we rescued at the same time as Lady Talia."

Their welcoming party started in surprise.

"I had no idea, otherwise I would have insisted you return with Talia to heal," King Sovex said.

"I think I ended up where I needed to be, King Sovex."

"In private, all of you, please call me Traxen. I don't require the formalities."

"Then you can drop the Ladies with us," Kara piped up.

"Where are my manners? This is my fated mate and Queen of Costonia, Lady Rachel."

"Queen?" squeaked Kara. "Are you shitting me?"

Rain rolled her eyes. Makai sighed heavily. Grulen silently thanked the Goddess for Kara's irreverent behavior easing his tension.

"Brinkman, decorum," Rain barked.

"Yes, Colonel." Kara straightened her posture and pasted a serious look on her face. She waited until Rain turned, then stuck her tongue out at her.

Queen Rachel smirked. Crax pulled Kara closer and whispered in her ear. Kara's face flushed.

"I can see you will all get along just fine with the other humans here." Lady Talia laughed.

"Can we get back to Grulen?" Morgan said quietly.

"Of course." Traxen exchanged a warrior's clasp with Grulen. "Welcome home, Grulen Jevax. We have been looking for you for *lunars*. We feared you perished in the explosion."

"Explosion?"

"Come, let us get comfortable and we'll talk more." Traxen gestured to the next room and the dining area's long table.

"It appears the Zuvgran attacked the shuttle you were temporarily assigned to."

"Given the data from the pod where Jevax was rescued, that makes sense." Makai crossed his arms.

"He must have suspected the danger if he was in a pod at the time," said Lezon.

"I've reviewed your medical records from the *Morning Star*. You were lucky to survive." Rivezt held his gaze. "Do you remember any of us?"

"With the exception of the king, all of your scents feel familiar, but no memories accompany the sensation." Grulen frowned. Morgan leaned into his shoulder and his tail wrapped around her ankle under the table.

"Hmm. Anything else?"

Grulen squinted at the healer.

"Like what?"

Rivezt leaned forward.

"You tell me."

"It sounds silly."

"Let me be the judge of that."

Grulen let out a long breath.

"Impressions."

"Please explain."

"A word or two."

"Curious. What words?"

"I do not wish to offend anyone." *This healer is tenacious.*

"You won't, Jevax. Think of this as a fact-finding mission." Queen Rachel's blue eyes encouraged him.

"Fine." He pointed at Durek. "Volatile, but fair." He indicated Rivezt. "Controlled, but compassionate." Dipping his chin at Lady Talia, he said, "Stubborn caretaker." For Queen Rachel, his words were "Warrior instructor."

At their silence, his shoulders drooped. Then Queen Rachel laughed, and the others joined in.

"Oh, Jevax, we've missed you." Queen Rachel wiped her eyes.

"Given your accuracy, I believe you will most definitely retrieve your memories at some point." Rivezt's fangs gleamed white against his bronze skin.

"Really?" Morgan leaned forward.

Rivezt nodded.

"I don't know how long it will take, but his answers suggest that the memories are there but misplaced or hidden somehow." *That's good news.*

"Are you a mind healer?" Abby spoke for the first time.

"No. I've had training because of my position on the *Invictus*, but it wasn't my primary focus."

"Our best mind healers believe that since Rivezt has treated you for over five years, you may find it easier to speak with him initially. They hope you may have retained a sense of rapport with him and that will reduce the time it takes to remember. Rivezt will report to them and discuss his own impressions. They will offer advice or suggestions as needed. There may come a point when you no longer feel Rivezt is not the one you need to speak with. They will intervene if that happens." Traxen gestured as he explained.

"Part of me feels there is something important I'm supposed to do, but I haven't been able to recall what that is."

"There was. However, the situation no longer exists," Durek said.

"Can you tell me what it was?"

Rivezt's ponytail swung as he shook his head.

"At this time, I would prefer not to. I'm concerned it will negatively impact your natural progress."

Crek. Even when there are answers, no one will tell me. Hopefully, they'll respond to the next question.

"The file you sent said I was unmated and under no contract. Is there a specific female waiting for me to remember her?"

Morgan tensed beside him and his tail rubbed along her calf. Queen Rachel and Lady Talia laughed.

"Oh, no. No one."

Morgan pursed her lips.

"What's so funny?"

"Let's just say our initial impression of Jevax when we first met several *lunars* ago was that he was a flirt."

Grulen frowned at Lady Talia's words.

"However, he treated all of us with respect and became a trusted friend." Queen Rachel studied Morgan's reaction.

"Hmm."

I hope Morgan doesn't change her opinion of me based on the females' words.

Chapter 22

Morgan finished unpacking her clothes. The room she chose was beautiful with its white and gold color scheme. Grulen suggested she have her own space, just in case. *I wonder if today's revelations shook him.*

They ultimately decided the Wing Raiders would stay at the palace for a few days so the Kara, Rain, and Abby could spend time with the newest women in this quadrant. Abby promised she'd tell Morgan all the gossip. *As much as I'd like to make new friends, I think Grulen needs me here.*

Rivezt planned to bring Grulen's father, Nurin, to the cabin after they got the Wing Raiders settled. *I'm sure Grulen is nervous. Maybe that's why he wants separate bedrooms.*

Grabbing some clean clothes from the drawers she just filled, she brought them into the sanitary facilities while she showered. Hot water rained down on her and she moaned. Steam rose as the water pelted her body relaxing her tense muscles. *I missed taking real showers.*

After soaping up with something that smelled like Earth's sandalwood, she ran her hands over her flesh. Tilting her head back and closing her eyes, she cupped her breasts and circled her nipples. She pictured Grulen's hands teasing her, coaxing pleasure from her. Her palms skimmed her waist and delved lower. Using her forefinger and thumb, she pulled her lower lips apart and let the water roll over her swollen clit. Not enough pressure to bring her to orgasm, but more than enough to make her squirm.

Finally, she stepped back and brought her hand back to her breast to pinch her nipple and gasp. Turning off the water, she clenched her thighs tightly. Her ass cheeks flexed as she walked, her clit tingling and keeping her arousal at the forefront of her mind. *Not going to let myself get off. I want to save it for later. Hopefully, there will be a later.*

She dried off, dressed, and combed her hair. A pink flush decorated her face. Her eyes looked too bright. She took some deep breaths letting her ardor cool as she finished getting ready.

Maybe I should make some snacks for Grulen and his dad. At least it will give me something to do.

Shit. I guess Grulen will age well. His father is gorgeous.

The older reddish-bronze Svesti greeted them both with a smile and relief in his pale green eyes. His dark hair showed streaks of silver. *Grulen's brown eyes must come from his mother.*

"Son. I'm relieved to see you hale and hearty." Nurin extended his arm for a warrior's clasp. Rivezt stood quietly behind him.

Grulen frowned.

"I'm sorry I don't remember you." He held onto his father's forearm.

"Yet, my son. You don't remember me yet. The healers are confident you will in time." Nurin pulled his son close and hugged him tightly for a long moment. Tears filled his eyes when he stepped back. "Even if you never do, you are alive and well. That is what is important to me." He turned to Morgan. "And who is this?"

"Morgan Calloway, a friend of Grulen's." She held out her hand.

Instead of a handshake, Nurin kissed the top of her hand lightly. *Oh my, he's a charmer like his son.*

"Lady Morgan, it is wonderful to meet you."

"Won't you come in and sit? I made some snacks if you're hungry."

"I would love to if Grulen finds that acceptable. I can wait to eat."

"Of course." Grulen's tail touched her back.

They moved into the living area. Grulen led her to a couch and sat close to her. His father rested across from them while the healer took a seat just outside their triangle. *He must not want to interrupt their reunion.*

"I'm not sure what to say." Grulen's tail wound around her ankle and his elbows rested on his knees with his fingers laced together.

"I am happy to answer any questions you may have or share memories if you want. Whatever is most comfortable for you." Nurin leaned forward. "I don't want to overwhelm you."

"Truthfully, information isn't an issue for me. Frustration at not being able to recall is."

"Maybe you can share events since you woke up instead. I have always enjoyed knowing what is happening in your life."

Grulen relaxed and relayed much of what he did after waking on the *Morning Star*. Morgan hadn't known some of it. She listened eagerly to his stories and his father asking questions. Her heart lifted as she watched them become more comfortable and noticed the similarities in some of their speech patterns and body language. *The males had a good relationship before the accident, I'm sure of it. They'll be close again.*

When Nurin began telling tales of Grulen's early childhood, the love for his entire family shone brightly. He spoke of his wife and daughters and their interactions with Grulen, his only son. Laughter rang out at some of the more outrageous shenanigans his children engaged in. Even Rivezt chuckled from his offset chair.

Nurin's expression turned somber.

"In some ways, I envy you at this moment, Grulen. You don't remember our grief when we lost all of them to the virus. So much promise and love gone within days of each other." Surreptitiously, he wiped a tear from his eye. "If it weren't for you, I'm not sure I would have survived their deaths."

Grulen reached out and squeezed his father's hand.

"I want the memories, even the pain. From what you've said, they deserve the honor of remembrance."

"You have always had a solid heart. No sire could be prouder of his son than I."

Oh, shit. I think I'm going to cry.

Needing a moment to collect herself, she rose to get the prepared snacks. Thankfully, both males had moved on to general conversation by the time she returned.

Several times during his father's visit, Grulen's tail moved to caress her absently.

When he rose to leave, Nurin said, "When you are ready, I would like to take you to Nestune and show you where you grew up."

Rivezt spoke for the first time.

"I think it's best if you wait several days before you schedule a trip, Jevax. Let today's information settle and see if it prompts any memories. Pushing too hard or too fast could impede your progress."

Grulen nodded and tentatively hugged his father.

"Thank you for being patient with me. When the healers approve it, we will gladly accompany you to Nestune."

"I look forward to it." Nurin clapped his son affectionately on the back.

Morgan said her goodbyes to Nurin and added a quiet "thank you" to Rivezt. Grulen's arm settled over her shoulders and tugged her closer to his side as they watched the males take off in a small flitter.

"I liked your father."

"Me, too."

"Did anything feel familiar?"

"His scent, mostly."

"Don't force it. It's only the first day."

He turned her to face him. Shivers traveled her spine as his finger traced her ear.

Gazing into her eyes, he said, "I told Rivezt I did not want any additional company for evening meal. However, if you wish, we can change that and invite anyone you like."

"No, I think a quiet night in for us is best. I can easily make something. Someone stocked the kitchen well."

Bending forward, he nuzzled her neck. *Damn, I didn't realize how sensitive I am there.*

"I hope we can revisit my giving you pleasure soon. Now that I know the truth, I wish to pursue you romantically." His voice deepened, and he licked her earlobe. She shuddered.

"I'm game if you are." She shrieked when he suddenly lifted her and carried her with long strides to his bedroom. Once inside, he let her body slide down the front of his slowly. Her eyelids fluttered at the contrast of his hard body against her softer one.

Large hands framed her face, and his fingers tunneled into her hair. *Did his brown eyes change to copper?*

"May I kiss you, *ciebala*?"

"Please." She wrapped her arms around his neck and tugged. Almost violently, their lips clashed and their tongues dueled. Long-denied passion erupted unchecked. She found the fastener on his shirt and flicked it impatiently. Her fingers clenched on his warm pecs. The scent of warm caramel and cinnamon made her dizzy.

His hands drifted underneath her T-shirt and contacted her skin. Heat flared between her legs, and her hips gyrated restlessly as he slowly caressed upwards taking her shirt with him. He broke off their kiss long enough to pull the fabric over her head and toss it aside. He stilled and licked his lips. A single finger dragged gently over the upper lace of her bra. Goosebumps followed his progress, and her breasts swelled. Her nipples hardened with his attention.

"You are even more beautiful than I imagined." His husky voice tapered off as he bent his head to trace his finger's path with his lips and tongue leaving her skin damp. His hands squeezed her ass while his tail swept along her back to tuck itself between her cheeks to tease between her thighs.

Her head fell back, and her digits dug into his muscular shoulders. Delightful shivers shook her body, and she moaned his name. The sensation of his lips smiling against her flesh shot electricity to her clit. Her knees became boneless when the tip of his tongue licked a nipple through the lace.

Her nails bit into his skin when he blew on her wet nipple. Noises she didn't recognize escaped her throat when his lips latched onto her and sucked. His fangs dug into her without breaking her soft flesh. *Sweet baby Jesus. So intense.*

He lifted her, and her legs wrapped around his waist. Carrying her to the bed, he sat her on the edge and moved his hands to fumble with her bra closure. He slid the straps down her arms and grumbled when he released her nipple with a loud pop to finish baring her upper torso.

"Does this give you pleasure, Morgan?" He kneaded her breast and brought it back to her mouth.

"Yes. More. Please."

"As you command, *ciebala*." Alternating between both breasts, he lavished attention on them until her nipples became swollen and red. He leaned back slightly and grinned at his handiwork.

"Even more beautiful now."

She gravitated toward him and kissed his pec. Licking her way to one of his nipples, she surrounded it with her lips and sucked. When she gently bit it, he hissed.

"Again," he growled.

Now it was her turn to smile at his reaction. She played with his hard little buds occasionally nipping. His stomach muscles contracted under her hands each time she surprised him with another nibble.

"Enough. You haven't had enough pleasure yet." Gentle hands pushed her to lie supine on the bed before pulling down her yoga pants and panties lifting her ass and legs to undress her. She toed off her shoes so he could slide everything off easily. He knelt at her feet, warm hands caressing her ankles after removing her sock before exploring higher. Raising up on her elbows, she watched as he intently investigated every inch he had exposed.

His wide shoulders pushed her legs apart. He inhaled and briefly closed his eyes.

"You smell delicious. I can't wait to have my fill." His fingers reverently spread her lower lips open. "So beautiful everywhere," he mumbled. His tail maneuvered upwards to rub against her nipple.

Her hair tickled her shoulders when her head tipped back at the first tender touch of his tongue where she was the wettest.

He growled low making her hips shift at the sensation. His tail left her breast to rest over her waist to hold her still. When he mouthed her opening and delved deeper with his tongue, her elbows flopped, and she lied flat on the mattress.

Voraciously he explored every nook and cranny, experimenting with movements and pressures. A heartfelt moan left her lips when he found her clit and he focused his attention there sending small shocks of delight throughout her body. At some point, his stiffened tongue darted left and right just under her clit and her toes curled with extreme rapture.

A small squeal preceded her breathy, "There. Right there. Oh, please don't stop."

Tears slid down her face when he added a rumble and continued teasing the underside of her bud. Her hands buried themselves in his hair and her fingers dug into his scalp. Trying to squirm, she didn't know if she wanted to get away from the unrelenting pleasure or press harder against him. His tail and hands held her firmly. Her body shook as the pressure inside her built to a crescendo, then shattered. She screamed his name and every part of her trembled. His tongue softened and slowed.

"Oh my god. I've never felt that good before."

His eyes raised to hers, and he licked his smiling lips and fangs. *Wow, his brown eyes really do turn copper when he's aroused. That's so sexy.*

"I want to do that all day, every day."

An exhausted laugh passed her lips.

"I'm not sure I could keep up with all day, but that was extremely wonderful."

"We'll have to build your stamina, *ciebala*."

Her fatigue passed quickly when he stood and divested himself of his boots and pants. His cock sprang free hard enough to slap his stomach. When he fisted his shaft, the lower position revealed his three head nodes. *I bet those bumps will feel incredible inside me.*

Attempting to sit up so she could return his oral attentions, she glanced at him in surprise when he shook his head and pressed her back.

"Not this time. I want you too badly to wait." He bent his knees slightly to rub the head of his shaft in the evidence of her orgasm. Leaning forward, he covered her body and tugged her legs around his waist while he placed the head of cock at her entrance.

Unexpectedly, her body tensed, and she pushed upwards on his chest. He frowned and immediately moved his body to lie by her side.

"*Ciebala?*"

She silently screamed in her mind and gasped for air. Unbidden, tears flowed down her face, and she turned away from him. Her hands grabbed her elbows, and she curled into a fetal position. *Oh, shit. Oh, shit. No. No. No. I want him, not a panic attack.*

Did they break me?

Chapter 23

Grulen's cock deflated at Morgan's distress. His tail caressed her outer thigh lightly. Her highly responsive nature delighted him, and he didn't doubt she'd experienced pleasure from his hands and tongue. He reviewed their interactions to determine what caused her panic attack. Concerned that she would faint from her rapid breathing, he sat up and cautiously tugged her naked body onto his lap.

Loosely embracing her, he softly said, "Breathe with me, *ciebala*. Slow and deep. Breathe." He picked up one of her hands and held it to his heart. "Breathe, Morgan. You're safe."

Her head fell forward onto his chest. Her damp face rubbed on his skin. Her flesh felt cold when only minutes before she burned with passion. *I hate when she cries. It hurts to see her pain.*

He tenderly rubbed her back attempting to warm her. Eventually, her respirations slowed. He continued his ministrations and maintained his silence.

"I'm sorry."

"Don't be."

Her silky hair tickled his chest when she shook it.

"I feel like a fool. I honestly didn't think sex would be an issue." One of her hands drifted lower. "Let me take care of you."

He seized her hand and pulled it to his lips.

"Not necessary, *ciebala*."

"I feel guilty you didn't get a chance to come." Her voice was barely audible.

"I don't need an orgasm for its own sake. I am happy I gave you pleasure."

"It doesn't seem fair."

"It's not an issue of fair." He paused. "Do you know what caused your panic?"

"Your weight and you looming over me." Embarrassment tinged her words.

"Okay."

Quietly thinking while her scent lost its acrid taint, he decided to pamper her. He stood and carried her to the sanitary facility.

"Where are you taking me?"

"I'm going to give you a bath and then hold you as you sleep."

"You don't have to do that."

"I want to help you relax." He started the water running in the oversized tub. After checking the temperature to ensure it wouldn't harm her satiny skin, he carefully set her down. He rummaged through the bottles on a nearby shelf and found a bath oil made with herbs known to aid in releasing tension. Planning to add it to the bath after he cleansed her body, he placed it on the ledge surrounding the pool.

"Would you like me to remain outside the bath while I tend to your hair?"

She lifted red-rimmed eyes to his.

"I don't understand the question."

Lifting a hand, he rubbed her cheek with his thumb.

"I'm going to be your ladies' maid this night. I will see to your every need. To start, I will wash your hair and body. If you prefer to have the water to yourself, I will do it from here."

Her eyes widened and her jaw dropped.

"That's sweet, but I don't expect that from you."

He tapped her nose with a forefinger.

"It is my honor, Morgan. My feelings for you are more than sexual. I want to care for you in any way you need or desire."

"I'm usually taking care of others—either by choice or being forced when I was kidnapped."

"Then you're long overdue to receive." He kissed her forehead. "Now lean back and let's get your hair wet."

She grabbed his hand.

"Join me in the bath, Grulen."

"Are you sure?"

"Yes. I have no bad memories associated with sanitary facilities."

"As you command." Water sloshed as he climbed into the pool and sat facing her.

She slid downward and wet her head. Droplets flew as she blew out a breath. She twisted to give him her back. He drizzled shampoo onto her hair, then worked up a lather with gentle fingers. Her head fell onto his chest as he massaged her scalp, and she sighed.

"That feels wonderful. The shampoo portion used to be my favorite part of visiting a hairdresser on Earth."

Suds landed on his cheek when he bent to kiss behind her ear.

"So we're bringing up good memories?"

"Even better, Grulen, we're making good memories." She squirmed and her ass snugged between his thighs. He mentally ordered his cock to behave. *This is about her comfort.*

He rinsed her hair before soaping his hands and tenderly washed her body beginning with her shoulders. Soft sighs filled the air as she relaxed. Using both hands, he cleaned and cleansed one arm. Taking his time, he worked his way to her hand, holding it in his palm and kneading each digit with his thumb and forefinger. Then he started on the other arm.

"Lean forward and I'll do your back."

She scooted to give him access and moaned when he rubbed her tight muscles as he washed her. His cock hardened at the sounds of her enjoyment. Savoring the experience, he continued downward ensuring each of her flesh received his devoted attention. He stopped at the dip in her back.

Voice husky, he said, "Turn around."

Maneuvering languidly, she rose and rotated to face him. She straddled him and rested her arms on his shoulders. Hazy blue eyes smiled at him. She cleared her throat.

"I want you, Grulen. I'd like to try again."

Goddess, she's so brave.

"We don't have to do more tonight, *ciebala*. That wasn't my intent."

"I know and I appreciate your patience and care. This isn't to reward you for your understanding. I want to take back my sexuality and own it. You are the only person I've wanted to be with since before I was kidnapped. The decisions about my body haven't been my own for a long time. I want my power back."

He searched her expression for any hint of distress and found none. Her fingers played at his nape.

"We can stop at any time. You are in control." Spreading his arms wide, he said, "Do with me what you will."

A self-satisfied look crossed her face. Her hands pulled him forward to kiss. His hands dropped to her waist and caressed the curves of her hips. Their mouths met and tongues collided. *Crek. She tastes so good.*

His fingers skated to the underside of her pert breasts and outlined them. She arched and brought them closer to him. Humming, he glided soft kisses and licks along the length of her neck and along the upper portions of her swollen globes. He flicked his tongue across an erect nipple and her hands clenched.

"Yes," she hissed. "Your mouth feels so good."

Surrounding the hardened bud with his mouth, he circled it with his tongue while cupping her breast. His tail snuck between them and delved between her legs. Seeking her other nub that enjoyed his attention earlier, he mimicked what his mouth was doing. Her breathing quickened and her moans filled his ears.

His tail slid lower to her entrance and pressed inward steadily. Supporting her weight on his free arm, he leaned her backwards to partially float on the surface of the water. She clutched his head as he switched breasts. His tail increased the tempo of its thrusts. A long, low groan left her lips.

"Grulen, your tail. More." Her hips gyrated and her insides clenched around him. *So crekkin' tight. The Goddess made her for me.*

Pumping faster and delving deeper, he gave her what she asked for. He lifted his head and watched her writhe on his tail. His digits played with her nipple, tugging and pinching lightly.

"Open your eyes, *ciebala*. Let me see your desire."

Her passion-filled gaze met his. He could see the effort she made to keep her heavy eyelids open.

"You are incredibly sexy and beautiful." He flattened his hand and drug it between her breasts to her core, then back again. "This body was made to receive pleasure from me."

"Grulen, I want your cock, not your tail. Please." *Does it make me a bad male to enjoy her begging for my member? If so, I don't care.*

Lifting her up, he gently placed her on the ledge and knelt in front of her. She cried out when his tail left her sweet hole and slid to playfully slap a stiff nipple. His engorged cock entered her slowly. Feeling her channel squeeze to accommodate him and watching her cunt swallow him sent his own desire rocketing wildly.

"You take me so well, *ciebala*. All pink and swollen sucking in my cock." He held her hips steady as he pushed further. He watched her closely to ensure she felt only pleasure, not pain from his intrusion.

"More. I can take it. Oh my god. Your head nodes. Jesus, that feels good." She panted and tried to push against him.

"I don't want to hurt you. Almost there. Goddess, your greedy cunt swallowing my cock feels like coming home." He seated himself and held himself motionless to give her time to adjust. His base node touched her clit, and he swiveled his hips to rub against it.

"Oh, yes." Squeals of delight left her mouth.

"As you command." He withdrew until only the head of his cock remained in her.

"Fuck me, Grulen. Make me yours."

In a single swift motion, he buried himself inside her again and ground his base node against her clit. Seeing only agonizing pleasure on his face, he repeated himself. Gripping her ass cheeks, his claws extruded and pricked her flesh. His fangs elongated.

Over and over again, he thrust into her welcoming warmth. She played with her breasts, tugging her nipples, and tried to push him deeper. His tail rested on her collarbones, and she grasped it in one hand and squeezed. Shockwaves of arousal spread throughout his body. Feeling him jerk in surprise, a lustful expression filled her face, and she lifted his tail to her mouth. Holding his gaze, she mouthed the end. He growled as she sucked the taste of herself from him. Heat and wetness embraced his cock and tail. He pounded faster.

She pulled his tail from her mouth long enough to shout, "Deeper. Harder."

His rhythm accelerated and sweat formed on their bodies. Their heat spiraled higher. When his base node hit her clit, electricity shot up his spine. Their scents combined and his ass clenched as he tried to hold back his release.

"Come for me again, *ciebala*. I want to feel your cunt strangling my cock." He pulled his tail from her mouth and pushed it under her ass seeking her other hole. She gasped as he tickled the opening without entering. Taking one hand from her hips, he thumbed her clit, their bodies slapping his hand between them when they collided.

A long wail filled the room as she shattered on him. Her entire body spasmed and her cunt milked his cock. His balls drew up and he came. His movements slowed as her insides clenched him. He roared her name as his vision whitened.

Eventually they slowed, gasping for air. Taking care not to put his weight on her or give the impression of looming, he lifted her back into the water and sat heavily causing her to bounce on his cock. They both hissed. Still filling her, his cock softened. He caressed her as their bodies recovered. He raised her chin with a forefinger and kissed her forehead.

"Thank you, *ciebala*, for sharing yourself with me."

"Thank you for being exactly what I need."

"Let's dry off and rest. It's been a long day for both of us."

In his bed, he positioned her between his legs, her back to his front and combed her hair with his claws. Her head fell forward, and her fingers traced patterns on his upper thighs.

"May I ask a question?" He paused when her fingers stilled momentarily before continuing her light caresses.

"Of course."

"Will sleeping in the bed with me cause you distress?" *I hope not.*

He watched her hair sweep across her shoulders when she shook her head.

"I don't think so, so long as you don't roll over on me. Most of the clients Slovis made me service, sleeping wasn't high on their list of activities." A bitter undernote to her deliberately light tone and darkness in her scent warned him to use caution.

"Please tell me if anything I do or say makes you uncomfortable. Your happiness is my priority." He ran his hands down her arms, and his fingers entwined with hers.

She tightened her grip on him.

"Talking about it isn't something I like to do, but I understand ignoring my issues won't help. Your patience helps." She twisted her upper torso, and a small smile brightened her face. "For my own sake, I'm glad there wasn't a female waiting for you."

"For my own sake, I'm happy you chose to wait with an open heart and understood my position." He kissed her tenderly.

They slid downwards, and she turned further to lie upon him. She shifted so her leg covered his, and her ear rested on his chest. He kissed the top of her head.

"For tonight, I think I need to face you so if I wake in the middle of the night, I'll recognize you and your smell."

"Whatever you like." His arm wrapped around her while his tail tucked over her leg. "What do I smell like to you?"

"Caramel and cinnamon, an Earth dessert topping and a spice. They bring me happy thoughts and memories." Her lips moved against his skin. "What do you smell in my scent?"

"*Trulet* and grass in a light rain or mist. Earthy, growing odors that bring me inner peace."

"Not sure that sounds very sexy."

His chest rumbled.

"Oh, trust me, on you, it's extremely arousing."

She giggled.

"Okay, I trust you."

"I'll never abuse that trust, *ciebala*."

"I know."

Tenderly, he played with her hair, marveling at how soft and silky it felt. He listened as her breathing leveled and soft snores reverberated against his pecs. *Thank you, Goddess, for watching over her. Please let her find lasting peace in her soul.*

Chapter 24

Morning sunlight woke Morgan from the most restful sleep she could remember. Her face lay smooshed against Grulen's warm pecs, and she felt the steady beat of his heart. Her head rose with his rhythmic slow breaths. His tail held her securely around her waist, and her right leg over his thigh remained as when she first fell asleep. His left leg bent to trap her right ankle between his legs. His right arm rested on her shoulders with his fingers tangled in her hair, while his left hand held her right one on his chest.

I trust him. *When I had the panic attack last night because of his position over me, instinctively, I didn't move far from him. I trusted him to help me.*

Even now in sleep he's protecting me and keeping me safe.

Her mind stalled at the thought. *Is that all of what's drawing me to him? That sense of safety and protection when I've been through so much?*

His heart thrummed soothingly against her ear. *No. He's thoughtful, kind, honorable, and is sexier than any male I've ever seen. He makes me laugh, and he patiently holds me when*

I cry. He makes me believe I'm stronger than I am. I want his words and company. The safety and protection are a bonus.

Relieved that she wasn't unconsciously using a good male for understandable, but wrong reasons, she blew out a breath. His fingers tightened, then loosened to comb lightly through her hair. She lifted her head and rested her chin on top of their clasped hands.

"Good morning." She tilted her mouth downwards to kiss his knuckles before returning to look at him.

"Good morn, *ciebala*. Did you sleep well?" Brown eyes affectionately smiled at her.

"Better than I have in a long time, thanks to you."

"Having you in my arms during the quiet hours soothed me as well." *He has a beautiful way with words.*

"I'm glad."

"Come closer and let me kiss you properly." His deep rumble under her breasts sent quivers through her nipples.

"As you command." She flashed him a cheeky grin before scooting upwards to peck him on the lips.

"Not good enough," he growled. The arm around her shoulders tugged her closer as his tail tightened to keep her in place. His gaze dropped to her lips. "Now, allow me to express my affection in minute detail."

Be still my heart.

Her eyelids closed as his lips lovingly smoothed over hers. Low purring sounds tickled against her breasts. She opened her mouth when he licked the seam of her lips. Their tongues lazily danced in perfect counterpoint. A contented sigh gathered in her chest and escaped when they broke for air.

"Much better," he said.

"I'm glad you approve." She caressed his face. "Do we have plans for today?"

"Not yet. Is there something you'd like to do?"

"Nothing specific. I'm happy to spend a quiet day here with you."

"I like that idea. This is the first time we've been truly alone."

"I..." she broke off when his comm chimed. She giggled at his exaggerated frown. He answered in audio only mode.

"Jevax."

"Jevax, this is Healer Rivezt. There are some more people hoping to see you and Morgan today."

"What time and where?"

"Two hours and we'll come to you."

Grulen looked at Morgan. She nodded in agreement.

"We'll see you in two hours." He disconnected the comm.

"That was rude hanging up so abruptly."

"Don't care. He interrupted us during our alone time."

"We only have two hours to have breakfast and get ready."

"How about a shower together to save time?" He arched an eyebrow.

"I like that idea. Just give me a couple minutes alone in the sanitary facility first."

His forehead wrinkled, and she laughed.

"I have to pee. After being kidnapped, I consider privacy during the act of relieving myself a priority."

Dropping a kiss on her forehead, he pretended to shoo her away.

"Go, take care of business. I'll be anxiously waiting to join you in the shower."

"You're the best, Grulen." She inwardly smiled when his cheeks darkened slightly. *How cute.*

Morgan grinned and swiveled her hips as she scrambled eggs. Earlier, Grulen took her hard against the shower wall making her scream out three orgasms before he groaned her name and emptied himself into her. Deliciously sore, her good mood could power Oklahoma City for at least a month.

Turning and tipping her head back when his hot breath hit her neck, she accepted his kiss. His arms embraced her from behind, and his hips matched her swaying. Inhaling his clean, familiar scent, she smiled and pushed her ass into his groin.

"Vixen. Tempting me again. Haven't you had enough this morning?" he teased as he ground his cock into her ass.

"Funny, you feel like you haven't had enough yourself." She turned off the heating unit and plated the eggs. "Let's get some food into us before we faint from exhaustion."

Humor brightened his brown eyes.

"We will need energy for later. I didn't get a chance to taste that delectable cunt earlier. I plan to make up for that."

She fanned herself before picking up the plates.

"You have to let go so I can feed us."

"I don't want to. You belong in my arms."

She kissed him again.

"A girl could get used to this adoration," she teased.

"You should expect it. You're worth it."

Happy tears caught on her lashes while her breath hitched in her throat at his sincerity. He took the plates from her and stepped away to place them on the table. She brought over a pitcher of juice. The breakfast meat and toast already sat waiting for them. She'd been surprised and happy to find fresh bread in the stores. There hadn't been any when she was last on Costonia.

They chatted amicably while they ate. His tail caressed her calf as he jokingly fought her for a piece of breakfast meat. Her cheeks hurt from grinning. The door chimed before they finished.

"Stay and eat. I'll get it." Grulen stood and kissed her before leaving to answer the front door. He returned with Healer Rivezt, two human females around Morgan's age, and another shorter Svesti male with caramel bronze skin, teal eyes, and multiple dark braids.

"Hi," the petite Asian female said shyly. Shoulder-length dark hair framed a pretty face with brown eyes.

"Grulen, Morgan, this is my fated mate, Lin Chang Rivezt."

"Hi, Lin." Morgan gave a little wave. "Please, everyone, sit and join us. I can make more if you haven't eaten."

Everyone took seats. Rivezt tugged Lin onto his lap.

Quietly, he asked, "*Bataavi*, are you hungry or thirsty?" The small woman shook her head.

"With us is Lieutenant Devik Tolvex, head security officer on the *Invictus*, and his fated mate, Emmy Norton Tolvex."

Emmy's brown curls bounced, and her fingers waggled a hello. Once Morgan got over her envy of Emmy's skin tone—so different from her own perpetually pale flesh—she got a good look at her T-shirt. She laughed out loud when she read "I'm not anti-social. I'm just not user-friendly."

"Oh my god. I just realized how much I missed graphic T-shirts." Morgan giggled.

Emmy grinned.

"I brought a bunch of them. Most are about coding." *She sounds Australian.*

"So, I'm guessing you're into computers."

"Yep." Emmy snagged a piece of breakfast meat and gestured it at the toast. "I see you found the fresh bread Ava sent over."

"Ava?"

"Six of us came over on the *Invictus*. Long story there for another time. Ava's a Canadian chef and found ways to make a number of Earth foods from ingredients out here." She tilted her head. "Let's see, you've already met Talia and Rachel. The other one is Natasha, she's a Russian physician."

"Morgan is an exceptional cook," Grulen said.

"I'm sure I don't have the training that Ava does."

"That doesn't negate how well you prepare meals, *ciebala*."

Morgan ignored his comment.

"Lin, tell us about yourself."

"I'm a botanist. I graduated from the University of Chicago." *English isn't her first language, but she sounds fluent.*

"That's a good school."

"Do I know you from before?" Grulen looked at Tolvex.

Tolvex grinned. *I'd forgotten how attractive most Svesti males are.*

"Obviously, you don't remember me. We've met several times. In fact, I was the last person you saw when you left *Invictus.*" He turned to Rivezt. "Ash'n, does he still have his tracker?"

The healer frowned. *Why did Grulen have a tracker?*

"I never checked. If I could now?" he asked Grulen.

"Of course." Grulen sat still when Rivezt pulled out a scanner and ran it over his head.

"Yes, his tracker is still there, inactive. I'll have to extract it later."

"Morgan, so you've been with the Wing Raiders for several months?" Emmy poured herself some juice.

"I didn't tell either of you. Morgan was the other female rescued at the same time as Talia." Rivezt glanced meaningfully. "She's also the human who volunteered with our healers during their research."

Tolvex exhaled heavily.

"That was you? I'm so glad you're okay. We should have found you sooner."

Morgan ducked her head in embarrassment.

"Thanks," she mumbled.

"We got drunk with the other women last night," Emmy said. "It seems to be the fastest way to bond. So, we know some background on Rain, Kara, and Abby, but you weren't there."

"Emmy, leave her alone. She doesn't have to satisfy your curiosity during our first meeting." Lin frowned at the woman.

"Aw, come on. You know it makes me itch when I don't know what makes people tick."

"*Milara*, please do not make our guests uncomfortable." Tolvex tugged on one of her curls.

"It's okay." Morgan drew in a breath. "How much did they tell you?" Grulen's tail moved up to her waist and gave her an encouraging squeeze.

"Only that you'd been kidnapped by Durelians, enslaved, rescued, captured by the Zuvgran, and rescued again. Oh, and you're very talented on aerial silks and thankfully you cook better than one of the Jalaxians." Emmy smirked. "But I'm more curious about before all that."

"Um, okay. How far back should I go?"

"Hit the highlights. I can wait for more detailed stories."

Rivezt rubbed his mate's back absently. Lin shook her head in exasperation.

"You don't have to tell her anything. She's like a nosy child sometimes."

"I'm from Oklahoma City. My mom raised me but became ill with cancer while I was in college. I quit school and worked as an exotic dancer in a high-end club to pay the bills while I cared for her. After she died, the job paid for me to get my degree. In fact, the Durelians kidnapped me when I was on my way to my new job in Portland, Oregon.”

“That sucks.” Emmy’s nose wrinkled. “What did you study?”

“Education.”

“You’re a teacher?” Lin leaned forward. “What grades?”

“I wanted to teach elementary school, but my training involved teaching older children, too.”

Lin glanced first at Emmy, then the Svesti.

“Are you thinking what I’m thinking?”

“*Bataavi*, we don’t know what Jevax’s plans may be once he regains his memories.”

“His plans shouldn’t take priority over hers. Not offering her the opportunity does a disservice to both of them.”

“What are you talking about?” Grulen’s tail left Morgan and flicked behind him.

Tolvex stared at the women for a long moment before nodding.

“Are you willing to take a short trip?”

“Where?”

“There’s a new group home on Costonia with Zuvgran hybrids. We’d like to show it to both of you.”

“Zuvgran on Costonia?” Grulen’s tail flicked again.

“Only one pure blood. The rest are hybrids with other species. King Sovex offered them refuge here. They are no threat to Svesti.” Tolvex pinned Grulen with a look.

“Actually, I’m more concerned about Morgan. Zuvgran experimented on her.” Lin bit her lower lip.

Morgan inhaled deeply.

"I think I'll be fine, but I guess we won't know until we try." She looked to Grulen for his opinion.

"If you're willing, we can go, *ciebala*. I admit I'm curious as to who the king would invite to stay on our home world." He glared at Rivezt. "If she becomes upset, we leave immediately."

"Agreed."

Morgan finished her juice and began collecting dirty dishes. Lin hopped off the healer's lap.

"Let me help."

Morgan nodded.

"I think you'll find it a happy visit." Lin smiled encouragingly.

"I hope so."

Chapter 25

Grulen followed their visitors out to their flitter. Larger than the one that brought his father, it easily fit eight. Which worked out well, as Yanz and Kragen appeared from the woods to join them.

"Have they been guarding us all this time?" Morgan settled into a seat.

Grulen shrugged.

"King Sovex ordered a team of two to ensure Jevax's privacy and your safety," Tolvex said. "Precautionary in nature. No specific threats."

"I wish I'd known. I would've made enough for them to eat with us."

"That's not necessary, Lady Morgan," Yanz said from the front. "However, we appreciate the kind thought."

"I guess I should've expected it. I was guarded the last time I was here, too," she mumbled low. Grulen wound his tail around her ankle and tucked her under his arm.

"While a surprise, I'm happy to see your safety is important to the king, not just me."

She reached up and held the hand draped over her.

"I wonder what is so important about where they're taking us?"

"We'll see soon."

A short flight later, they landed in front of a huge building. Grulen blinked in surprise when he saw a Svesti-Zuvgran male approach with an older Zuvgran male. *I didn't think Svesti and Zuvgran could have young.*

They disembarked.

"Grulen Jevax. Lady Morgan. Allow me to introduce Largon d'Ayen, the leader of Phoenix House. With him is Ronan d'Olorg, first cousin to Commander Durek and second in command of this facility." Tolvex dipped his chin in greeting to the two males.

"Welcome, Jevax. Lady Morgan. We are pleased to have you visit. Please call me Largon, and I'm sure Ronan would prefer his first name as well."

"So formal." Emmy snorted. "Give me a hug." She embraced each male, as did Lin. *Curious.*

"Is Natasha here?" Lin asked as she returned to the healer's side.

Ronan shook his head. *It's so strange to see Svesti skin in gray.*

"No, she's at the main healing hall training on other species."

"Oh, that's right. I forgot that was today."

"I'll be honest, I have no idea what Phoenix House is," Morgan said.

"Would you like the long answer or the short one?" Largon's green eyes twinkled. *I'm not sure I've ever seen a Zuvgran smile that wasn't cruel before.*

"Short is fine for now." Morgan glanced between the two new males.

"We're a home for Zuvgran hybrid children and adults."

"Most are orphans or in some cases, wish they were orphans." Emmy's face looked like she drank sour milk.

"Oh."

A Mostiffian-Zuvgran male youngling bounded out the front door holding hands with a younger Crestillian-Zuvgran female.

"We have guests!" The young male with three oval eyes grinned widely. Four-fingered hands on long, gangly arms were another Mostiffian trait. His short, thin tail waved excitedly.

The small reptilian female smiled shyly.

"Hello."

Morgan squatted and smiled.

"Hello, I'm Morgan. This is Grulen."

"I'm Yostal. I'm four, and I like science. This is Zela. She just turned three."

"Wow, Yostal, I'm glad you told me that." She tapped her lower lip with a forefinger. "Are you supposed to be out here alone?"

Yostal looked confused.

"But we're not alone. You're here and so is Largon and Ronan and everybody."

The adults laughed.

"True, but did you have permission to leave the building?"

Yostal peered up at Ronan.

"Do we need permission?"

"To go out front without an adult? Yes, you do. If you're going into the courtyard, not really. We just want to ensure you're safe."

Yostal's oval eyes filled with tears.

"I'm sorry."

"Oh, honey, please don't cry. You just learned something new you didn't know before so you can do better next time. There was no harm done." Morgan reached out to pat his hand. *She has a natural talent with younglings. I can see why she wants to be a teacher.*

"You're nice," Zela whispered.

"Thank you. I think you're nice, too." Morgan stood in a fluid motion. "I think I'd like to see more of Phoenix House."

Grulen followed her and listened as she asked numerous questions. Amazed at the amount of thought and care that preceded the construction of Phoenix House, he saw happy younglings throughout. Older Zuvgran hybrids, which Largon said he and Ronan had rescued *solars* prior now helped care for the younger ones.

They only met one other purebred individual. Talos, an older Pellotian teacher who spent twenty *solars* on Pellotia rescuing and hiding hybrids from Zuvgran patrols. The male had scars on his green skin between his wings. His flat yellow eyes lit up when he discovered Morgan also trained as an educator. The two of them wandered to a corner in one of the classrooms and spoke animatedly.

After checking that Morgan felt comfortable with him leaving, Grulen found himself wandering alone as the other couples broke off. He noted recreational rooms, the library, large dining area, and kitchen before he walked outside to the courtyard. Various play areas, an outside garden, and several training areas filled the spaces around smaller tables and benches.

Grulen noticed an older youngling who wasn't gray in one of the outside training areas. Brown skin, high narrow forehead, and no hair signified the other portion of his heritage was Romittel. The younger male experienced difficulties with the climbing portion of an obstacle course. Grulen watched for several minutes before approaching the trainee.

"Hello, young warrior. My name is Grulen Jevax."

Sweat poured from the youngling's bald head.

"Crutaw."

"You are persistent, and that's a good quality."

"Thank you." Crutaw huffed. "The climbing portion keeps hindering me."

"May I make a suggestion?"

"Please."

Grulen demonstrated how to determine the best hand and foot holds.

"Concentrate less on going straight up. You want to make progress, but a straight line is not always the fastest. If you find easier holds to the side, so long as you're still moving upwards, you'll find you won't work nearly as hard lifting your body weight, and you'll be faster."

Crutaw bit his oversized lower lip.

"Really?"

Grulen nodded.

"Try it and see how it feels."

Crutaw began hesitantly. The Svesti smiled as the youngling gained confidence and speed and reached the top.

"Yes, I did it!" Crutaw raised his arms to the sky. "Finally." He hopped down the ramp at the side.

"Thank you, Grulen Jevax, for your help."

"Any time, Crutaw. You're the one who did the hard work to achieve success."

The youngling looked over Grulen's shoulder and his face brightened further.

"Did you see me, Largon?"

"I most certainly did. You should be proud of yourself." Largon smiled. "Why don't you go get a snack and cool down? Rumor has it Tolvex and Emmy brought cookies."

"Thanks." Crutaw ran indoors.

"You gave him good advice. You're a natural instructor." Largon slapped Grulen's back.

"Anyone could have done it."

"However, you did it without hurting his confidence and pride."

Grulen shrugged.

"If you decide you wish to help here, we would be honored to have you."

"I'm not sure what or where I'll be." Grulen frowned. "I don't know how much you know about my circumstances."

"Quite a bit. After you contacted Traxen and Rachel, all the human females and their mates could talk about was how excited they were you were found and coming home. All of them had stories to share about their interactions with you. You are well respected and liked, Grulen Jevax. What I saw today with Crutaw reinforces the impressions they shared."

"It's frustrating that everyone else knows more about me than I do." Grulen's tail flicked.

"Understandable. Walk with me." Largon led them through more of the courtyard and explained several of their security procedures. Grulen made a suggestion about the branches of a tree outside the courtyard being a security risk. Largon nodded.

"I have to be honest. This refuge would not be nearly as good as it is if not for the human females. They have provided cogent input and volunteered their time and energy to make it a home for the younglings. I will never be able to thank them enough." Largon dipped his chin at a Wrestikan-Zuvgran female wrangling several younglings to one of the play areas. She waved one of her four red arms before she caught an energetic youngling by the tail to keep him with the group. Laughter rang out.

"That's Herrah. Ronan rescued her when she was eleven *solars*. Until recently, she and a number of others lived in caverns. She advocated for relocation because she wanted the younger ones to experience freedom in the sunlight. She was correct." Largon smiled. "Traxen surprised me with his offer to build and support Phoenix House. Even more surprising was the number of *Invictus* warriors that helped to make the younglings comfortable. Simple respect and courtesy would have been enough for them to feel safe. Receiving all that kindness after so much Zuvgran cruelty filled the younglings with joy."

"I'm proud my people have aided you."

"There are still some factions that want us gone, but we're not going anywhere. When I see the younglings free from their anxiety about being found and returned to slavery or killed, I can't take that from them again."

"No youngling should have to live in fear." Grulen's tail flicked.

"You are correct."

"I'm curious about Ronan's heritage. I've never seen a Svesti-Zuvgran hybrid before."

"You probably never will again either." Largon sighed. "Ronan's father, Jorn, was a geneticist and my best friend. He rescued Saletta on Himita Prime during the Zuvgran invasion. There's a long story there, but he wanted young with his mate and worked to find a way to make it happen. They had Ronan and his younger sister, Marris. Eventually, the Zuvgran caught up with Jorn and took everyone but Ronan, who was hidden in a safe room." Largon's eyes watered and his tail drooped. "I was able to rescue Ronan and care for him. It took me longer to find the others. Too long. By that time, the Zuvgran had experimented on Saletta and Marris with the virus they eventually used here. I arranged an escape, but they all died in great pain soon afterwards. I raised Ronan as my son. As far as I'm aware, all of Jorn's research was destroyed before the Zuvgran captured the family."

Grulen's tail stilled, and his heart broke at Largon's pain.

"I'm sorry. I shouldn't have asked."

"It's fine, Grulen. Zuvgran cruelty is a common theme in our backgrounds."

"What do you think will happen now that Emperor n'Tuli is dead?"

"We're all waiting to see. I do not know much of the Commander who leads now or if he will be strong and crafty enough to retain power." Largon frowned. "There are factions of Zuvgran who disagree with n'Tuli's treatment of other species. Whether or not they'll band together to make sweeping changes in the Empire only the Goddess knows."

Tail swaying, Grulen looked at the younglings playing happily.

"I'd like to imagine a galaxy where cruelty no longer exists."

"I'm not sure it will ever happen, but it is a worthy goal to strive towards." Largon squeezed the Svesti's shoulder. "Come, let us find the others and see if any cookies remain."

Grulen chuckled.

"Lead the way."

Chapter 26

Morgan buzzed with excitement. Phoenix House impressed her, and the children were adorable. Despite how difficult their lives started, they still found happiness and joy in small things.

Talos told her they needed teachers. With the wide age ranges and only him, he had to assign too many of them digital courses. He worried they weren't receiving enough personal attention. While others taught them gardening or warrior training, their academic education was suffering. His dedication inspired her, especially once she learned that he only recently became a part of their contingent. If she wanted to work at Phoenix House, he believed Largon would hire her without question.

She knew King Sovex would allow her to remain on Costonia. He offered the option before, so that wasn't an issue. One of the reasons she'd chosen to go to a colony was because no children lived on Costonia at the time. But now there were and according to Emmy, they expected more women and children to relocate to the planet from Earth once treaties were signed.

The only issue was Grulen. Without his memory, he would probably remain on the home world, but once it returned, he most likely would return to the *Invictus*. Lin said she thought the space cruiser would be making regular trips to Earth for the foreseeable future with short stays on Costonia in between.

Emmy suggested Morgan could travel on the *Invictus* and teach whatever children traveled or even lead the training for adults relocating to or visiting the planet. While the compromise would allow her to use her degree, she wasn't sure she could make a real difference if she only taught a child for a month or two. Not like she could on the planet where she'd have time to form meaningful connections.

If things worked out with Grulen, then she would definitely consider it to stay together, but she was concerned it might not be enough for her now that she knew a better option was available. She didn't know what to do with that.

Yanz and Kragen reentered the woods once the flitter returned to the cabin. She and Grulen said their goodbyes to the visitors and making vague assurances to get together again at a later date.

"Are you hungry?"

She shook her head at Grulen's question.

"Not really. I am thirsty, though."

"Let's get some beverages and sit outside. We can watch the sun set." His hand rested at the small of her back as he escorted her to the kitchen.

"Okay." She grabbed some water pouches from the cooling unit. "These work?"

"Yes, but I think I'm going to want something stronger."

"I'll meet you outside." She wandered out the kitchen door and smiled. *I didn't know there was a firepit and grill out here.*

She found a couple chairs and moved them closer to the firepit. Locating the firewood pile, she grabbed a couple logs and arranged them in the center of the pit. She raided a box of kindling and added her find to the pit. *I'll wait and see if Grulen wants to have the fire now or later.*

His fangs gleamed in the sunlight as he held up two bottles.

"Estalan liquor. One smoky, the other sweet."

"Oh, the good stuff."

"Yes." He placed the bottles on the small table between the chairs. "I forgot glasses."

"I'll get them. If you want a fire now, feel free to light it now."

"Let's wait until the air cools a little."

"Okay." She made quick work of finding glasses. Deciding to grab a throw from the living area for when the temperature dropped, she tossed it over her arm and returned. Taking the empty seat, she placed the glasses on the table and the colorful afghan over the back of her chair.

"Which one?" He arched an eyebrow.

"How about smoky?"

"As you wish, *ciebala.*" He poured some in the glasses and handed one to her.

She swirled it and sniffed. *Oh, this smells divine. I hope it takes as good.*

Taking a small sip, she moaned as the full-bodied liquid slid smoothly down her throat. It reminded her of some of the best whiskey on Earth.

"This is wonderful."

"I agree." He took another sip. "What did you think of Phoenix House?"

"They did an awesome job making it a safe, enjoyable home for the children. I can see a lot of human influence in some of the setup."

"How so?"

"Well, Emmy grew up in foster care and it was her idea to have multiple bedrooms with their own sanitary facilities instead of dormitory style rooms. They prioritized everyone feeling they have their own safe space over ease of maintenance or oversight. That tells me their primary mission isn't just to keep them safe, healthy, and educated, but they want them to thrive and be loved." Morgan hummed as she swirled her liquor. "And the smaller seating areas in the dining area and elsewhere makes me believe one of the women probably suggested it."

His brows drew together.

"Why?"

"Most large institutions on Earth tend to go with long tables and benches or chairs to accommodate big groups. When I was in high school, neurodivergent needs began receiving a lot of attention."

"Neurodivergent? I'm unfamiliar with the term."

"It simply means someone's brain might work a little differently from what people perceive as 'normal.' Truth is, no one's brain could meet the supposed definition of normal, even if we knew what that was. Many neurodivergent individuals might have more extreme reactions to various stimuli—be it sound, light, texture, taste, etc. Some might get distracted by too many details or process information in a different manner or need a little more time to understand. It's not an issue of intelligence, but their brains sometimes file the new information in multiple places. While it can frustrate them or those around them, I believe it's one of the reasons they can be as creative as they sometimes are or see new solutions others miss. Anyway, some find it difficult to be in settings that can overwhelm them. Many find it easier to interact in smaller groups."

"So, more than the difference between introverts and extroverts?" Interest lit his eyes.

"Absolutely. In fact, neurodivergent people can be either. There's a huge range of behaviors and each person is different. Even how they might react to stimuli can be affected by whether they're tired, ill, or a whole host of other factors. Honestly, once I understood neurodivergence better, I thought it must be exhausting for them." Her forefinger traced the rim of her glass. "In some cases, a person's neurodivergence can affect things like balance, clumsiness, and, unfortunately, their self-esteem and confidence."

"Now the smaller seating areas around the edges of the dining area make sense to me." He smiled at her. "I like how you become more animated when you're discussing something you care about. And you seem to have a natural rapport with younglings."

Heat crept up on her cheeks.

"Thank you." She watched as he moved to crouch in front of the firepit and light the kindling. "What did you think of Phoenix House? And so many Zuvgran hybrids?"

"I found it a warm and welcoming environment dedicated to younglings. I wasn't expecting to like Largon or even Ronan, but I admire them. They've worked for decades saving younglings at risk and genuinely care about their well-being. Not behaviors or attitudes I expected from Zuvgran, even without my memories intact." He returned to his chair and reached for her hand. "Largon offered me a position there if I wanted it."

She wove her fingers with his.

"Really?"

"I helped one of the older younglings with some tips about an obstacle course. Largon said my interaction with Crutaw, along with stories the others have told about me, makes him believe I would be a good fit for their mission." *Oh, that would be a perfect solution.*

"What are your feelings about his offer?"

"I'm flattered, but I don't know if it would satisfy me. Until I remember more about myself and my life, I don't want to decide one way or another." Staring into the flames. "Then there's you."

"Me?"

"What do you want? You have so many options. Where do I fit in?" His voice trailed off. *I don't think I've ever heard him uncertain before.*

Tightening her fingers on his, she said, "Until I talked with the younglings today, I thought I would be happy returning to the

Wing Raiders or living on another ship. But I believe I would eventually become dissatisfied if I couldn't teach. If you don't think you'd be happy remaining planetside, then I would see if I could teach on the *Invictus* as more people from Earth are transported here." She sucked in her lower lip, then said, "That's assuming you'd want me with you."

"Of course I want you with me." He tugged her hand. "Come sit with me."

She rose and sat on his lap.

"We haven't known each other very long. Your feelings could change." She wrung her hands.

He brushed the hair from her face. His tail smoothed along her thigh while his other hand gently stilled her fingers.

"I expect my feelings for you will grow deeper and stronger, *ciebala*. You continually amaze me, and I feel whole with you." His lips twisted. "That sounds strange given I have missing memories leaving gaps in myself. You make the gaps matter less."

"We don't have to decide anything tonight."

"No, we are simply discussing how we feel and what other information we need to consider." Leaning forward, he kissed her. "No need to be anxious. Let's watch the sunset and enjoy the fire."

Kissing him back, she scooted to sit with her back to his front. His cock prodded her ass, but they ignored it. Kicking a small log closer, she rested her feet on it. He wrapped his arms around her and nuzzled her neck.

"This is where you belong, Morgan. In my arms."

"You really are a sweet male." Her hands caressed the corded muscles of his forearms. The smell of burning wood mixed with his scent. *I want more moments like this.*

The periwinkle sky turned pink, before deepening to a dark purple. The smoke smudged the last rays of sunlight, and the flames danced orange, yellow, and red. The air began to cool, but Grulen's body kept her warm. She sighed in contentment.

"I should think about making us something to eat."

"Not yet. I'm enjoying this." His hands stroked her legs and moved closer to the junction of her thighs. "Let me give you pleasure." He licked her earlobe, and she shivered as his hot breath tickled her sensitive skin.

"The guards..."

Grulen grabbed the throw from her chair and spread it over her. One hand rested on her waistband. His other arm banded under her breasts.

"Better? May I continue?" His fingers drew circles under her belly button. *I can't believe I'm being so naughty.*

"Yes." She spread her legs over his thighs. He pushed her pants and panties down past her ass.

"I wish I could see you." Long fingers pet the outside of her pussy softly. Gradually increasing the pressure, his thumb found her clit and two fingers slid into her. "You're already wet for me. I'm imagining your beautiful cunt glistening in the firelight."

"Oh..." She wriggled and spread wider.

"My *ciebala* wants to be filled, doesn't she?" His voice lowered and rumbled in her ear as he whispered, "Should I fuck you with my tail right here under the stars?"

Her pussy clenched on his fingers, and she moaned.

"You like that idea, don't you? I'm going to make you come on my tail and watch you light up the night sky." Withdrawing his fingers and replacing them with his tail, he sucked her wetness from his digits. Her eyelids drifted lower. *Shit. That's so fucking hot. I love his dirty talk.*

Slowly, he slid his tail deeper, and his hand returned to her clit. Using his middle finger, he circled her nub in time with his tail's thrusts. Squirming, she tilted her hips to take more of him and increase the pressure. She whined when he didn't take the hint.

"Harder, Grulen."

A dark chuckle raised the hair on her neck.

"So impatient. Savor this, *ciebala*. I am. Your scent is rich and heavy. Your naked ass is rubbing on my cock, driving my desire for you higher." The arm under her breasts moved to sneak under her shirt and bra. He plucked her nipple. "Despite your toned muscles, your flesh is soft against me, but these..." Simultaneously, he lightly pinched both her nipple and her clit making her gasp. "These are as hard as valadium. Such contrasts delight me."

Her moans grew louder. His attention to her body was as dedicated as a master musician to his instrument. She reached up to circle his neck with her hands, arching her back and encouraging him to do more.

"You are so magnificent in your passion, Morgan. Watching your take pleasure from me makes me feel strong and worthy." His hand kneaded her breast. "I only wish I could drink from your body from this position."

His name left her lips in a tormented gasp. Rubbing herself harder against him, she panted.

"That's it. Take what you need." He groaned as her movements quickened. "The things you do to me."

His tail pushed deeper. His slippery finger began flicking the underside of her clit. Her orgasm rushed through her. Her body stiffened before shaking uncontrollably. Her pussy clenched so hard his tail couldn't move.

The intense pleasure left her breathless, and her mouth opened on a silent scream.

"Yes, *ciebala. Crek*, you are so beautiful."

She turned her head, and his mouth crashed onto hers. He frantically kissed her, and her tongue sloppily dueled with his. They broke apart and gasped.

"I want to be inside you. May I?" His strangled voice filled her ear.

She nodded and he lifted his hips to push down his pants. Grabbing her by the waist, he elevated her high enough to where his cock could replace his tail. He lowered her onto his shaft and they both groaned when their bodies sat flush together.

"*Crek*. So tight. Hot and wet for me. Only me." Inwardly, she preened at his disjointed sentences. *Me. I do this to him. I make him crazy with desire.*

"Take me, Grulen. Give me everything." Her inner muscles squeezed his cock. His groan was the perfect counterpoint to her moan.

Sliding lower in his chair, he withdrew slightly before thrusting upwards hard and fast. His head nodes dragged inside her, but his base node hit her rosebud. The sensitive nerves there reacted by sending shivers throughout her limbs. Gripping her waist, he lifted her before dropping her as he plunged deep. He repeatedly rammed into her as hard as he could. Her body shook with the undeniably erotic force of his body filling her over and over. His tail moved over her slippery clit bringing her closer to another orgasm. Desperately, she squeezed her breasts in an erratic rhythm.

His cock swelled and sweet pressure built. Darkness dimmed her vision as she spasmed and clutched his shaft. He roared as he came. Hot liquid bathed her insides and set off another round of shuddering ecstasy. Her head fell forward, and her hair brushed her sensitive breasts. *Holy fuck, that was intense.*

His grip loosened and his hands smoothed over her rising to cup her breasts. Tugging her back against his heaving chest, he nuzzled her neck and kissed her shoulder. She shivered as the cool night air met her naked flesh. She weakly pulled the afghan up to cover her torso again. She had no idea when it fell to begin with. *I hope Yanz and Kragen didn't get an eyeful.*

"I have no words to describe how amazing you feel." His fangs dragged across her skin.

Breathlessly, she laughed.

"You had plenty of words earlier. I really like your bedroom talk." Tilting her head to give his mouth better access, she moaned. "No one has ever turned me on with words like you do." She smirked when she felt him grin against her flesh. *Mmm, positive reinforcement is always the way to go.*

"I live to serve, *ciebala*." They both chuckled. "Hold on to that throw. I'm going to move us indoors."

She clasped the fabric to her chest. A startled moan escaped her when he stood with her still impaled on his cock. Aftershocks moved through her as he carefully carried her to bed.

Chapter 27

Grulen opened his eyes when Morgan left the bed. Naked, she padded to the sanitary facility. It wasn't long before he heard water running while she brushed her teeth. His hand lazily tugged on his morning erection as he relived the previous evening. His *ciebala's* passion made him feel like he was twelve feet tall.

He smiled at her when she crawled back into bed and kissed him.

"It's another good morning," she teased.

"It always is with you." His fingers combed her hair from her eyes. "Did you sleep well?"

"Like a rock." Her nimble fingers circled his nipple.

"Vixen. Are you trying to entice me?"

She arched an eyebrow and pointedly looked down at his erection.

"I think you're already enticed."

They both laughed. Releasing his cock, he hugged her.

"Thank you for last night."

"No need to thank me. I benefited as much as you did." She giggled.

His comm chimed and he growled.

"Why is it they interrupt us first thing? Can't they wait a few hours?"

"Grumpy, grumpy. Just answer the comm. No video, please."

"No one gets to see you like this but me." Tapping his comm, he said, "Jevax."

Rivezt said, "There's someone who wants to meet with you. He's been on the southern continent but returned last night."

Grulen sighed.

"When and where?" His brows knit when Morgan mouthed something that looked like 'day-ja vu.' *I'm not sure what she's trying to say.*

"We'll bring midday meal with us."

They coordinated a time and Jevax disconnected the comm.

"Now where were we?"

"Thinking about a shower?"

"No, that's not what I was thinking."

"Oh, what did you have in mind?" She squealed when he flipped her onto her back.

He slid lower on the bed before shifting to settle between her legs.

"I'm going to enjoy my morning meal." His tongue flicked her clit, and her hips jerked. "Behave and allow me to savor this delicacy." He grinned and lowered his head.

"You have the best ideas." Her fingers tunneled into his hair as he licked her.

Goddess, I love the taste of her.

Sated and showered, they tidied up from the night before. Having some time before their guest arrived, Grulen suggested she teach him another Earth card game. The rules of Gin Rummy were similar to those of a Jalaxian one, even though the cards were different, so he learned it quickly. Evenly matched, they tied after four games and were partway through the fifth when the door chimed.

She tossed her cards down.

"Guess we'll have to finish this another time. I'll go let them in." Kissing him, she let her hand drift across his shoulders as if reluctant to leave.

He smiled and gathered the cards. Hearing footsteps, he looked up and saw Rivezt and Lin followed by a human female with curly red hair and green eyes. Behind them was a large male with reddish bronze skin like his own and gray eyes.

His head spun and images flashed in his mind. Green crackers and water pouches. Black stone sculpted. Cookies. Shoulder slaps. A dusty planet. Looking down at a console and knowing the Zuvgran captured his teammate. Running for an escape pod.

Dizzy, he fell heavily onto a chair. His breaths accelerated and sweat dotted his brow. His vision dimmed and Morgan's voice sounded far away.

"Grulen, are you okay?" He felt her hand on his shoulder. "Can you talk?"

More memories crowded his brain. Names, places, events. Trembling, he gasped and dropped his head into his hands. His fingers tangled in his hair. He groaned as pain throbbed in his temples.

"I'm here, Grulen. You're safe." Her voice rose. "Who the fuck are you? What did you do to him to make him react like this?"

Clumsily, he reached for her hand, shaking his head as he squeezed her fingers.

"No, *ciebala*. It's okay. Just give me a minute." He forced the words out.

Tears gathered in his eyes as he recalled his mother and sisters. Thousands of emotions hit him simultaneously, and he felt battered, body and soul.

When his brain finally settled into a semblance of normality and he could see again, he lifted his head. Rivezt lowered the scanner. Everyone but Morgan sat at the table. She stood behind him with her arms embracing his shoulders. He glanced up at her. Worried blue eyes gazed back at him.

"I'll be fine, *ciebala*. It was just a great shock to my system. Please sit."

She kissed his forehead and released him. He realized he was still holding her hand. He let it go so she could take her seat. Then he reached for the one closest to him and entwined his fingers with hers.

Squaring his shoulders, he faced their visitors.

"Morgan, this is Lieutenant Karid Wurvez and Lady Ava Taylor."

"Ava Taylor Wurvez now, Jevax." The redhead smiled at him. "Are you feeling better?"

"A headache and far too much information, but much better than a few minutes ago."

"Wurvez, the last I saw you, the Zuvgran captured you. I knew we shouldn't have split up."

The large male's gray eyes darkened.

"I'm glad you weren't with me. No reason why both of us had to suffer at their hands." A pained look crossed his face. "But it sounds like you didn't have it easy either."

"No."

"Can you remember what happened?" Rivezt watched him intently.

"Am I allowed to speak about everything? The mission was classified."

Wurvez nodded, his ponytail bobbing.

"Yes."

"After I returned to the *Tenacity*, I immediately engaged the cloak, departed Millus, and headed for the asteroid field. I cursed you when I saw you'd been captured, but I knew I couldn't rescue you on my own. My plan was to contact the *Invictus* with the traitor's name and arrange for assistance retrieving you. Scans alerted me that two Zuvgran fighters left the planet and were coming my way. I grabbed the bag of equipment, as well as some food and water, and took it all with me into the escape pod. My intent was to hide in the shadow of a mid-size asteroid until the Zuvgran cancelled their search."

Morgan handed him a water pouch. Gratefully, he wet his dry mouth.

"Before I could reach my target, there was an explosion behind me which threw the pod forward into the rock. I'm assuming the Zuvgran somehow found the *Tenacity* despite the cloaking device and destroyed the ship. I awoke to alarms blaring. I was sluggish and certain I had a concussion. I remember trying to fix the hull breaches with blood running down my face. That's the last I recall until I woke up on the *Morning Star* two weeks later."

"What made you think to lower the oxygen flow?" Rivezt asked.

"I didn't. Or at least I don't remember doing it. I know I passed out at some point."

"You must've bumped it when you lost consciousness. The Goddess truly watched over you. I'm glad." Wurvez grinned. "I'm still going to recommend you transfer to security. Of course, there's still those computer courses so you can code a synthesizer."

Morgan frowned.

"He can code a synthesizer already. I taught him." *That's right. She did. But I used to find it all so confusing.*

Wurvez eyebrows raised high.

"Really? Interesting."

"What happened with the traitor?"

Wurvez growled.

"Pluvi Frulix is in custody. The male is insane. He murdered his nephew, Lerix Sproid, and doesn't remember doing it. We found evidence that he was being brainwashed as well."

"By whom?" *Is there another traitor?*

"Unknown."

Grulen looked at Ava.

"Congratulations on your mating. You know he pined for you while we were on our mission. And he raved about your cookies."

He wrinkled his nose in confusion when Morgan snickered.

"Is cookies a euphemism for something else?"

Ava giggled at Morgan's question.

"I don't think so, but with these guys you can't always tell." The human females smiled at each other. "I made food for midday meal." She pointed at the units they'd placed on the edge of the table.

"Oh, that's right. You're the chef. I'd like to compare notes with you."

"I'm looking forward to it."

Grulen ate quietly and let the others carry the conversation. He filtered through his memories recalling he'd made a vow to himself to never take a mate. His gaze settled on Morgan's face as she chattered with the others. His heart heavy, he realized he should extract himself from their romantic relationship to keep the promise to himself. He rubbed his chest over his heart.

I thought waiting until I knew if I had a female waiting for me was the only possible dishonor. But it seems I've behaved dishonorably anyway. Goddess, forgive me for the pain I will cause her.

After their guests left, Morgan cleaned up the dining area while Grulen sat in silence.

"Karid and Ava are a fun couple. Lin opened up more today."

He nodded.

"How are you? It must be disorienting to experience forty-one years of memories in such a compressed time frame."

He drew back when she placed a hand on his face. Her frown pierced his heart.

"What's wrong, Grulen?"

"Morgan, I think we should stop seeing each other."

Shock filled her eyes.

"Why?"

He stood and paced. His tail flicked sideways repeatedly.

"My father was devastated after my mother and sisters died. All the adult males became shadows of themselves at the loss of their mates. It was *solars* before things got better."

"That's understandable. They experienced an inordinate amount of loss in a short period of time. I imagine everyone was in shock and grieving. Usually, people have others who aren't also grieving to help them through it. They didn't have that luxury. I'm not sure what that has to do with us."

"When I got older, I vowed never to take a mate. I never want to be in a similar position."

"So you want to break up so you won't feel grief or pain?" Her face fell.

"I want to keep my vow. It's the honorable thing to do."

"There's nothing I can say or do to change your mind and give us a chance?"

"No."

"You were a child."

He shook his head. She inhaled a shuddering breath.

"I think you're making a mistake. I guess I made one as well. I trusted you not to hurt me," she whispered as she walked out of the room.

Crek.

Chapter 28

Eyes watering, Morgan comm'd Makai to tell him she wanted to move to the palace. Her instincts screamed she should yell and throw things. Instead, she mindlessly packed her belongings, most of which were still in her original room. *I'm not going into his bedroom to collect anything from the refresher. He can throw it all away.*

Taking a last look at the room, she realized they never made love in here. *No, not making love. We fucked, nothing more. If we'd made love, he wouldn't be able to let me go so easily.*

At least on Delizas I expected hurt and pain from males. Maybe Grulen has it right. If I never risked acting on my feelings for him despite my past, I wouldn't be feeling my own grief now.

Her anger tasted bitter. She swallowed the lump in her throat. *This isn't the worst thing that's ever happened to me. I will survive.*

Makai comm'd and told her to meet Kragen outside and he would escort her to the palace. She picked up her bag and descended the stairs slowly. She didn't see Grulen in the living area, so she left through the front door. *No need to say goodbye.*

Kragen waited by a small flitter. He opened the door for her. Neither of them spoke. Makai met them when they arrived at the palace.

"Morgan," Kragen said softly as he helped her out of the flitter. "I don't know what happened, but I do know he is a fool."

"Thank you," she whispered. "I appreciate your kind words."

He nodded. She didn't hear the flitter leave until she and Makai entered the palace.

"Did he hurt you?"

"Not physically." Her lips trembled. "I'm not ready to talk about it, but he remembers everything now."

"If you need anything, just ask." He eventually stopped in front of a door. "These are your quarters. I'm there." He pointed to the door on one side, then a door across the hall. "Tren's there. All the couples are at the other end of the hall."

"Thanks." She opened the door and realized she had a suite of rooms. Dropping her bag, she wrapped her arms around her waist.

Makai dropped a beefy hand onto her shoulder.

"Do I need to beat him?"

She gave a teary laugh and shook her head.

"The irony is his reasons have nothing to do with me specifically."

He tugged her closer and hugged her. Her tears flowed freely.

"You're strong. You'll get through this and be stronger still. We're here for you when you want to talk."

She pulled back and tipped her head to face him.

"I should tell you I don't think I'll be staying with the *Fortitude*."

"Even before the Svesti showed up, I guessed you'd leave us sooner rather than later. You are meant to take a different path." He bopped her nose with a finger. "That doesn't mean we don't care about you."

"You are a good male. We're all lucky to have you in our corner."

His brow furrowed. She gave him a sad smile.

"It means fighting for someone. I think it came from boxing—a sport a little more civilized than sparring."

"I understand. Do you want me to send the females to you?"

"I think I'd rather be alone right now."

He gave her a gentle squeeze then stepped back.

"We'll check on you later."

"Thanks."

When she was alone, she kicked off her shoes and found the bedroom. She turned off her comm, threw herself onto the bed with a hard plop, buried her face in a pillow, and cried.

"Knock, knock."

Morgan groaned. Heart battered and body sore, the thought of lifting her head made her brain ache.

She mumbled, "Go 'way."

"Not happening. Get yourself up. You need some girl time."

Rolling sideways, Morgan opened one eye partway. Kara stood grinning like a fool next to her bed. Rain had her arms crossed and foot tapping, while Abby gave her a sympathetic smile.

"Fuck you. Let me be miserable in peace."

"Nope." Kara drew out that single word with an exaggerated pop. "Take a shower, get dressed, and meet us in your living area. We brought food, alcohol, and company."

"You're a bitch."

"Yep." Another pop of the 'p'. "You've had enough time to wallow. Now it's time to trash talk."

Morgan's eyes felt swollen and gritty, and she was sure she looked like death warmed over. *Damn, I should've at least taken off my bra before I fell asleep. The damn thing is strangling my tits.*

"I'm not in the mood."

"That's what we're for."

"You know I can see your roots. Soon you'll be ordinary like the rest of us."

Kara hissed.

"Now you're just being mean. So unlike your normal behavior."

Morgan reluctantly laughed and closed her eyes.

Throwing her arm over her face, she said, "You're really pushing this?"

"Don't make us undress you and put you in the shower. We don't swing that way. I don't need the trauma."

Another chuckle was forced out of Morgan.

"How did you get in here?"

"Seriously? You think an electronic door can keep me out?" Kara's voice sounded indignant. *She's got a point. She's a fucking savant.*

"In this instance, Kara's dubious abilities were unnecessary. Rachel overrode security," Rain said.

Morgan dropped her arm, and her eyes flew open. *Ouch.*

"The other women are here, too? Are you crazy?"

"You'll like them, Morgan. Trust us." Abby sat on the bed next to her and squeezed her knee. "We all just want to help you feel better."

Eyes darting between the women, Morgan gave up her protests. *They're right. I can't stay here forever.*

"Fine. I'll get up. But I want it on record that I'm complying under protest."

"So noted." Rain smirked.

"No need to dress up. Just pick something comfy. You have ten minutes," Kara ordered.

Morgan forced herself upright. *Ugh.*

"If your head still hurts after you shower, I'll give you something for that headache," Abby said.

"How did you know I have a headache?"

"It's obvious you had a crying jag, and your face just winced in pain. I know how I usually feel after a good cry."

Her bag sat on the end of the bed, and she looked at it curiously.

"We brought it in with us from the living area. Figured you'd need it." Kara opened the bag and rummaged carelessly. She tossed some yoga pants and a T-shirt at Morgan. "I'm not touching your underwear. Either find it yourself or go commando." She turned to leave, and the other women followed. "Nine minutes."

Morgan shook her head cautiously. *I can't decide if I love or hate her at this moment.*

Eight minutes later, she gazed upon her reflection in the viewer. Her eyes looked clearer. The hot water took care of most of the redness and swelling. She brushed her teeth and hair. *Might as well leave it down.*

Forgoing socks and shoes, her bare feet sunk into the plush carpet of the bedroom. Straightening her spine, she reluctantly left the peacefulness of the room. She halted at the living area and stared at the nine women talking quietly. Food and drinks littered the flat surfaces.

"We brought comfort food," Ava said from where she sat on the floor.

"And chocolate." Lin smiled from her perch on a couch arm.

"Hi, I'm Natasha." Next to Lin, sitting on the couch, a slightly older woman with long blonde hair and brown eyes held up a bottle. "We have wine, liquor, and some fruit concoction Talia whipped up. Unfortunately, we finished off my cases of vodka a month ago."

"I've been experimenting." Talia shoulder-bumped Rachel. They shared the opposite couch. "Until we can find acceptable substitutes or bring more familiar alcohol back from Earth, we need a reliable supply here."

"Hey, don't spill my wine. I'm on my last bottle of Chardonnay. It'll be months before I can get another."

"You lushes drank all my Pinot Noir two months ago. I still haven't forgiven you for that." Emmy sat cross-legged on a chair and pursed her lips as she looked into her glass. "This Estalan stuff is good, but I get drunk too fast."

"Ooh, hit me with that," cooed Kara from the floor near Emmy. "I prefer the hard stuff."

Rain munched on a cookie. Her long legs stretched underneath the coffee table.

"Like you need another excuse to be socially unacceptable."

Kara stuck out her tongue.

From another oversized chair, Abby sighed as she sipped from a water pouch.

"And this is your support group, Morgan. What would you like to drink?"

"Uh, hi, everyone. Thanks for coming?" Morgan looked at Abby. "If Rachel doesn't mind, I think a glass of wine."

"I'm happy to share." Rachel's blue eyes perused her. "Did the shower help?"

"Some."

Abby handed her a glass of Chardonnay.

"You can share the chair with me or pick somewhere else to sit." The nurse scooted over to make room.

"Thanks." A plate of cookies passed by, and she took one. Biting into it, it tasted like oatmeal raisin but with a different texture. "This is good."

"Ava introduced the Svesti to cookies. They can't get enough of them." Talia grabbed one for herself.

A few minutes of idle chitchat went by before Emmy addressed the elephant in the room.

"So what idiotic thing did Jevax do?"

"I'm not sure I want to talk about Grulen." *Damn, it hurts so much.*

Talia tipped her head to the side.

"It's weird to think of him by his first name. We all were friendly with him on the *Invictus*, but he wasn't in the inner circle with some of our mates."

"Are you all mated?"

Everyone nodded.

"Every single one of us found our fated mates out here. Me and Vared, Emmy and Devik, Lin and Ash'n, Natasha and Ronan, Karid and Ava, and finally Rachel and Traxen. We've got the clan markings to prove it." She pulled at the collar of her knit shirt and revealed an intricate gold design. "Vared, Devik, Karid, and Ash'n have been best friends since the Warrior Academy, and all serve on the *Invictus* together. Oh, if you didn't know, Vared and Traxen are cousins." Morgan tried to keep up with Talia's explanation.

"So you got tattoos to match their clan markings?"

Rachel shook her head.

"No, they just appeared on our skin and kinda look like Earth. It's weird and makes you wonder if their Goddess is real."

"So far, I haven't found a scientific explanation for the spontaneous change in our bodies." Natasha frowned. "I don't believe there is one."

"Back to Jevax. Do we need to take a baseball bat to him?" Emmy persisted.

Natasha snorted.

"You are like a dog with a bone."

"This surprises you why?"

Morgan found herself relaxing at the easy banter between the women.

"None of us had an easy time with our mates in the beginning." Kara's blue eyes were serious. "We really do want to help you. Whether it's to come up with a plan to illustrate to him how stupid he is or to let you move on depends on you."

All the women nodded and waited. Morgan's fingers twisted in her lap.

"Does it have to do with him getting his memories back?" Ava asked.

"Yes."

"Don't tell us he had a sidepiece we didn't know about." Rachel's eyes narrowed.

"No, that would be too easy." She inhaled deeply. "His mother and five sisters died within days of each other when the virus hit."

"That's sad," Lin murmured.

"Grulen saw how devastated the adult males were and how long it took before they began to recover. He vowed never to take a mate so he would never be in the same position."

"That's some fucked up logic," Kara took a sip of her Estalan liquor.

"He would've been a child," Natasha said. "And viewed the loss and grief from a child's perspective."

"That's what I told him."

"The destruction caused by the virus was like a planetwide trauma. Imagine a tsunami sweeping over every inch of Earth. No one could remain unaffected." Talia grabbed some green crackers and cheese from a plate before passing it on.

"What happened?" Abby asked quietly.

"He told me his honor demanded he keep his vow, and we shouldn't be together romantically. I asked if there was anything I could say or do to change his mind. He said no. So I packed and left." Morgan took a piece of chocolate and popped it into her mouth. *God, I've missed chocolate and right now, I need it.*

"Do you love him? Do you believe he loves you?" Ava poured some of the fruity drink from a pitcher.

"Yes, I love him. I thought he loved me. At least he acted that way." Tears welled up in Morgan's eyes.

"Then we need a plan to bring him crawling back to you." Kara punctuated her words with a burp. "Excuse me."

"Dress you up and can't take you anywhere," Rain teased. Everyone laughed.

"I'm not sure he'll change his mind. If I get my hopes up and it doesn't work, I'm not sure I'll survive it."

"With or without Jevax, what would make you happiest? Going back to the Wing Raiders? Staying here? Going to a colony? Going back to Earth? Something else entirely?" Natasha listed her options.

"I could go back to Earth?"

"I can arrange that. My biggest concern would be how Earth's leaders would treat you. They might keep you under wraps and interrogate you under the guise of protecting you."

Rachel frowned. "I would know. I was an MI6 agent. We'd have to have safeguards in place before Traxen or I would allow you to go."

Morgan nodded. *She makes sense.*

"I honestly wouldn't want to return to Earth to stay, although I would like to visit and reassure my friends that I am safe."

"Do you have anything in mind?"

"I've been thinking seriously about teaching at Phoenix House."

"That's a wonderful idea. It's not common knowledge yet, but after we sign some treaties, we're going to set up some communities specifically for domestic abuse victims and their children. I think the plan for the first one will be near Phoenix House," Talia said.

"Are you sure having battered women so close to a variety of aliens would be good for them?" Lin bit her lip. "It might make them even more afraid."

"Traxen and I have been discussing this. We believe we'll set up a small village with housing and shops between the two. The new arrivals will be in a gated community with everything they need, but as they gain confidence, they'll be able to venture out into the village. We're thinking of setting up a joint school so the children can begin interacting right away. From a logistical standpoint, it is easier to provide security for the women and children, the village, and Phoenix House from a central location. An added benefit is that the humans would transition away from largely populated areas."

"That would be good, not only for their own healing, but I remember how pushy some of the Svesti males were at Court not long ago." Ava shuddered.

"Pushy? I didn't have that experience, and I spent a year here." Morgan's forehead wrinkled.

"When you were here before, they didn't know humans could spark fated mate bonds. Even though they don't appear like they have historically, some of the males still believe they can convince the bonds to show up if they touch a woman. I got so tired of males wanting to touch my arm. Beyond being irritating, I felt bad each time their hopes were dashed." The edges of Ava's lips dipped down.

"I was ready to stab someone," Rachel grumbled.

Natasha laughed.

"How many knives are you wearing now?"

"Three."

Morgan's eyes grew wide at Rachel's answer. *I guess she really was MI6.*

"So, should we have Morgan push Grulen to confront and deal with his trauma like you did with Karid, Ava?" Lin timidly spoke up.

Ava's red curls bounced as she rejected that plan.

"Karid was self-destructing and needed immediate help to keep from hurting himself. Grulen is just being obtuse and not seeing the trauma's effects on him fully. He believes he's dealt with it."

"So what do we do?" Kara propped her chin on her fist.

"Morgan goes to Phoenix House and lives her best life without him. It's somewhere she wants to be, and when he comes around, he'll have to take that into account." Ava gave the others an evil grin. "I think we utilize our mates for the rest of it."

"How so?" Talia leaned forward.

"We visit the stubborn male and act all lovey-dovey with our mates, not-so-subtly reminding him he could've had the same thing with Morgan. And we convince our mates to slap some sense into him in their own unique ways. Do you think any of our mates would choose to let us go now even though they know they would experience pain if something happened to us?"

A chorus of no's filled the room.

"Exactly. Their reasons for loving us despite the unknowns are their own and only they can express it. I believe it would be more effective if the males share versus us females."

"So I do nothing?" Morgan glanced at each of the women who wore satisfied expressions.

"Just do what you would do without him. Let us take care of the rest." Rachel stabbed a piece of fruit with one of her knives. *Where the hell did she pull that from? I never saw it.*

"Damn, I'm so glad I ended up with you as my friends," said Emmy. "We always have each other's backs."

"Yeah, you were a tough nut to crack, but we figured you out." Natasha tossed a piece of cheese at the Australian.

Morgan's shoulders relaxed, and she realized her head no longer hurt. Even if Grulen never changed his mind, she could get through this. *I can't regret loving him. He gave me back my sexuality and reminded me there's more to life than surviving.*

"Thank you, all. I actually do feel better than I did an hour ago."

"Any time, Morgan. You're one of us now, and we take care of our own." Talia grinned. "Even if you don't want us to."

Morgan laughed along with others. *Kara was right. I needed this, and I needed them.*

Chapter 29

The silence in the cabin deafened Grulen. Morgan left not long after their discussion without a word. Wrapped up in his own misery, he didn't even realize until later. He searched for her and attempted to comm her without success. Finally, he noticed all her belongings gone from her room. He stalked outside to find the guards.

Stony-faced, Yanz informed him she departed hours prior. When Grulen asked where she went, both males shrugged. *I guess I know where their loyalties lie.*

He couldn't blame them. He would react the same way to someone causing her pain. Only this time, it was him. Even though he didn't plan to go after her, he didn't like not knowing where she was or if she was safe. Being unaware of her whereabouts ate at him.

He spent the remainder of the day punching a heavy bag in the training area, then he swung an axe splitting firewood. The burn of his muscles felt like penance, but his mood did not improve. Kragen's eyes flashed when he asked if either guard would spar with him, but both declined. *I think he wanted to beat me. I wish he would.*

For evening meal, he programmed the synthesizer. Lost in the memories of Morgan teaching him how to do so on the *Fortitude*, the food became cold, and he had to reheat it. Although there was nothing wrong with the stew, it tasted like dust in his mouth. At first, he thought Morgan's training as an educator was the reason she was able to instruct him when so many others had failed. But then he realized that his memory of his sister Fliva trying to teach him interfered. It was as if something in him believed if he learned how to do it, he dishonored her memory. Without his subconscious creating difficulties, he easily gained the skill. *Strange how the brain works.*

The sanitary facility seemed to emit soft echoes of their grunts and moans as they took pleasure in each other's bodies, haunting him. *Before I didn't have enough memories. Now I have too many.*

Later, he tossed and turned in his bed which retained the scent of them combined. The long night saw him drifting into sleep only to wake abruptly later when his arms felt empty. He groaned the fourth time it happened. *I miss her. Her company, her warmth, her laughter.*

The morning found him sitting in a chair outside, staring blindly at the trees as the sun rose. Even out here, he swore he smelled her on the breeze. His comm chimed several times before he blinked rapidly and answered it.

"Jevax."

"Son, good morn. Healer Rivezt informed me your memories returned. I hoped we could visit Nestune today." *I'm not sure I want to, but I do want to see my father.*

"I'm available."

"Good. I'll be there soon."

Disconnecting his comm, he rose from his seat and headed inside to change. His stomach protested at the thought of eating. *Maybe food will appeal later.*

He went out the front of the cabin to wait. His back against a tree, he lazily pulled at the grass by his side. *Crek. The smell reminds me of her.*

Frowning, he rose and watched a flitter larger than expected land. Yanz and Kragen appeared silently from the trees. The ramp opened. His father smiled when he saw Grulen waiting.

"Excellent. We can be on our way immediately."

Grulen embraced his father and followed him onto the flitter with Yanz and Kragen in trail. His tail stiffened when he saw all the males already onboard. The four friends from the *Invictus*—Durek, Wurvez, Tolvex, and Rivezt—sat next to the king and across from Makai, Ronan, Lezon, and Crax. Glancing toward the cockpit, he recognized Kriven Tesix and Slaiv'n Westov, two *Invictus* security officers, manning the controls. Toward the rear of the craft, two additional royal guards greeted Yanz and Kragen and they conferred in low voices.

He sat in the seat between Makai and his father. He nodded to everyone at large. *Why are all of them here?*

"Jevax, you look tired. Did you not sleep well?" Durek leaned back, crossed his ankles, and rested his hands on his thighs.

"I was restless last night. Nothing to be concerned about."

Durek's fangs flashed.

"I understand. I have difficulty sleeping when Talia isn't there."

"I have to exhaust Kara to keep her next to me. The female has too much energy at times." Crax's eyes were closed, but he wore a small grin.

"Emmy's the same way. Maybe their affinity for technology has some strange effect on them. However, I have my ways to ensure she remains abed." Everyone but Grulen laughed at Tolvex's jest.

"I've never slept better or as deeply as I do with Natasha in my arms." Ronan seemed young compared to the other males who nodded in agreement.

"It's as if their presence quiets all the worries of the day," Traxen said quietly.

"Now you're just trying to make me jealous," Makai grinned. "But with no mate, I have no one to harangue me or cause me worry. The lack of commitment allows me to offer my sexual prowess to any female who desires a taste. I sleep just fine without a mate."

The other males chuckled.

"Someday you'll understand, Makai. Rain makes everything brighter and better. There's no comparison. Making love to your mate is a hundred times better than casual sex with a stranger." Like Crax, Lezon's eyes were closed.

"I'll take your word for it. In the meantime, I'll enjoy my bachelorhood." Makai turned to Grulen. "I'm looking forward to seeing where you grew up. I'm glad your father invited us."

"There's not a whole lot of activity in Nestune. It's a quiet agricultural village." Grulen shrugged.

"It still had a role in shaping you." *That it did.*

For a short time, the conversation still focused on their mates, but instead of waxing eloquently about sleep, the males joked about how inebriated the females were the previous evening. From what Grulen could understand, the females periodically had what they called a girls' night and consumed liquor and food in copious amounts. Despite sometimes suffering ill effects the next morning, all swore they needed the girls' nights to maintain their friendships and sanity. The males appeared indulgent of the activity and both Crax and Devik made comments about how needy their mates became afterwards—in a good way.

Topics changed to the Zuvgran empire and speculation about its leadership with n'Tuli dying without a successor, the faster engines being installed on the *Invictus*, Phoenix House improvements, and the upcoming diplomatic mission to Earth. Grulen listened intently, but he chose not to comment. When he leaned his head back, he felt the gentle thrum of the engines reverberate in his skull and closed his eyes.

A hand shaking his shoulder woke him. Bleary-eyed, he looked at his father's smiling face.

"I hope you enjoyed your nap. We've arrived at Nestune."

Grulen unfastened his safety restraints and realized everyone else had already disembarked. He followed his father down the ramp. Tesix landed the flitter in a clearing outside the village. *We're not far from our old home.*

The other males waited quietly as he took in the familiar sights and scents of the area. To his right, large fields extending as far as he could see contained growing vegetables and fruits, their dark blue leaves dancing in the light breeze. *That field holds lobile, while that one holds yeddom.*

The field closest to him had knee-height plants with large yellow globes hanging from its sturdy stems. *The shurlix should be harvested in the next several days for peak taste. Maybe we should find the owner and ask to buy some for Ava. Karid could take it back.*

Briefly, he considered that Morgan might like the fresh fruit and vegetables. Then he remembered he didn't know where she was...and sighed.

The village lay directly in front of him, while some dwellings spaced further apart along the path to his left were closest to where he grew up. His father gestured for everyone to follow him as he took steps along that well-worn trail. He absently listened to his father expound to Traxen and Ash'n about the vagaries of the dirt and what foods did not do well here.

There. That's path to the lake. I remember playing with my sisters and parents and having so much fun.

Underground irrigation pipes ran from a single pumping station at one of the lake to every field. The villagers cordoned off the station for safety, but other areas along the lake's border were designed for water activities—fishing, boating, swimming, and more. He tilted his face to the periwinkle sky. A slight smile rose the edges of his lips as the warmth of the sun brightened his mood. *This really is a peaceful place close to the Goddess. I regret Morgan isn't here to share it.*

"How are you doing?" Lezon asked quietly as he dropped back from the others.

"Fine. Lots of good memories here, not just the painful ones of our females dying."

"I understand. When the Zuvgran destroyed our home world, I remember elders speaking of the beauty and bounty of our planet. While many Jalaxians raged for *solars* and became bitter and vengeful, others ensured the good memories of the home world passed on to those of us too young to have experienced it for themselves. They wanted us to know that while the loss was heinous, the joy should live on so that we might experience it again."

Grulen glanced at him from the corner of his eye.

"I never heard you speak of it before."

"Not much point, is there? I was born in space long after the destruction. But walking here, it reminds me of the stories telling us that the lifeblood of our planet was its peace generated by its closeness to the Goddess and its ability to provide sustenance for all." Lezon looked around. "I imagine this is what it felt like, even if the plants, dirt, or sky is different."

"Perhaps you should have been a poet instead of a medic."

"Maybe."

They reached the others. His father shared a story of their family when Grulen was but eight *solars* which resulted in much laughter. A reluctant smile lifted his lips. *I did have a habit of getting myself into trouble back then.*

"Are you ready, my son?"

Grulen met his father's eyes and nodded. They traveled side by side to the resting place of his family. The others fell back and gave them privacy when they finally reached the patch of riotous flowers under a huge *trulet* tree. Small markers with their names dotted the area.

"Do you ever imagine what they would be like now?" Grulen's tail swept fast enough that the heads of the flowers near them fluttered.

"Every day. I envision your sisters finding mates and raising their own young. Holding your mother and feeling her joy each time a new grandchild arrived." His father's voice lowered. "Your mother was the love of my life and the brightest light in my world. I hate that she didn't live to see our younglings grow to adulthood or see the fine male you turned out to be."

Grulen spoke words he'd never said to his father before.

"I remember you broken after their deaths. All the village males were."

His father nodded. The silver in his hair glinted in the sunlight.

"To have so much taken from us so fast was a shock. It upset everything we knew and believed. Even worse, I think, was the pain they suffered that we couldn't alleviate." Nurin's eyes shadowed. "Nothing is worse than seeing your loved ones in constant pain. Not even their deaths."

"That's why I vowed never to mate. I will not put myself in a position to feel the same. Our family line will not continue."

His father's tail stilled, and his shoulders fell. *Dear Goddess, he looks like he did the day we buried them.*

"Then I'm glad your mother is not here to see my failure as a father. To know I raised her son to be afraid of love would kill her anew." The quiet words pierced Grulen's heart, and his hand rubbed his chest.

"You believe I should embrace the pain?"

"No joy exists that has no risk of pain or loss, son." Nurin gazed into the distance. "Do you think I ever wished to not have met your mother?"

Grulen shook his head.

"I treasure every moment the Goddess blessed us with. I would relive the pain of her suffering and death a thousand times over to gain more of those joyous, loving memories. Her love and place in my heart was worth all of it. Just as every hug, laugh, or tear from each of your sisters was worth it. Pain can be overcome or accepted, but love cannot be manufactured or replaced. Facsimiles are hollow." His father paused. "Is your vow the reason Morgan did not come with us?"

"She left yesterday when I remembered my vow and told her I would never mate her."

"Oh, son, I wish you hadn't done that."

"The only honorable course is to uphold my vow."

"No. That vow caused you to dishonor yourself and her. A vow made as a youngling experiencing grief and pain is like a temper tantrum. Violent and sudden but with no true weight behind it. It's a reaction to big feelings and emotions the youngling has no understanding of. It's a bid for control over the emotions that is never successful long-term."

"Your father is correct, Jevax." Wurvez moved next to him. "I tried to send Ava away because I thought she deserved a better male—one who was whole. Had she listened to me, my life would be much sadder and poorer. If she died tomorrow, my life would be shattered, and I would feel her loss every day afterwards. But to temper that loss would be every beautiful memory we're making together now to sustain me. The love of a good female is priceless."

"None of us would give up our mates just to save ourselves possible grief. We would rather bear their pain, if necessary, so their lives are happy," Traxen said.

Crax slapped him on the back.

"Tell me, how do you feel?"

"Confused."

"That's not what I meant. Are you pain-free now that Morgan is no longer a potential mate for you?"

"No. I miss her. I hate that I'm not by her side, protecting and keeping her safe. Everything's duller and muted."

"And if you find out in a year she died in shuttle crash? How would you feel then?"

Grulen's tail slapped the ground stirring the flowers. The thought of the universe without Morgan's light squeezed his heart until he gasped for breath.

Crax's hard visage softened.

"So you would feel the pain of her loss regardless?"

Grulen conceded the point.

"Then why should you both suffer for something that may never happen or occur when you are nearing the end of your time in this body? Why not fill your hearts and souls with love that makes you better than you are?" *The Jalaxian may look like a brute, but he's a deep thinker.*

Grulen turned Crax's words over in his mind, as well as those of the other males. He looked at all of them...seeing their support. Love and encouragement shone from his father's eyes.

Makai said quietly, "If I found my mate, I would hold onto her and never let go."

"*Crek.* I did this to myself...and her. How do I fix it?"

"Groveling," said Durek.

"Lots and lots of groveling," Tolvex agreed with a smile.

"But then afterwards, you have make-up sex. That's a whole other category of pleasure of its own." Wurvez waggled his eyebrows. The other males nodded with huge smiles.

"I need a plan."

"Let's help you with that."

Chapter 30

Rachel arranged for Morgan to meet with Largon at Phoenix House. All the women went with her. She suppressed a laugh when Rachel rolled her eyes when several royal guards accompanied them.

Even though her heart still hurt from Grulen's stance, it lifted when she entered the building. The sounds of happy children soothed her rough edges. Largon smiled at them.

"Welcome, ladies."

"Hey, Largon, how's it hanging?" Emmy smirked.

"The same as always, Emmy." Largon grinned at her. "Don't let Devik hear you ask another male that question."

"Pfft. I know how to handle him."

"Yeah. Let us know how that works out for you," Natasha said. "I'm going to head to the infirmary. If anyone needs medical care, I'm available for a bit."

"I'm off to the kitchen." Ava followed Natasha down the hall.

The other women split off to pursue their own interests.

"I can stay with you if you want," Talia said.

"I think I can handle it, but thanks." Morgan appreciated the offer of support.

"Okay, comm if you need me." Talia walked confidently toward the library.

"Walk with me, Morgan."

She fell into step beside the Zuvgran.

"I don't know if anyone told you, but I earned a degree in education on Earth." Morgan kept her gaze forward.

"I heard that. Do you have suggestions for Phoenix House?"

"Actually, I was hoping to hear more details about what you have in place, your goals, and where I might fit into all of that."

"What a relief. Talos has been hounding me to offer you a position. He's excited to have another teacher to help." Largon let out an exaggerated sigh.

Morgan laughed. *Well, that was easier than I thought.*

"Would you need me to live on site?"

"Not necessarily. Rumor has it Traxen may build a small village nearby. I'm sure we can request a domicile for you so you're close but not always in the thick of things."

"I think I'd like that."

"Will Jevax be joining you?"

Her breath caught in her throat. She swallowed hard.

"I'm not sure what Grulen's plans are. I'm making my own without him. If he chooses to reenter my life, I'll address it then."

Largon halted and turned to face her.

"I'm sorry, Morgan. I had the impression you were mates."

Her eyes filled. She blinked rapidly.

"He took me by surprise by severing our relationship. I have to do what's best for me now."

He patted her forearm. *His skin is cool.*

"If you need to talk, I'm willing to listen."

"Thank you. For now, I'd rather talk about helping with your mission here."

After a productive meeting with Largon where they decided she would move into Phoenix House in a week and begin her duties, she wandered into the kitchen. Ava pulled a fresh batch of cookies from the oven. She pulled off the high-tech potholder and motioned for Morgan to sit.

Grabbing a plate of cooled cookies and some milk, Ava joined Morgan at the small table in the corner.

"Have some."

Morgan groaned.

"Oh, snickerdoodle. Where did you find the flour?"

They discussed ingredients and various food and spice combinations each had discovered.

"How'd it go with Largon?"

"I move in next week."

"Wonderful. The kids here are great. You'll find several Svesti come by regularly to help, too."

"Grulen will come to his senses eventually."

"Maybe. I'm not sure I can trust him after this, though." Morgan glared at her cookie.

"He's male, Morgan. It doesn't matter what species they are. All of them make stupid decisions thinking they're being noble or something. It's our job to make them see the error of their ways and forgive their idiocy." Ava grabbed the cookie from Morgan's hand. "She didn't mean it, sweetie. She's just pissed at her male."

Morgan giggled.

"You're talking to a cookie?"

"Made you laugh, didn't I?" Ava winked.

"You women are insane."

"Maybe, but we're loyal." The redhead pursed her lips. "We've been lucky. Not a mean bitch in the mix so far. As more humans relocate here, we're bound to see that change. We need to set the example. Most of us have experienced some sort of trauma or hardship, either on Earth or out here. I think it makes the bonding tighter between us."

"I haven't really heard the stories about how you guys ended up on the *Invictus*."

"Oh, girl, let me fill you in."

When Ava finished, Morgan blinked.

"Holy shit. All of that happened?"

"I'm sure I probably forgot a thing or two, but for the most part, it's pretty much how it went."

"No wonder you guys are close."

"You're part of our ride or die group now. We're equal opportunity here."

Morgan laughed at Ava's outrageousness.

"I'm glad I came back to Costonia."

"We're happy you're here." Ava clinked her milk glass to Morgan's.

Back at the palace, Morgan made a face at the women in her living area.

"Really? A Court dinner tomorrow?"

"Yes, Traxen insists all of us are there." Rachel waved a hand.

"I don't have anything to wear." *I don't want males touching me like Ava mentioned.*

"That's why we're here." Natasha held up some samples of fabric. "I can whip up something quickly. Or we can synthesize something."

"Kara's synthesizer is working now on our gowns," Rain said.

"I really have to go?" Morgan whined.

"If I have to dress up, so do you." Emmy's foot tapped. "I hate getting all dolled up."

"But Devik loves it," Lin said with a smile.

"True." Emmy sighed. "The last time we almost didn't make it back to our quarters before he..."

Lin covered her ears.

"No, don't tell us. None of our business."

The women laughed.

"We get the idea, Emmy." Natasha sorted through her samples and held up a dark copper silk. "I think this will look stunning against your pale skin and with your hair color."

"Oh, that's beautiful." Talia fingered the cloth. "And it's incredibly soft."

Morgan stood there as Natasha held it up to her face. She tilted her head, and her tongue stuck out of the corner of her mouth.

"In the stores, I think there was a walnut-colored fabric that would work for accents." Her eyes glazed over before clearing up. "Yes, I think that will do it."

Morgan looked at Ava and raised her eyebrows.

"Natasha loves to sew. She's taken our gowns to the next level, even with staying within the Svesti parameters of acceptable Court attire. She really has a gift for making us look good." Ava grinned. "Of course, she's not fond of my rolling pin earrings, but who cares?"

Giggling, Morgan gave up.

"What do you need from me?"

"Let me take some measurements, and we'll do a fitting in the morning so I can finish it in time." A tape measure appeared in Natasha's hand. "I'm assuming you want me to build in a bra."

"If you think I should."

Natasha took her measurements and Emmy tapped on her tablet.

"Sent to your comm," Emmy said.

"Thanks."

"Come on, Traxen's expecting us in his quarters for evening meal," Talia said.

"Do I have to change for that?" *I'm not used to this.*

"If you have dress pants or jeans, they'd be better than the yoga pants." Rachel smiled. "Your shirt's fine."

Morgan rushed to throw on a pair of jeans and quickly brushed her hair and pulled it into a bun. *So many changes in my life all at once. I'm not sure I can keep up.*

During dinner, Morgan ended up enjoying herself immensely. The sense of family she experienced on the *Fortitude* was magnified with the larger group. Lots of teasing and humor punctuated some of the more serious conversation. She observed all the couples and how they interacted with each other. *They're all so different, but the depth of caring and emotion is similar.*

"Largon tells me you'll be moving to Phoenix House soon," Traxen said.

"Yes, next week. I'm looking forward to teaching the younglings."

"Would you be willing to add teaching human younglings in the future?" *I guess the rumors are true.*

"Of course." She looked down at her plate, then took a deep breath. "Largon mentioned you might be willing to add a house for me nearby when you begin building a new village."

"That's a good idea. Think about what you'd like, and we'll make it happen." He tugged Rachel onto his lap and kissed her. "*Belgella*, if you have any suggestions about security concerns, please make sure they're addressed before Morgan moves in."

Rachel snuggled into her mate and grinned.

"Yes, Your Highness."

Traxen rolled his eyes. *I didn't know kings did that.*

Morgan savored her dessert and realized she could handle Grulen's loss with her friends' support. She still hurt, but she wouldn't give up. *Survive. I can do that.*

Staring in amazement at her reflection in the viewer, Morgan raised her eyes to meet Natasha's.

"I can't believe you made this in a day. It's a work of art."

The gown appeared deceptively simple at first glance. The basic design followed the usual single shoulder and floor length pattern preferred by the Svesti. The copper fabric comprised the majority of it. Natasha added a narrow, dark brown metallic trim for the shoulder and outlining the sweetheart neckline and low back. A wider band circled the waist. But the true beauty was the skirt. Small pleats widening as they reached the floor were hidden in the copper. When Morgan moved, flashes of the shiny brown emphasized her legs, then tucked away when she stood still. Even with the pleats, Natasha incorporated a high slit along her left thigh to tease with a hint of skin. Morgan raised her arms and realized there were tiny brown pleats underneath her breasts in the bodice.

"I really enjoyed this one. I knew that walnut fabric would work." Natasha wore a self-satisfied look. "Let me fix your hair."

Brown high heels and jewelry completed Morgan's outfit. Natasha had pulled Morgan's hair up in a messy bun with wisps of curls near her face. A copper scroll bracelet and a matching necklace accompanied long, dangling copper earrings that swung as Morgan turned to hug the doctor.

"Thank you, Natasha. I was hesitant about attending, but this gown screams self-confidence."

Natasha hugged her back. *She looks awesome in that navy silk, too.*

"Let's go wow some males."

Morgan paused at the doors leading to the main dining area. Ronan and Largon waited for them. Ronan held out his arm to his mate, and she elegantly slid into position next to him.

"May I escort you, Lady Morgan?" Largon offered her his arm.

"Please, Largon. Don't let me trip and embarrass myself." She took a deep breath.

"You look beautiful."

"Thank you."

They entered the room and faces swiveled in her direction when people realized someone new was in their midst. Her stomach roiled briefly, then she lifted her chin and walked confidently with Largon.

"That's it, don't let them intimidate you."

Loud whispers followed her progress. *Guess there's not much difference between crowds no matter the species.*

Largon led her to table where several seats were open near Karid and Ava. He pulled out her chair and as she stepped forward to sit, the scent of caramel and cinnamon made her dizzy. Hastily, she sat, and her chair was pushed forward. Hot breath stirred her hair and earring.

"You look stunning, *ciebala*. You take my breath away."

Her eyes widened as Largon took the chair to her right. She turned slightly to see Grulen sit on her left. *Oh my god, he's here.*

Chapter 31

In the corner, Grulen anxiously waited for Morgan to appear. Traxen assured him she would attend, and the other males arranged to have seats available for them to sit together at the meal. He had a lot of groveling to do and wasn't sure the best way to do it.

When she entered the room on Largon's arm, his heart pounded. She was always beautiful to him, but that gown highlighted how truly magnificent she was. He couldn't wait to be near her, but he forced himself to sidle cautiously in her direction while remaining out of her sight. He'd hurt her badly, and he was afraid she'd run in the opposite direction before he could apologize.

Part of him felt guilty ambushing her this way, but the other males convinced him this was his best option. *I hope they're correct. I don't want to upset her more than I already have.*

Largon moved aside so Grulen could push in Morgan's seat. Her shoulders stiffened when she heard his voice.

"You look stunning, *ciebala*. You take my breath away."

He took his seat on her left, hoping she'd turn so he could look into her eyes. However, he was disappointed.

Facing Karid and Ava, she said quietly, "Grulen, I wasn't expecting to see you again. You made your decision quite clear."

"I am an idiot and a fool, *ciebala*."

"Please don't call me that anymore. I won't answer to it." *Ouch. She's not going to make this easy for me.*

"Morgan, I wish to apologize for my words and actions."

"Apology accepted. You may leave now." She turned and said something to Largon.

His tail drooped. Consciously, he kept his shoulders from falling. Karid gestured for him to keep talking. He tried again.

"I made a mistake and hurt you. I hope you will give me another chance. I want to make it up to you."

"There's no need. Will you be returning to your duties on the *Invictus* soon?"

"That depends on you."

"It shouldn't. My decisions about my life no longer depend on you." *Crek.*

"*Cie*...Morgan, please. This coldness is not you, nor how we interact."

Her head whipped to face him, and her blue eyes flashed. *How can she be so glorious in her anger?*

"This coldness is exactly how you treated me when you informed me our relationship was over," she hissed. "I didn't like it much either, but I'm just following your example."

"Fair point. However, I'm no longer treating you that way. Perhaps you might consider doing the same so we can talk. Please." His tail wound around her ankle under the table. Her fingers strangled her napkin.

"I don't want to discuss this here."

"May we speak in private later?"

She opened and closed her mouth several times but said nothing. Finally, she bent her head and simply nodded.

"Thank you."

He didn't attempt to speak to her again during the meal. He left his tail where it rested on her flesh when she didn't acknowledge it or demand he stop touching her.

He chatted with Abby who sat on his other side. She gave him sympathetic glances and once leaned closer to say, "Give her time. You hurt her badly."

"I know," he whispered back.

As difficult as it was to sit next to Morgan with her stiff spine and lack of conversation, watching her after evening meal speaking to several males who found excuses to touch her arms infuriated him. One Svesti crowded close to her and Grulen's claws extruded. He took a step toward them when a blue hand grabbed his forearm. He glanced upwards to see who it was attached to.

Crax shook his head in warning.

"Don't do it. I understand the impulse, but you gave up the privilege of being her protector. Until she allows you to do so again, all you will do is make her angrier."

Grulen's tail flicked wildly. He wanted to eviscerate the male standing too close to Morgan. Crax's grip remained firm holding him in place. He watched as Morgan stepped back from the male with a few words. The male's tail flicked once, and he replied. She crossed her arms and glared at him. He finally moved away. She found Largon and he escorted her from the room.

Grulen looked pointedly at Crax's hand. The Jalaxian removed it, and Grulen wasted no time following Morgan. He caught up the couple as they climbed the stairs.

"Morgan, may we speak now?"

One hand on the railing, she paused midstep. Largon bent his head to speak quietly to her. Her shoulders dropped, and she turned her head.

"Join us."

Grulen had to consciously control his eagerness to be near her and keep his approach measured. *It's only been days since I screwed up, and I feel like it's been forever.*

Largon searched his expression before nodding. They walked silently to the residential guest quarters.

"Morgan, if you would prefer to speak with Jevax on neutral ground, I offer the living area in my quarters for your use," Largon said.

She gave the older male a sad smile.

"I appreciate it, but my quarters will be fine."

"As you wish."

At her door, she thanked Largon and entered without saying a word to Grulen. He followed her. She kicked off her shoes and started taking off her jewelry. She glanced at him.

"Go ahead and say what you want to say so I can get some rest."

He dropped heavily onto the couch. His elbows dug into his thighs, and he rested his head his hands.

"What can I do to prove I love you?"

Her arms raised taking pins from her hair, she froze at his question.

"How did we get to love?"

"Oh, *ciebala,* I became infatuated with you the first time I saw you on Nulorn. Once I got to know you, I prayed to the Goddess that no female waited for me so I could show you how I felt. I had every intention of asking you to true mate with me when you were ready." He pounded a fist into his thigh. "Then I regained my memories, and that stupid vow tripped me up. I reacted badly trying to reconcile my feelings about mating before and after my accident."

"If you love me, how could you just turn away?' The pain in her voice hurt his soul. *I did that. I'm such a naroon.*

"I know you don't believe me, but I thought I was doing the right thing. The way I felt, I believed I would always hold some of myself apart from you to spare myself the pain I saw in my village. That wouldn't be fair to you. You deserve to be the sun, moon, and stars to a male."

She moved closer, and he held out his hand. His heart clenched when she gingerly took it. He tugged lightly and had her sit next to him. Her scent and warmth seeped into his soul, and he immediately felt hope.

"You hurt me badly."

"I know and I can't apologize enough. If you give me a chance, I will never turn you away again. I don't think I can. I've been miserable without you. I don't want to live it again if I have a choice."

"Bad things could still happen, Grulen. I could die from some weird disease in a decade or get hit by a flitter."

"I know, but my father and friends helped me realize that I was already in pain, and you were alive. If you died too early, even far from me, I would still feel your loss. But if we spend the intervening time loving each other instead, I would have beautiful, happy memories to ease my loss rather than regrets."

She reached up to caress his face. It dawned on him that not once in all their interactions had she ever given any indication she saw his scars from the accident. *One more reason to love her.*

"I don't want to live on a ship. I'm going to work at Phoenix House."

"I thought you might feel that way. I'd like you to consider a compromise." His fingers rubbed hers.

"What?"

"Durek asked that I complete one last round trip to Earth on the *Invictus*. We'll be picking up Earth delegates to visit Costonia and finalize treaties. He wants me to transfer to security and participate in high-intensity training with Tolvex. Once we return, I'll be part of the team providing security for Phoenix House, the gated community, and new village. I can also teach part-time at Phoenix House. I'd like you go with me for that last trip before we settle here. Durek assures me he'll approve it."

Tears filled her eyes.

"You're okay with giving up travel?"

"Yes, so long as I'm with you. I just don't want to be apart from you for the three or four months it will take to go back and forth to Earth."

She leaned forward and kissed him gently.

"Does this mean I'm forgiven?" he whispered.

"Yes. I've been miserable, too. I love you, Grulen."

He slid to the kneel on the floor in front of her. He held her hands in his.

"Will you true mate with me, Morgan Calloway? Will you be mine for as long as the Goddess blesses us? Which I sincerely hope is forever and beyond."

"Yes, Grulen Jevax of House Midnar. I would be honored to true mate with you."

He rose to kiss her. Her arms wrapped around his neck, and she arched into him. Her breasts rubbed against his chest. He growled as his hands found her ass and squeezed.

"Take me to bed, Grulen. It's been too long." She tugged at his shirt. He ripped it from his body and tossed the ruined fabric aside.

Holding her tightly, he stood in a fluid motion. He kicked off his shoes and stumbled forward, his mouth dragging across every inch of flesh he could reach.

Finally, they reached the bed. He sat her on the edge and stripped. His cock dripped with precum. Kneeling, he found the fastener for her gown and pressed it. He reverently slid the shoulder of her dress downward and exposed her heaving breasts. One finger traced her mounds before circling her nipples.

Leaning forward, he stiffened his tongue to flick at her hard peaks while his hands kneaded her soft flesh. Her fingers clutched at his shoulders and back, then her hands flattened and stroked large swaths of his skin. His mouth moved lower.

"Lift, *ciebala*, so we don't ruin your spectacular gown." He gently tugged the fabric from her when her hips rose. Her scent tickled his nose, and he wanted more of it. "Lean back, let me love you."

Placing her legs over his shoulders, he licked along her seam. His tail tugged her ankle and spread her further open. He wrapped his arms underneath her thighs and used his hands to hold her there.

"This beautiful cunt has a starring role in my dreams and fantasies. I love tasting you." His tongue circled her opening softly. Over and over again, he teased her flesh. Her core began to weep, and she tried to press closer. Delving into her, his tongue explored her before sliding out to find her clit. Loosening one hand from her thigh, he inserted two fingers into her cunt and thrust slowly while he licked her clit. Her moans filled the room, her thighs squeezed his ears, and her hands clutched his hair.

Finding a spot and rhythm that made her shake, he heard her moans rise in pitch. He crooked his fingers and pressed upwards. Finding a spongy spot, he explored, and she wailed. Her cunt spasmed on his fingers and her body fought against his hold as she succumbed to pleasure. When her body calmed, he slowed his tongue and slid his fingers from her. Sucking his wet digits, he groaned. Peering up at her, he inwardly preened at the pink flush of her skin. A soft smile resided on her face. *She should always look so sated.*

"Come here," she said huskily.

He rose to lie next to her. His tail caressed her hip, and he kissed her gently. She pushed him onto his back.

"My turn."

Ripples of pleasure spread outward from every spot her mouth kissed or her tongue licked. She started at his earlobe and slowly worked her way downward. Her hands stroked and fingers pinched his nipples while her lips drug wet lines along his neck and collarbones. She sucked on his hard little buds, occasionally nipping at them with her teeth. Her palms smoothed his abdomen, and she reached between them to stroke his erection while she kissed along the path her hands had taken. Kneeling beside his hip, she held his cock firmly and licked its length keeping her eyes on his. *Crek.*

Never looking away, her tongue explored his head nodes and the vein running underneath his shaft. Her other hand cupped his balls and rolled them gently with her fingertips. A groan erupted from his throat when she closed her mouth over the head of his cock. She hummed, and his hips bucked. Wet and hot, her mouth loved his member while her hand continued to stroke him in time with the bobbing of her head. He cupped her cheek with his hand and felt the movement of his shaft in her mouth. His vision centered on her—her hazy eyes, the stretch of her reddened lips around his cock, and the flare of her nostrils. Tension built in his spine, and his balls drew up tight.

"No more, Morgan. I don't want to come in your mouth tonight." He reached down to pull her up and couldn't help the groan that escaped when her mouth popped off his cock.

Chapter 32

Morgan allowed Grulen to pull her from his cock. She'd never really enjoyed giving blow jobs, but sucking on him was intensely arousing. He maneuvered their bodies higher on the mattress and lay beside her, his head propped on one hand.

"How can you taste like you smell?"

His eyebrows raised.

"You taste like cinnamon and caramel." She licked her lips.

His chuckle made her smile. He drew patterns on her skin with a single claw and his tail. Goosebumps raced across her flesh.

Leaning forward, he dropped butterfly kisses on her face as he whispered low.

"I love you, Morgan Calloway. You are my moon, sun, and stars, my *ciebala*, my sky dancer." His words flowed into her soul, and it wept at the love in his voice and touch.

"Your beauty is more than your soft, silky skin or your brilliant blue eyes, or even these plump breasts or welcoming cunt. Your beauty is your intelligence, your kindness, your unrelenting strength in the face of adversity, your loyalty, your caring, and your joy in the world around you."

Her back arched as his kisses moved to her neck. Shivers sprinkled electricity to her nerves.

"I will never take your love for granted. I will strive each day to be worthy of your attention. I will care for you and meet as many as your needs as I can. I will hold you when you are afraid. I will be your biggest supporter in all you do. I will respect you. I will protect you. I will try to keep my male stupidity from ever hurting you again." She giggled at his last sentence, then moaned when his tail pushed into her pussy and thrust slowly.

"My body is yours. My soul is yours. My love is yours for all eternity." His tail withdrew, and he rolled onto his back pulling her on top of him. His fingers burrowed into her hair, and he gazed into her eyes. "I ask you again, will you true mate with me?"

"Yes, Grulen. I want to be your true mate. I want to love you, care for you, and support you. I will hold you when you're in pain. I will laugh with you. I will cry with you. I will be your friend, your lover, and you will be my everything."

His eyes watered as she spoke.

"I don't deserve you, *ciebala*, but I am greedy and will keep you anyway. Ride me."

She stared down at him for a long moment. *It's time to face this.*

"No."

"No?"

She rolled off him and tugged him over her body with her legs spread wide. He rested his weight on his elbows.

"I want you to true mate me in this position."

"But I do not wish to cause you any distress." His tail flicked once.

"I'm asking you to trust me, Grulen. I'll be fine."

His eyes searched hers.

"Are you certain?"

She caressed his face and smiled.

"I want to take back this huge part of my sexuality. Can you think of a better way than true mating with the male I love and trust?"

He dropped his forehead to hers and they breathed each other's air.

"Your wisdom and strength continue to amaze me."

"Make me yours in all ways, Grulen."

He shifted his hips, and his cock unerringly found her pussy. He pushed in slowly never taking his eyes from hers. She moaned when he seated himself fully within her.

"There you are," she said and gyrated her hips. Her hands gripped his upper arms. His corded muscles pulsed against her skin with every movement of his body.

They settled into the age-old rhythm of lovers everywhere. His head nodes created ripples of pleasure, while his base node slid on her clit. She began exploring more of his body with her hands. Her palms loved the surging muscles on his back. When her fingers moved lower, they lingered on his glutes enjoying the sensation of them tightening and form those sexy side dips. Her fingernails dug into his ass as his speed increased.

Sweat dripped from their bodies as they crashed into each other over and over. Her moans grew louder. His tail played with her nipples, and her orgasm took her by surprise. She shuddered and shook, her pussy clutching as his cock as he continued to move.

"That's it, *ciebala*. You are so *crekkin'* glorious." His voice rasped in his ear. "I want you to come again for me."

He thrust faster and harder, and her hips met his with equal determination. His tail snuck between them and was crushed between his base node and her clit each time their hips met. The little slap of it and additional pressure pushed her higher and higher. *Oh, so good.*

He licked her neck where it met her shoulder. His fangs dragged on her skin and quivers radiated outward. She panted trying to get enough air. Her pussy began to ripple, and he bit her. *He just bit me.*

She screamed as a myriad of colors blurred her vision, and she bucked beneath him as her orgasm took over her body. Mindlessly, she bit his shoulder trying to ground herself. *What the...?*

Her mouth fell open when his cock began to vibrate within her and more pleasure racked her body. She couldn't tell where he ended and she began. The rapture seemed endless. They gasped as their lower bodies eventually stilled. Aftershocks shot through her with no warning.

He rolled them so she was on top of him. His hands and tail stroked her. Her head rested heavily on his chest.

When she could talk again, she said, "Did your cock vibrate?"

Rumbles of laughter jostled her.

"It certainly felt that way. I wasn't expecting that."

"Wow. I wonder if we can make it do it again, because that was intense."

"I don't know why it happened to begin with, but I'm certainly willing to recreate the circumstances." His fingers combed her hair in long, soothing strokes.

She smiled against his pecs. From the corner of her eye, she could see part of clan marking. She frowned and lifted her head to look at it closer.

"Grulen?"

"Yes, *ciebala*?"

"Your clan marking just turned gold."

He sat up abruptly.

Looking down at himself, his jaw fell open. His hands gently gripped her shoulders, and he stared.

"Morgan?"

"Hmm?"

"You now have a clan marking." His finger traced it.

She twisted her neck to see it. When she looked back at him, tears filled his eyes.

"Are you okay?"

Wonder filled his voice.

"We're fated mates, *ciebala*. The Goddess has blessed our union." He huffed. "And to think I came close to *crekkin'* it all up for good."

"Fated mates," she whispered.

His head bobbed and a single tear ran down his cheek.

"I think we need to celebrate."

"Okay. What would you like to do?"

"I think we need to test that vibrating cock in another position." She cupped her breasts and plucked her nipples. "You game?"

"If that means am I willing, the answer is always yes." He growled and tickled her.

She squealed with laughter.

"Then let's start our lifelong experimentation."

"As you command, *ciebala*."

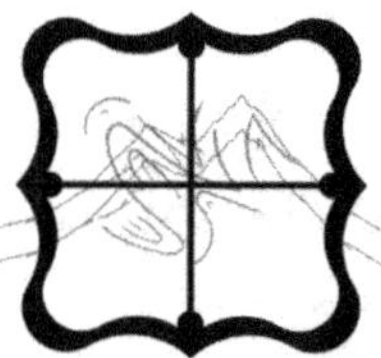 

Recap

Races thus far

Human - Enough said.

Svesti - Warrior Race. About seven feet tall, skin in various shades of bronze, semi-retractable fangs, tails, and retractable claws. Ruled by a King. Honorable race protecting many regions of space from the Zuvgran, including near Earth. Most Svesti females died or were rendered infertile thirty Earth years prior due to a virus released by the Zuvgran. Plural is Svesti.

Cephation - Cephalopod Race. Averages six-eight feet tall. Green skin, six tentacles, two arms and a single eye.

Crestillian - Reptilian Race.

Durelian - Mercenary Race. About seven feet tall, orange skin, three bulbous black eyes.

Ermipa - Mining Race. About four feet tall, furry, round head, oval eyes.

Estalan - Sybaritic Race. Known for its quality liquors and drugs.

Frezzian - Mercenary Race. Adverse to personal risk. Considered dishonorable.

Jalaxian - Warrior Race. About seven feet tall, blue skin, fangs, retractable claws, and tail. Considered honorable. Many work as mercenaries after the Zuvgran decimated their world fifty Earth years ago.

Ladortan – Hunter Race. Eight-nine feet tall, long fur, resembles Earth's Yeti.

Mostiffian - Mammalian Race.

Nulorian - Mammalian Race.

Orkite – Mammalian Race. Large, muscular, green skin, tusks, and horns.

Pellotian - Avian Race. Green skin and wings.

Praxite - Mammalian Race. Lavender skin and tails. Females have three breasts.

Romittel - Mammalian Race.

Rumaskan - Mammalian Race. Female-dominated. Pink skin, cat-like ears, retractable claws.

Straxian - Mammalian Race. Brown skin.

Urdite – Arachnid Race. Non-space-faring.

Wrestikan - Mammalian Race. Four arms and red skin. Home planet was Himita Prime.

Zuvgran - Warrior Race. About seven feet tall, gray skin, fangs, claws, and horns. Ruled by an Emperor. Dishonorable race that invades planets to strip them of their resources and take the inhabitants as slaves. Considered violent. Plural is Zuvgran.

Planets and Space Stations thus far

Earth - Really not the center of the universe as humans might believe.

Costonia - Svesti Home World.

Arona – Orkite Home World.

Bralia – Colony planet.

Crestillia - Crestillian Home World. Zuvgran-controlled.

Delizas – Pleasure planet.

Dianthia – Costonia's moon.

Gladdeus – Gambling world known for its fighting pits and slavery.

Himita Prime - Wrestikan Home World. Zuvgran-controlled.

Ladorta – Ladortan Home World.

Millus - Unoccupied planet outside of Costonian galaxy.

Nulorn - Trading planet halfway between Pellotia and Talonka Six.

Pellotia - Pellotian Home World. Zuvgran-controlled.

Praxis - Zuvgran-controlled.

Romitte - Zuvgran-controlled. Closest planet to Lestanus system.

Rumaska – Female-dominated planet known for their bremmite mines and male subjugation.

Straxis - Agricultural and trading world. Sixth planet in the Lestanus system.

Talonka Six - Mining world closer to Costonia than Earth. Fourth planet in the Lestanus system.

Theron - Space Station approximately one quarter of the distance from Earth to Costonia.

Urdita – Planet in the Quon system.

XB9428B - Uninhabited planet, home to a Zuvgran lab.

Svesti Houses

Davelk - Ruling House of Costonia.

Binova - Primarily merchants.

Fresida - Primarily educators and scientists.

Glixon - Primarily merchants.

Kreliz - Primarily scientists.

Midnar - Primarily agriculture.

Nuxar - One of the two Houses that strictly adhere to the old ways of worship.

Ruxila - Primarily agriculture.

Srotix - One of the two Houses that strictly adhere to the old ways of worship.

Troliv - Primarily merchants.

Vramel - Primarily warriors and educators.

Yula - Many Svesti healers come from House Yula.

Terran - New human clan marking.

Characters

Humans

Morgan Calloway – American, former exotic dancer at the Manor House, teacher.

Jake Broussard – American, bartender at the Manor House.

Tony Dixon – American, bouncer at the Manor House.

Penny Lockhart – American, waitress at the Manor House.

Sophia Pratoria – American, owner of the Manor House. Morgan's best friend.

Faith Roberts – American, social worker.

Danae Stefano – American, waitress at the Manor House.

Candi Torres – American, exotic dancer at the Manor House.

Beth Weston – American, exotic dancer at the Manor House.

Jim, Lisa, Bree, Evelyn, Moe, Renee, Kiki, Colleen – Slaves.

Lin Chang - Chinese, botanist.

Rachel Llewellyn - British, MI6.

Emmy Norton - Australian, hacker.

Natasha Petrov - Russian, medical doctor.

Talia Sullivan - American, U.S. Ambassador of Interplanetary Relations.

Ava Taylor - Canadian, chef.

Daniel Taylor - Canadian, detective, Ava's adoptive father.

Svesti

Grulen Jevax of House Midnar - Warrior.

King Traxen Sovex of House Davelk - King of the Svesti.

Arinna Brexis of House Midnar – Traxen's grandmother.

Lieutenant Triv'n Brauvix of House Kreliz - Communications officer on the *Invictus*.

Lieutenant Hozan Crulex of House Yula - Science office on the *Invictus*.

Yan'n Dralix of House Troliv - Warrior.

Rostrox Dresiv of House Troliv – Weapons shop owner in Trezoura.

Canaan Durek of House Ruxila - Vared's father, House Ruxila representative in the King's Court, manages the family estate. Also Main Agricultural Advisor.

Commander Vared Durek of House Ruxila - Commander of the space cruiser, *Invictus*, the flagship of the Svesti military. First cousin to the king.

Pluvi Frulix of House Srotix – Council member.

Hil'n Glopiz of House Nuxar – Council member.

Bavin Hossix of House Binova - Royal Guard.

Merix Hunnek of House Nuxar - Head of aquiponics area on the *Invictus*. Rank - Major.

Fliva Jevax of House Midnar – Grulen's deceased older sister.

Hadili Jevax of House Midnar – Grulen's deceased younger sister.

Muri Jevax of House Midnar – Grulen's deceased younger sister.

Nurin Jevax of House Midnar – Grulen's father.

Riba Jevax of House Midnar – Grulen's deceased older sister.

Yopa Jevax of House Midnar – Grulen's deceased older sister.

Gal'n Kalix of House Binova - Security officer.

Besix Kloir of House Kreliz - Warrior.

Jespan Kragen of House Yula – Royal Guard.

Oriba Lunex of House Binova – Headmaster of the Warrior Academy. Rank - Commander.

Rexus Markham of House Yula - Healer on the *Invictus*. Rank - Captain.

Nerid Mantoor of House Glixon - Warrior.

Yistax Minnet of House Troliv – Council member.

Reesa Naturu of House Davelk – Head cook at the palace.

Prixo Naxxar of House Yula – Healer.

Talen Previv of House Fresida - Warrior. Head Cook on the *Invictus*.

Wanon Reccix of House Midnar – Council member.

Boriv Ristan of House Davelk – Healer.

Ash'n Rivezt of House Yula - Head healer on the *Invictus*. Rank - Captain.

Narilla Rivezt of House Yula - Council member, Main Medical Advisor, Master Healer, Ash'n's grandmother.

Klero Rovex of House Glixon - Warrior.

Nerob Sinoaz of House Troliv - Healer on the *Invictus*. Rank - Captain.

Aldis Sovex of House Davelk – Traxen's grandfather.

Grissa Sproid of House Kreliz – Lerix's mother.

Lerix Sproid of House Kreliz - Warrior.

Krivez Tesix – Security officer on the *Invictus*. Pilot.

Lieutenant Devik Tolvex of House Vramel - Head security officer on the *Invictus*.

Marek Tolvex of House Vramel - Council member. Devik's father.

Pex Tolvex of House Vramel - One of Devik's older brothers.

Rassix Tolvex of House Vramel - One of Devik's older brothers.

Solen Tolvex of House Vramel - One of Devik's older brothers.

Clen'n Vepiv of House Nuxar - Warrior and medic.

Lieutenant Leriv Volax of House Kreliz - Supply Master on the *Invictus*.

Slaiv'n Westov – Security officer on the *Invictus*. Specialty – computers.

Lieutenant Gat'n Wrox of House Fresida - Head engineer on *Invictus*.

Drikon Wurvez of House Binova– Merchant, Karid's father.

Lieutenant Karid Wurvez of House Binova - Head tactical officer on the *Invictus,* second in command of the space cruiser.

Brestov Xoriv of House Fresida - Security officer.

Wexan Yanz of House Srotix – Royal Guard.

Saletta Yemez of House Ruxila - Ronan's mother.

Ari Zunnax of House Davelk – Spymaster disguise.

Wing Raiders

Captain Makai - Leader of the Jalaxian mercenary group, Wing Raiders.

Crax - Jalaxian Wing Raider, specialty is weapons.

Kara Brinkman - Human female in the Wing Raiders, specialty is technology.

Lezon - Jalaxian Wing Raider, specialty is medical.

Rain Oakhurst- Human female in the Wing Raiders, pilot.

Abby Quinlan – Human female in the Wing Raiders, nurse practitioner.

Tren - Jalaxian Wing Raider, engineer.

Yaz - Jalaxian Wing Raider, pilot.

Zuvgran

Largon d'Ayen - Jorn d'Olorg's best friend and surrogate father to Ronan.

Jorn d'Olorg - Ronan's father.

Emperor Prigon n'Tuli – Zuvgran emperor.

Commander Rufen d'Urfan – Interim leader of the Zuvgran.

Orkites

Dablar – Technology merchant in Urzo.

Fraddar – Niksen's guard.

Heggar – Lord of Urzo.

Krinir – Niksen's guard.

Lollek – Niksen's assistant; covert operative.

Niksen – Heggar's daughter.

Rumaskan

Mistress Akka – Planetary communications worker.

Mistress Hower – Hotel owner.

Mistress Linoro – Fishery owner.

Mistress Lyet – Senior member of the Rumaskan Ruling Commission.

Mistress Overly – Bremmite mine owner.

Mistress Pitman – Bremmite mine owner.

Mistress Relim – Planetary communications supervisor.

Mistress Summi – Fabric manufacturer.

Mistress Thespa – Bremmite mine owner.

Ryost – Mine worker.

Other

Ronan d'Olorg -Svesti-Zuvgran hybrid. Son of Jorn and Saletta.

Marris d'Olorg -Svesti-Zuvgran hybrid. Ronan's deceased younger sister.

Annika - Pellotian-Zuvgran hybrid.

Brenos - Pellotian-Zuvgran hybrid.

Creet – Healer on the *Morning Star*.

Kito Dresine - Wrestikan. Shop owner on Nulorn.

Flitos - Pellotian-Zuvgran hybrid.

Gromm - Wrestikan-Zuvgran hybrid.

Herrah - Wrestikan-Zuvgran hybrid.

Krutus – Captain of Durelian slave ship.

Manx – Jalaxian body servant to a Rumaskan female.

Molla - Jalaxian female.

Reeva- Wrestikan female slave at *Fantasia*.
Rina - Pellotian-Zuvgran hybrid.
Ordan – Captain of the *Morning Star*.
Overseer Roho - Ermipa on Talonka Six, head of the Veba Mine.
Slovis – Cephation owner of brothels on Delizas.
Talos - Pellotian teacher.
Tarqel – Slovis' assistant. Ladortan.
Yostal - Mostiffian-Zuvgran hybrid.
Zela - Crestillian-Zuvgran hybrid.

Svesti Words thus far

Bataavi - Cherished one.
Bloniv - Spice similar to Earth's turmeric, but grows in tube-like clusters.
Brellia - Small, rumik-filled pastry.
Caliana - Beautiful female.
Ciebala – Sky dancer.
Cold season - Comparable to Earth's winter in the northern hemisphere.
Crek - Fuck.
Drelix - Spice similar to Earth's ginger, but grows in tube-like clusters.
Estrecaro - Beloved grandson.

Forliza - Flower similar to Earth's jasmine, but with purple petals.

Harvest season - Comparable to Earth's autumn/fall in the northern hemisphere.

Horicar - Vegetable with a texture similar Earth's carrots, but shaped like blue potatoes.

Hot season - Comparable to Earth's summer in the northern hemisphere.

Kirani - Female feline found in the wild. Similar to Earth's lioness.

Leringa - Fruit that has a hint of spice when ingested.

Lobile - Purple tuber, cross between Earth's potato and sweet potato.

Lunar - Month.

Maxiem - A large animal that resembles a hybrid between Earth's ox and cow. Used as a source of meat, milk and beasts of burden.

Mentok - Similar to Earth's myna bird, but larger and with plumage reminiscent of an Earth's peacock. Chatters incessantly.

Milara - Small brown bird with periwinkle/white chest and underside of wings. Known for its cunning.

Naroon - Large furry animal, similar to Earth's ape, with blue fur. Gregarious and known to be silly in their family groups.

Nestune – Village in House Midnar territory on Costonia.

Pertiza - Creamy yellow sweet yogurt made from maxiem milk.

Picana - Little one.

Plostiv - Meat similar to Earth's chicken.

Raralumia - Rare light.

Renewal season - Comparable to Earth's spring in the northern hemisphere.

Ristern - Ermipa organ that filters dangerous gases.

Rulah - Small, furry animal similar to Earth's cat.

Rumik - Meat similar to Earth's ground beef. Comes from maxiem.

Sedapi - Vegetable similar to Earth's celery, but white.

Shurlix - Similar to Earth's tomato, but yellow.

Sibella – Vegetable similar to Earth's onion, but tubular in shape.

Solar - Year.

Tempika - Green berries that taste tart, but also sweet.

Trezoura - Capital city of Costonia.

Trulet - Similar to Earth's oak tree, but with dark blue leaves and orange bark.

Valadium - Steel-like ore when tempered is one of the hardest substances known in the universe.

Wimma - Blue citrus fruit similar to Earth's lime.

Woolah - Red flower that blooms on Costonia during Harvest season.

Yeddom - Orange bean-like vegetable that tastes like Earth's asparagus.

Young – Baby/infant.

Youngling – Child.

Yuffa - Plant similar to Earth's aloe, but with orange ball-like leaves.

Other
Ermipa

Ristern - Extra organ that filters out air impurities.

Pellotian

Annum - Year.

Zuvgran

Grak - Fuck.

Author's Note

Did you see that coming? Morgan let me know who she really was in *Vared*, but all the other stories needed to be told first. I originally thought Grulen would die in the asteroid field, but he was just too adorable to not find a happy ending.

I apologize that their story took as long to get to you as it did. Quite a bit has happened in my personal life this past year which negatively impacted my mental stamina. Hopefully, things are settling into a new normal where I can continue bringing characters to life on a timeline we'll all enjoy.

- Wavy

Thank you for reading Grulen and Morgan's story. If you enjoyed this book, please leave an online review where you purchased it. This lets other readers know whether they might enjoy it, too!

If you'd like to hear about Wavy's other books, you can sign up for her newsletter or find her social media links at wavymartin.com.

www.ingramcontent.com/pod-product-compliance
Lightning Source LLC
Chambersburg PA
CBHW070204310726
48976CB00001B/210